SUPERPOWERS
OF THE
SHY GIRL

SUPERPOWERS OF THE SHY GIRL

AMY C. GORMAN

Shy Girl
PUBLISHING
ASHBURN, VIRGINIA

Shy Girl Publishing LLC
43300-116 Southern Walk Plaza, #641
Ashburn, VA 20148

www.shygirlpublishing.com
www.facebook.com/shygirlpublishing

Ordering Information:
For information about special discounts available for bulk purchases, sales promotions, fundraising and educational needs, contact Shy Girl Publishing Sales at sales@shygirlpublishing.com.

ISBN 978-0-9991461-0-1 (HardCover Edition)
ISBN 978-0-9991461-1-8 (Paperback Edition)
ISBN 978-0-9991461-2-5 (eBook)

Printed in the United States of America

Library of Congress Control Number: 2017951708

First Edition 2017

For Elizabeth and Alex

SUPERPOWERS OF THE SHY GIRL

My parents always start long car trips in a goofy mood. They become giddy once they are finally buckled into their seats, with sweat on their foreheads from loading the car and running into the house for one thing or another. That click of the seat belt is the refreshing sign that the hard work is finished. Now all they have to do is sit back and drive sixteen hours with their two adoring daughters, myself, age ten, and my sister April, almost fourteen. Either they're the most optimistic people in the universe or the most forgetful. April and I never do well on long car drives. Sometimes even just driving around town with the two of us can put my parents over the edge. Heck, we've been threatened with no more television for the rest of our lives on the short trip from our house to the bus stop when it was raining. Even before April became a teenager and started hating me, we were not good in the car. Yet here they sit, seat belts buckled, giving April and me hopeful grins from the front seat. "Here we go," my mom says with her eyes shining.

"Florida or bust," my dad says and starts the car. I look closely at them. They're so filled with hope, but I can sense it. They're silently praying that this car trip will be different than all the others. They're hoping that since we're older, we can sit for long periods of time with nothing to do. My cousins live in Florida. Every few years, my dad forgets how awful this car trip is and decides to visit his brother. Their plan had been that they would wake us up before the sunrise and pack us in the car so we could get a head start. April and I even slept in our clothes last night. However, my parents aren't organized packers so they're always getting things ready at the last minute. They also like to sleep. So, we end up rolling out of the driveway at 10:30, full of false hopes and pretend sunny dispositions. They will not make this mistake on the way home though. Thoughts of this journey will be fresh in their minds. They'll make sure to be up and out hours before the sun rises if it means giving them some peace and quiet while April and I sleep. Maybe they'll even ditch the car and splurge on plane tickets home.

The first hour of the car trip was the finest. April slept. She sleeps really soundly. I was able to finagle her *Tiger Beat* magazine out from under her hand so I could read the small section about Henry Thomas. I've never seen the appeal of *Tiger Beat* before now. Last month, my dad dragged me to see *E.T.* with him. I didn't want to go because I saw a picture of E.T. and he looked gross but my dad promised he would buy me Reese's Pieces. My dad is pretty passionate about movies—not many, but what he likes, he loves. He's convinced me to sit through lots of John Wayne. We have to watch *The Quiet Man* as a family every Saint Patrick's Day. He also made me see *Star Wars* when it played at the drive-in theater. Our speaker wasn't very clear and I fell asleep during the middle but when he woke me up for the ending—that ending was great enough to make me love the whole movie. I had lots of questions about it as well. Mostly, I wanted to know if that was real. My sister still makes fun of me for this and tells her friends that I believe *Star Wars* really happened. In my defense, I wasn't even in kindergarten at the time.

When we went to *E.T.*, people started clapping before the movie began, so I knew it had to be good. It felt like the line to meet Santa Claus. Everyone was excited and knew they were about to see something better than real life. My dad was right. By the end of the movie, I wished I were Gertie because she was so cute, I loved E.T., and I no longer trusted the government. Why did they come to take E.T.? How is it possible to wrap an entire house in plastic? I don't think Ronald Reagan would allow such a thing to happen but my dad said the government would want to know all they could about an extraterrestrial. It was fantastic. I keep thinking about it. When I asked to see April's magazine last month, she scoffed at me and told me I would wrinkle it. When I said I just wanted to see if there was anything about E.T. in it, she accused me of having a crush. I don't really. I loved E.T. so much, part of me wishes it were real. I want to read that Elliott and Gertie and Michael are all like family in real life. It's a difficult thing though. The more I read, the less real the movie becomes as the magazines give me more facts about the actors' real lives. Yet I can't stop reading what I can find in hopes that the movie E.T. is real in some way. If April knew that, she would really never let it drop. My dad's brother still calls him Heinz because the only way he would eat anything was if it was covered in ketchup when he was a child. Now, he eats ketchup like a normal person, just on French fries, hamburgers or hot dogs. It still doesn't stop Uncle Tom from calling him Heinz. I'll be forty with two kids and April will tell them how I don't know the difference between movies and real life. At least she hasn't come up with a nickname for me though.

I was engrossed in reading about Elliott so I missed April's eyes fluttering open. She yanked the magazine from me causing the bottom corner of one page to rip, beginning the first car fight of the trip. Many fights followed along with lots of Hostess cupcakes, stomachaches, bathroom stops, possible throw-up stops, and one missed exit. By the time we were ten hours in, everyone was done. That's when my mom said something deep and meaningful in an effort to shut us up. Anyway, it was something like how if you can't change your situation, you should change your attitude. Since they told us to be quiet for the next hour, I had time to think about that.

I have lots of fears. I wish I didn't but I don't see how to get rid of them. Instead, I organize them into two baskets in my head. The basket I've labeled *Terrifying Fears I Think of at Night* include three things mostly: Darth Vader, vampires, and our attic. Darth Vader because he chokes people without even touching them. I know he isn't outside my window at night, but what if he was? I have stickers of Luke and Leia in my room. He could choke me while I sleep just for having an allegiance. Vampires, because I saw a wax vampire man biting the neck of a wax woman in a store window on a visit to Niagara Falls last year. Blood dripped from her neck like my uncle's wax candle lamp. He has this lamp that when it heats up, wax drips down its base that is shaped like a mermaid. I think I'll include that lamp in this fear basket actually. It's very strange and disgusting as over the years, lint and dust have stuck to it. My attic because, well, attics are creepy. I know all of these fears are silly, but at night, they scare me so I feel better sleeping with my stuffed animals around me. The pink bear I've had since I was a baby covers my neck, warding off both Vader and vampires. The two purple snake pillows I won at last year's church fair line either side of me to scare off any other monsters or space evildoers. I check under my bed and keep my closet doors open at night. I've thought lots about this one but there's simply nothing I can do about the attic. I can only check that it's closed and place a small note next to my door that says, *Keep Out*, in case anything makes its way down to my room at night.

The other basket is much larger. I've titled it, *The Annoying Basic Life Fears*. Included within this basket are fears of meeting new people, of raising my hand in class, or trying new activities that I want to try. Though the other fears are more intense and keep me up at night, these fears are the ones I wish I could lose first. You can hide the fact that you are scared to death of Vader if you are just walking around earth and not the Death Star. You cannot hide the fear of ever speaking in public though. In fact, everyone from my parents to every teacher I've ever had wishes I would just drop those fears. So while these fears don't wake me up at night, they're the ones that cause me to look like an idiot practically everywhere I go since every other kid my age doesn't have them. I think when I was younger, they were socially acceptable. "Oh, she's shy," people would gush. "How adorable." Now that I'm in fifth grade, it's just awkward. "Oh, she's shy. So she doesn't speak ever? She hasn't outgrown that?" My parents even introduce me that way. "Here's Jenny. She's our shy one." It feels as if they are saying, "Here's Jenny, she has really bad breath and pimples—do you see them? Right here on her cheek and over here on her forehead." In their defense, when I was younger, I liked for them to announce my shyness. It let me off the hook. No one expected me to answer them. Other kids would have to come over and introduce themselves to me if they wanted to play. As I've gotten older, as much as I still wish to hide, it's just not acceptable. I no longer think of shyness as something cute or just me. I see it as a big burden. I asked my parents to stop telling everyone I'm shy but it's been a hard habit to break, especially for my dad. He's never known a moment of shyness in his life. He speaks to everyone and anyone from tollbooth operators ("How are you this fine evening?") to the principal at my school ("Kids behaving?"). Now when he introduces me, he says, "And this is Jenny. I'm not supposed to tell you she's shy." Seriously? That's no better. I give up though because he's my dad and he means well.

I decided at the end of last year that when I start fifth grade next month, I'm going to finally empty the *Annoying Basic Life Fears* basket. I have no idea how to do that though. However, thinking about what my mom said, maybe if I start to look at these fears in a new way since I cannot change them, I could make my life better. Maybe I need to see my shyness in a new way. Since I can't change being shy though, I will change my attitude and find all of the good things about being shy. Shyness won't be seen as some freaky thing. I take out my new notebook and grab a pen, still planning how this new attitude will change my life.

"Why are you smiling out the window?" April said. "You look like an idiot."

"April, you are not supposed to talk for an hour," my mom says.

"But she's making me uncomfortable just staring out the window and smiling. It's creepy."

I smile even creepier, crossing my eyes and widening my mouth. I don't care what she thinks. I daydream my new self-complete with Princess Leia hair and a cape for good measure. I write one sentence on the top of the first page of my notebook: *Superpowers of the Shy Girl.*

SUPERPOWER #1: THE ABILITY TO REINVENT YOURSELF

Let's say you're funny. Everyone at school knows you're funny. You are so funny, sometimes you get sent to the principal because you just can't stop being so amusing. Now, you can't just show up at school one day and not be funny. People would keep asking you what was wrong. Or, say you are a great athlete and you always win kickball for your team. You couldn't just decide to not be a great athlete one day. Kids would still always pick you first for their team knowing that you are the best player. You can't let them down.

Now, for a shy person, people haven't really been noticing you much anyway. Nothing can stop you from seeking out a new identity. You're still a blank slate. People don't know if you're funny or not. Mostly, they probably think you're serious, so isn't it refreshing for them to find out you're funny? With this thought in mind, I developed my first step to a good school year. For starters, I'm no longer going to go by my first name of Jenny. Instead, I'll use my middle name, Emily. I came up with the plan on the long car ride back from Florida, but I haven't told anyone yet.

Today is the first day of school so I feel a bit shaky. I pop out of bed forcing myself to get back to that feeling of hope I had when I started trying to think of shyness differently. I feel embarrassed to tell my mom about my name change for fear that maybe it's not a good idea. It really seemed like a fantastic idea when I thought of it. I've been daydreaming about it ever since, but now, I'm sensing maybe it's weird. However, the whole point of changing my name to Emily is that Emily is a whole different person than Jenny. It's my reinvention. Emily isn't shy. Emily makes friends easily. Emily knows how to dress and what's cool and what's not. And, Emily is not a nickname for Jennifer. The prettiest and most popular girl in my grade is named Jennifer and that's what she goes by. Not Jen or Jenny. Jennifer Pendel. She spells it with a heart dotting the *i* and a curl under the *f*. This year, she's in my class. I figured it would be easier for everyone if there was only one Jennifer. So, I'll be Emily and then Jennifer and I can become friends. In fact, I'm going to her house after school today. My mom and her mom took a cake-decorating class together over the summer and thought it would be fun to "get the girls together."

I've practiced facial expressions in the mirror and jotted down a few topics of conversation for the get together. I think my face gives me away at times. If faces can look shy, that's what mine does. Right off the bat, I look scared. I think it's because of my eyes. So, in order to take on Emily's personality, I thought I should practice some un-shy faces. I looked through the magazines in the house at the pictures of all the beaming, confident smiles like the ones you see in every toothpaste commercial. Then I practiced the ones I liked best. I want to go for confident but sweet. Of course I locked my door when practicing so my family wouldn't stick me in the loony bin April always tells me I belong in. For conversation topics, while they're unoriginal, I think they'll work: what's your favorite school subject, what did you do this summer, what season do you like best. I read that you shouldn't ask questions that can be answered with a yes or a no if you want to keep a conversation going. I feel prepared for today. I run downstairs, excited with the possibilities of leaving my days as Jenny behind me and becoming best friends with Jennifer.

"That was fast," my mom says as she places a toasted frozen waffle drenched in Mrs. Butterworth's on the table for me. I begged to have Mrs. Butterworth's forever but my mom always said it was too much money and that I only wanted it because the bottle moves and talks in the commercial. She bought it with a coupon this week as a special back-to-school treat. It tastes fine, but I must admit, it is disappointing she doesn't talk. "Ready for your first day?"

I smile. The waffle tastes perfect; crunchy on the sides and mushy in the middle. April saunters into the kitchen, already dressed with her hair feathered on both sides. She slumps down into her chair at the table. She's in middle school and she hates me and everyone else who isn't in middle school. We used to be best friends but that changed around the time she began using Aqua Net and spending hours listening to her *Freeze-Frame* record in her room. I do kind of hope when I enter middle school I change just like she did. She has long straight brown hair and blue eyes and her face isn't covered with freckles. Her clothes always match outfits I see in her *Tiger Beat* magazines. The big fight in our house lately is between her and my mom over Jordache jeans. April wants another pair with the zippers at the hems but my mom thinks her old pair is fine and the Jordache are too expensive. To my surprise, April tried to involve me in it saying at some point I would have stylish hand-me-downs. She always tells me I don't know how to dress.

"Good morning, sweetie," my mom says to her as she places a bowl of Captain Crunch before her. April doesn't answer, she just picks up the spoon and starts eating.

"Ow," she says. "I told you these hurt the roof of my mouth."

"Well, wait until the milk softens them," my mother answers.

"Then they'll be soggy. I'll just have a Pop Tart."

April pushes the offending bowl of Captain Crunch away from her and crosses her arms. My mother sighs, which she does often lately. She searches through the cabinet and then lobs a silver package of chocolate Pop Tarts to the table. "Here," she says. "Enjoy."

I clear my throat and sit up straight. "I've been thinking that this year, I will tell the teacher to call me Emily."

April glares at me. "Excuse me?"

"Who?" my mom asks as she pours coffee into the purple ceramic cup April made her two years ago.

"I think I'll use my middle name this year."

"That's not strange at all," April says.

"Why do you want to use your middle name?" my mom asks.

"Well, there's another Jennifer in my class so I thought this would make things easier. And I like the name Emily better."

"A rose by any other name is still a nerd," April said.

"April, stop it," my mother said.

I scrunch my face and glare at her. "That's not funny."

"It's Shakespeare."

I don't know what that means but I'm not going to let her know that.

"I wish I had known before I filled out all of the school paperwork," my mom says. "It might be difficult to change your name now."

"Or just stupid," April says under her breath.

"April, you promised, remember?" my mom asks.

"Promised what?" I ask.

April rolls her eyes. "Jenny, I think changing your name to Emily is just a great idea. Gosh golly, no one at school will think you are trying too hard by changing your name. How do you come up with such fantastic ideas?"

"April, finish your breakfast somewhere else," my mom says.

"I was being nice," she protests, but my mom glares at her. "Fine. With pleasure. Bye Emily." April grabs her Pop Tarts and leaves.

I try not to show how embarrassed I am but my stupid face gives everything away all the time. I hate that I can't figure out what are good ideas and bad ideas. My mom places her arms around me. "Don't listen to her, honey. She's just going through a mean phase." I sniffle into her sleeve. "If you really want to be Emily, I can write a note to your teacher. However, I named you Jenny because it's a beautiful name and you are a beautiful girl. Since you go by Jenny, I don't think there will be much confusion. And Jennifer sounds like a nice girl so I'm sure she won't mind sharing a name with you."

I nod. I knew it would never work. If I could go back in time, I wish my mom had named me Emily. I can't help but think that if I was Emily, I'd be different. Everyone is named Jennifer or Jenny or Jen and it's embarrassing to have more than one in a class, especially when the other one will have more authority to it. If you're less popular than another person with the same name, you live a life of non-existence as if you have no right to the name in the first place. When I was in CCD with another cooler Jennifer, the teacher kept calling me Jennifer W. instead of Jenny. When she said just Jennifer it was known that she was calling on the other one. But April is right. Changing my name when everyone already knows me as Jenny will just look strange. I have no choice but to be the unpopular Jennifer in the class. I most likely would have been that anyway.

"I guess I'll stay as Jenny."

"Okay. Now, finish up your breakfast and be happy you didn't have to go to grade school as Vicki."

"Why?"

"They called me Icky Vicki the entire third grade just because there was a worm on my shoe when I got to school one day. It's not as if I put it there."

I laugh. I cannot picture my mom as a third grader. Note to self: check shoes daily to make sure there are no worms. I run upstairs to get dressed. Two days ago, I picked out my first-day outfit. Of course, the outfit was going to be something Emily would wear. I'm hoping Jenny can pull it off. I want to look perfect. I wear my favorite yellow dress with the large white polka dots with my E.T. shirt over it and my blue corduroys.

"What on earth?" April says when she sees me. "You cannot go to school wearing that. Blue corduroys? It's September, not January. And a shirt over a dress? It's like you don't even try.

You're so . . . " She turns and walks away. A lot of her sentences go unfinished. She's always had this habit but it wasn't bad when she was younger. When she was younger, her thoughts would casually go away. She may say, "Wow, what a beautiful rainbow, I've never seen one so . . . " Now when she lets a sentence trail away, you are usually meant to fill it with an insult.

My face flushes, which I wish it wouldn't. I had thought this outfit would be April-approved. I scramble out of the corduroys, take off E.T. and pull up my pink socks and follow her down. She sees that I have followed her advice and rolls her eyes, now disgusted at me for listening to her. My dad loves the expression, "You're darned if you do, you're darned if you don't," regarding April, Mom, and his boss.

"Okay, girls. Picture time," my mom says as she shuffles us toward the front door. "Get together." I move toward April but she takes a step away so I stop, close enough to be in the picture but far enough from her. "On the count of three. One, two, oh wait, I need to forward it." My mom twists the camera to forward the film.

"Mom!" April says. "We're going to be late."

"Got it. Count of three. One, two. Cheese!" The flash blinds us momentarily.

"Ready?"

"You are not coming to the bus stop with us," April said.

"Really? Not even for the first day?"

"No."

"Jenny?"

"You don't need to," I say. "It's okay." My heart is pounding though. Here we go. Back to school. Summers are much easier to be shy.

"Oh. Well, have a great first day." She kisses us both on our foreheads before we head out the door.

We live in the most perfect house in the most perfect state, Connecticut. I finally learned how to spell it by heart this year. Our house has an A-frame because part of it looks like an A. An apple orchard surrounds our neighborhood so it's called Apple Hill. We live on the hill. Lots of people don't realize there are houses up where ours is. There are only four houses and they're all on the right side of the street. The pond, or swamp, as my mom calls it, takes up the other side of the street. Thousands of tree frogs live near the pond during the summer. At night with my window open, I hear their croaking noises. I have a swing set in my backyard. April and I used to spend hours playing on it together. My room has green walls and a pink shag carpet. April's room has orange walls with bright yellow carpeting. It's not as pretty as mine. She agrees. When we moved here three years ago, she ran right upstairs and chose that room because it was bigger. Now she complains that it's like sleeping in a McDonald's.

We walk down our driveway and I make sure to step in the pothole like I always do. I was nervous on my first day of kindergarten and April used to help me through some of my worries. She told me to step in the pothole for good luck. In fact, she held my hand all the way to the bus stop then and had me do all sorts of things for luck such as touch a tree branch, skip, sing. Now, I just step in the pothole.

"You're so weird," April said when she sees me.

"You used to step in the pothole, too," I said.

"I never did that." April walks two steps ahead of me. If I

try to keep up, she just walks faster. When we get to the turn at the end of our street, we can either continue down the hill on the street or take the shortcut through our neighbor's backyard. April never lets me know which way she wants to go. She just chooses a way and huffs when I follow her choice but we are supposed to walk to the bus stop together.

Today, she's chosen the neighbor's backyard which is my favorite way to go. Behind my neighbor's house is a small dirt path through the trees that leads straight to the bus stop. My dad told me that all around the country are Indian trails—trails made by Native Americans when they used to live here. I like to believe this was their path, though I realize they were not going to the bus stop.

It may still technically be summer, but you can feel fall on its way. The leaves rustle above us and some flutter to the ground. Another great thing about Connecticut is that with all the big trees, there's always a creepiness to the weather. You always hear rustling from leaves or branches. The path is a bit of a scramble near the end. April skids on some rocks and catches herself before she falls. "Stupid," she said. I try to distance myself from her more, knowing she won't want for me to have noticed. "You're supposed to ask if I'm okay."

"Darned if I do," I said.

"What?" She faces me.

"Are you okay?" I ask sincerely, but nothing ever sounds sincere after someone tells you to say it.

"Like you care." She huffs, turns and continues walking, but this time she's even faster causing her backpack to bounce up and down, looking as if it's running after her. I take my time and pick up a shiny rock for my collection. At the end of the path are drooping tree branches we need to duck under and more than once we've gotten scratched. April is already in a circle with Cammy and Robbie. They're both middle-schoolers in our neighborhood. April and Cammy were in the same Girl Scout Troop. Cammy is always nice to me. Robbie is kind of crazy and gross but he's nice to my sister and me since we're his next-door neighbors.

"Watch this," he tells the girls, unwrapping piece after piece of Hubba Bubba, placing them in his mouth. His cheeks are stuffed and he chews loudly, trying to get a handle on all the gum. I can smell the grape flavor from where I stand near the path. He pulls at the gum, drawing it up and out of his mouth, patting it onto his nose and then around one eye. "Check it out. I'm the Monopoly guy," he says.

"Yuck," April says. Cammy giggles.

The gum falls from his face and onto the dirt. Robbie picks it up and layers it back into his mouth. The girls gasp. "Robbie, that gum has dirt all over it," Cammy says.

"Yum," he says. "I think there's even a worm in there. Delicious. Here, have some." He pulls out some from his mouth and puts it near Cammy's face. She shrieks and runs. Then he does the same to April. She blocks his hand with hers. "Quit it," she says.

He folds the gum back in his mouth. "Your loss."

Our buses come around the same time each day since April's school takes longer to get to. Today, the middle school bus comes first and they all get on without looking back at me. I can see my bus coming down the street so I walk to the curb once my sister's bus rolls away. "Darn," I hear from the path. I look back and my mom is there, still in her pajamas, forwarding the camera. "Keep forgetting to forward this thing. One more smile?"

I smile. She gives me one last hug before running away, suddenly aware that she's still in her pajamas. My bus passes me and stops a few feet away. A wave of heat hits me as soon as the bus driver opens the door. It's like an oven on wheels all year. You can never get the windows open without hurting at least one of your fingers on the clasps. The driver has her own personal fan blasting. I sit in the first open seat I see. The windows are fogging up so I draw a smiley face on mine.

"Hey," I hear someone say. "Hey." Frankie Myers. Actually, the Horrible Frankie Myers is his full name. I think he's supposed to be in sixth or seventh grade but keeps failing.

"Hi," I said, unsure of how to respond. The Horrible Frankie Myers has never picked on me before which I suppose was just a matter of time. I thought since I never say anything or do anything controversial, he would leave me alone. Jess Finkers always sits in the back of the bus and picks her nose. She's nice enough and I feel bad for her when Frankie the Horrible targets her, but, as my mom always says, don't give someone like that the ammunition.

"Did you eat too many hot dogs?" he asks me.

"No."

"Too many hot dogs with ketchup?" He starts laughing.

"No."

"Your hair looks like you ate too many hot dogs with ketchup."

I turn my back to him. I can feel my face flush. What he said is stupid. You can't get red hair from eating hot dogs with ketchup no matter how many you eat. If he says it again, I will tell him that.

"Look," he says to the boys sitting near him. "She ate so

many hot dogs with ketchup that her hair turned red. How disgusting." The boys near him don't say anything. They just watch me. "Hey." I don't turn this time. "Hey, do you have freckles, too?" I don't answer. I concentrate on the back of the seat in front of me. In the dark green leather of the seat, the word Thomas is embossed with a fancy T. The kid leans over to the side of my seat. "Yuck. You do have freckles. She does," he tells the boys. "You should wash your face."

I hate my freckles and I wish I could just wash them away but that doesn't work. I tried lemon juice which only stung my eyes. I hate my red hair but there's nothing I can do about that either. Grown-ups always tell me that one day I'll love it, and then it will turn brown. I hate this kid, too, and I just want to get to school.

"Don't you know freckles are ugly marks?" I stay quiet. "She has freckles." He laughs as if it's the funniest thing in the entire world that I have freckles. He stomps his feet and holds his stomach and laughs louder and louder. When we reach the school, I stand up the second the bus screeches to a halt. As I shuffle behind the other kids, I can feel his breath on my neck. I walk faster. He's trying to flat-tire my shoes. He succeeds and I stumble forward into the backpack of the girl in front of me. "Sorry," I mumble. I wipe tears from my eyes. Would this have happened if I were Emily? Maybe I'm not meant for school. Maybe I should just stay home with my mom all day. She's smart. She could teach me whatever I need to know.

I walk down the steps of the bus and he hurries behind me, pushing me aside and running into the school. I don't want anyone to see me fixing my shoes, since then other people will know I was picked on, so I walk through the hallways with the heels of my shoes under my feet. It causes me to walk slowly and makes it look as if I'm trying to walk in high heels which is hard to do in a sea of kids. Nurse Barb sees me and pulls me over to the side. "Fix your shoes, dear." I bend down and fix them. She has a funny way of being nice but mean at the same time. She calls everyone dear but her voice is gruff. If she likes you, she's pretty nice, but if she doesn't like you, she's mean. You can't really do anything about how she will feel about you. She's kind of like a dog. If your scent doesn't smell good to her, she just won't like you. I've heard her yell at some of the older kids for running in the hallway. I think she likes me, but I try to stay out of her way. "All set?" she asks. "Off to class then." I merge into the hall again.

I'm in classroom number 10, Miss Lotti's fifth-grade class. I was allowed to come in and meet Miss Lotti last week when she was setting up the room. My mom started arranging these special teacher meetings with me before I started second grade. I felt so nervous all of first grade, I would pretend I was sick all of the time or run away from the bus. It was pretty awful really. From what I remember, I would kick and scream all the way to the bus. Knowing that I did that completely embarrasses me now and I can't believe I would actually do it. However, I still get the feeling. Even now, inside of me, every part of me is kicking and screaming, telling me to just run home and try again tomorrow. When I see Miss Lotti, my heart stops pounding and I remind myself to take deep breaths. *I am not a nervous first-grader, I am not a nervous first grader.* Nope. I am a nervous fifth grader. Miss Lotti is beautiful with smooth skin, no freckles and arched eyebrows. She looks like Jaclyn Smith from *Charlie's Angels.*

Our classroom looks out into the small courtyard where we

plant flowers every spring. A bench dedicated to a former student is out there, too, but other than the day when we plant flowers, no one goes out into the courtyard except Janitor Henry.

"Hello Jenny." Miss Lotti stands outside her classroom and greets me. The Emily thing wouldn't have worked.

I know just where my desk is. I'm not near Jennifer, which is good and bad. If I had been right next to her, I may have felt shyer but maybe we would have become friends easier. Still, I feel some relief that I'm across the room. Less pressure.

"Look, look!" someone whisper-shouts. I look over and see Gwinnie with one hand covering her mouth and the other pointing to the hallway. Miss Lotti is talking with Mr. Housely, the gym teacher. He's handsome and fun. I don't think he's too old for Miss Lotti. "They're boyfriend and girlfriend." The class keeps sneaking over to look. "I think they are talking about a date!"

As Miss Lotti says goodbye to him, the kids all rush to their seats. The morning bell rings, she closes the door, and I remind myself not to be shy this year.

We spend the morning doing usual first-day of school set-up. I raise my hand once to try to shake off the old shy me. Miss Lotti smiles at me when I do and actually calls on me to answer the easy question of "Who knows our state capital?" It feels good to raise my hand, but I'm not sure that I'll do it again. I can't seem to get my heart to stop pounding.

At recess, I find my friend Anna and we swing on our usual swings, away from the chaos of the other kids. Today, the girls are chasing the boys, trying to tag them in freeze tag but the boys run away and won't freeze when the girls tag them. "Want to play two-square?" Anna asks me. I look at her closely. She's even quieter than me but she's lucky because I don't think it bothers her to not have friends as much as it bothers me. Anna is a friend, one of my only ones, but she is never allowed to play after school and she's even quiet with me. Usually, we just swing and sometimes she passes me notes folded in the shape of swans that say, "Do you like chocolate or vanilla? Circle one." Now she's asking if I want to go to the center of recess in front of everyone and start a game of two-square. Maybe she's trying to reinvent herself this year, too. I actually happen to love two-square. April and I used to play it all of the time at home since I was too shy to play it at school. In gym class, we've played it and I've done really well, surprising everyone.

"Okay," I say.

We lightly drag our feet along the dirt to stop the swings. When I stand up, I take a deep breath and push my shoulders up and back. Ready. As we walk toward the blacktop, I can't deny that I hope the bell rings, saving us from this moment of bravery. Anna moves quickly to pick up a ball while not disturbing anyone playing nearby, nor alerting them that we are playing two-square. "Okay?" she says.

"I guess so," I say.

Bounce, pass, bounce pass, bounce, pass. Soon, I forget about the kids around us. I notice that no one is even watching us. We actually start to giggle a bit. The ball bounces past Anna. She runs a silly, quiet girl run to get it.

"Can I play?"

I turn and see Jennifer and her two perfect friends looking at me. Her blond hair is feathered perfectly away from her face. Mine is sticking to my forehead. Jennifer looks like the girl that

Elliott kisses after releasing all of the toads in *E.T.* My dad loves that part because it shows a scene from *The Quiet Man.*

"Sure," I say, and move from my square.

When Anna returns, she finds Jennifer in my spot and another girl in hers. She hands the ball over to them. We stand and watch for a few minutes on the off chance they mean for us to play with them. Instead, they keep rotating between the three of them as players. When the ball rolls away, they ask us to fetch it for them noting that we're closer to it. Anna gets it for them. Then we make our way back to the swings without talking until the bell rings.

With the first actual day of school over, I cross my fingers and keep them crossed all the way through the halls and to the bus, wishing the Horrible Frankie Myers will not bother me on the bus ride home. I take a seat close to the bus driver. When he comes on, I look away, but it doesn't matter. He doesn't even notice me. Instead he heads to the back of the bus. Reinvention may be a superpower of the shy, but it's certainly not a quick one. My mom's car is waiting for me at the bus stop ready to take me over to Jennifer's house. She rolls down her window and starts waving at me as if I couldn't already see her in our blue station wagon. "Hi honey," she says. I get in the backseat. "How was the first day?"

"Fine."

"How was Miss Lotti?"

"Good."

"Did you get to know Jennifer at all?"

"Not really."

"Well, you will now," she said. "It'll be fun, I promise."

"Okay." Now I feel like looking out the window and not talking. Jennifer lives in one of the newer sections of our town so it takes some time to get there. I like riding in the car with my mom. She always has the radio turned on to an oldies station and she hums along to Elvis songs and gets so happy when they play the Beatles song, "Penny Lane."

"Let's see. It's number fifteen. All these houses look the same, huh?" my mother asks but I don't think she's really talking to me. "Eleven, thirteen, fifteen. Here we are." My mom pulls a compact from her purse and checks her face. "All set?"

We walk up to a house. It's big with a small yard and lots of flowers. The door opens before my mom even knocks.

"Hi Vicki." Through permed blond hair and sparkly makeup, Jennifer's mom smiles warmly at us. "Come in, come in. Aren't you a beauty?" She says this to me while lifting up my chin ever so gently. "She could be a model with this red hair, Vicki."

"I know but she's my sh . . . " my mom catches herself. "Oh, she can be anything she wants to be, this one."

"I bet she can," Jennifer's mom says. "Well, I bet you are eager to play. Jennifer! Come on down." She listens for any sound of her daughter as she ushers us inside the house. I've never seen an entryway so big and so white. The walls are bright white with a white bannister surrounding fluffy white-carpeted stairs, rounding up to a white hallway. The floor is a white tile next to rooms with bright white carpet. And then hanging on the wall is a white-framed giant mirror reflecting all of the whiteness. I imagine the evil queen watching through the glass, jealous at all the perfection. "You know, she's up there with Susie and they're probably listening to records. Do you know Susie? She goes to Howard Elementary, too. Well, go ahead upstairs to play. Vicki, come over and look at this cake I decorated. It looks positively terrible! I tried to make a grass-shade of green, but instead it looks like dirt. Let's eat my mistake, shall we?"

My mom gives me an encouraging smile so I walk upstairs. With bright lighting coming in through a giant window over the front door, I feel as if I'm ascending up to heaven with each shining, fluffy white step. Her stairs are those ones with no back: very modern and slightly scary in a nonsensical way. I know it would be impossible for me to somehow fall through the space between each step, yet my mind isn't so sure. The evil queen is probably watching to see if I fall so she can laugh her evil laugh. As I reach the top, it feels less like heaven and more like painful reality. All of the doors are closed. I do know Susie. In fact, she's one of the girls who played two-square today. But Susie always acts like she doesn't know me. I find Jennifer's room since there's a nameplate on her door hanging with a ribbon. I need to get one of those. I don't hear any music or talking so I tap on the door. No one answers. Now I don't know what to do. I knock. Again no one answers. I take a deep breath. I need to act like I'm not shy. I exhale and reach for the door, opening it just slightly. Two pairs of eyes look up at me. "Hi," I stammer. "I'm Jenny."

Jennifer and Susie look like one another but Jennifer's features are softer while Susie always holds her face in a mad, something-is-smelly way. They both have long blond hair and preppy Forenza pink sweaters over turned-up collars. I look down at my clothes, feeling completely awkward. "Hi," Jennifer says. Susie says nothing. They're both coloring pictures.

"Those are nice," I say. "I like to draw."

"It's a little rude to just walk in without knocking," Susie says.

I nod. "Sorry. What are you drawing?"

"We're making a book that lists all of our friends."

"Okay." I wait to be offered a piece of paper but they continue coloring as if I am not there. "I like the way you write your name." Jennifer looks at me. "On papers. At school. Jennifer is my name, too."

"You go by Jenny though."

"Mmmhmm."

"Yuck," Susie says. "Don't you think that's kind of babyish?"

"You can call me Emily," I stammer.

"Why?" asks Susie.

"It's my middle name."

Jennifer and Susie look at each other with their eyebrows raised. I'll have to practice that look later. They go back to drawing.

"Did you include Sylvie in your book?" Jennifer asks Susie.

"No, she and I aren't speaking now."

"I won't put her in mine then. Hey, Jenny, do you spell your name with an ie or a y?"

"A y," I say, hopeful that this means they are including me in their book.

"I think ie would be cooler," Susie says.

"Maybe I'll try that."

"Just because I said you should? That's strange."

Okay. Don't panic. Reinvention Commence. Be cool. I pull my hair away from my face and take a breath.

Jennifer looks like she's writing something. "All finished."

"Let me see," Susie said. Jennifer hands her the pages. "That's everyone. Help me with mine then."

Susie puts Jennifer's pages spread out on the floor in front of me. I scan them, trying to look like I'm not. My name isn't on them. I think of what April would do. In the corner, there's a record player. I decide April would walk over and look through the records next to it. I feel like leaving, but I need to try acting more like April. I do the shy-girl-trying-to-be-cool walk over to her records, swinging my hair a bit as I bob. I flip through them, wondering if I should have my own records.

I put them down and ask, "Can I draw, too?"

"Well, you could, but we need all the pages for our book," Jennifer says.

"Can I help you with your book?" I ask.

"Well, it's complicated and we don't want anyone to steal our idea," Jennifer says.

"I know what we can do," Susie says, smiling at Jennifer. "Why don't we play hide-n-seek? You two hide and I'll find you. Get going. One, two, . . . "

Jennifer and I jump up. Once we get outside her room, she tells me to hide downstairs while she hides upstairs. I agree and head downstairs into the living room. I hide under their piano. No lights are on in the room. A fluffy white cat peers at me from under the couch. The room is one of those fancy ones with the plastic covering on the royal-looking furniture, all white, and vacuum marks you can see all over the padded white carpet. I start wondering if maybe this room is off limits for kids, but I hear the door upstairs open so I stay where I am. I'm not convinced

Susie really wants to play this game but even if she doesn't come find me, it's better under here than in that bedroom. I hear my mom and Mrs. Pendel talking and laughing, with the occasional clinking of forks. Mrs. Pendel is complaining that Jennifer is growing up too fast and has started to be a handful. I know I'm a handful to my mom, but Jennifer and I are the exact opposites of handfuls. Mrs. Pendel has a handful of beautiful confidence with a book filled with friends. My mom has a handful of hiding under a piano in an off-limits room for a game of *Just Get Away From Us, You Loser*. After a few minutes pass, I lie down under the piano, confident that no one is coming to find me. The cat stretches out next to me. I hear the evil queen cackling as I begin to doze off. I wake to my mom's voice.

"Jenny? What are you doing?" I sit up and hit my head on the piano, sending the cat darting away. I rub my eyes, trying to adjust to the light that is now on in the room. "Were you sleeping?"

"We're playing hide-n-seek."

"Really?" Mrs. Pendel said with an edge to her voice. "I'm so sorry, Vicki. I have a feeling Jennifer wasn't being a very gracious hostess. Jennifer! Get down here now." This time, Jennifer does come when called. "Is this anyway to treat someone?"

"We are playing hide-n-seek. There you are. Good hiding."

"And how long have you been looking for her?" Mrs. Pendel asks.

Jennifer's face changes from innocent to annoyed. "Mother, I told you I didn't want to play with her today. Susie and I are working on something important."

"It's really okay," I say as I get out from under the piano.

My mom looks like she doesn't know what to do. "Olivia, we

have to leave anyway," my mom says finally. "Maybe we can try another time."

"I'm just . . . I'm so embarrassed. Yes, another time. Jennifer, go tell Susie she needs to go home now. You and I are having a talk. Tell Jenny goodbye."

"Bye Emily," Jennifer says and runs back upstairs.

When we leave, my mom puts her arm around my shoulders. She seems even sadder than me. "So, that didn't work out so great, huh?"

"No," I say. "It's okay though. I think they really just wanted to make their book."

"That's no excuse. Her mom is a sweetheart. Is Jennifer nice?"

"I think so. Everyone at school loves her."

"Well, maybe next time we can get together without Susie. Three girls is never a good number. How long were you under the piano?"

"Not too long."

"Really? So did they include you at first?"

"I don't really want to talk about it." I feel the tears start and I just don't want them to so I'm hoping my mom drops it. You know what's worse than being excluded? Having my mom see it. I always felt since forever, that my mom is super-connected to me. She always says she was just like me growing up though I find that hard to believe. If she was just like me though, I don't want her to have to feel like I do. One childhood of shyness and exclusion is really enough.

"Want to go out to Wolfie's, just the two of us?" she asks. Wolfie's is my favorite pizza place. I nod. I try shrugging away the thought that fifth grade will be like every other year in my life. I'm incapable of reinvention. It's easier to see the beauty in who you are when you don't have to interact with other people.

SUPERPOWER #2: THE ART OF LETTER WRITING

've noticed one very important fact about Frankie Myers: he's a shark. Some days, he's not hungry so he stays in the back of the bus. Other days, he's hungry and out for blood. Keeping out of his way is my main goal. When I get on the bus, I slouch in a seat so that my head doesn't appear over the back. This system has worked for now, but like all small fish, I live in constant fear of the shark attack. This morning goes pretty well, minus the flat tire he gives me in the hallway as he runs off laughing. No one saw though.

Miss Lotti told us today was the day we would get letters back from our pen pals. Last week, we filled out questions on an index card: *How old are you? Do you have brothers and/or sisters? Do you have pet(s)? What is your favorite animal? What is your favorite color?* I love a good questionnaire. Filling them out makes you feel interesting even when you're not. We brought pictures in from home to tape on our index cards. I looked through all of our photo albums. My mom gets annoyed when the school needs pictures of us since it always means we'll take one of the good ones and then she needs to search for the negative to replace it for her album if she remembers. I chose a picture of me from my birthday last summer.

Miss Lotti and her friend who teaches fifth grade in Chester Town, one town over from us, came up with this idea. They're going to use our questionnaires to match us with our pen pal. Then we'll write back and forth for the year and get together twice, once in the fall and once in the spring. It's as if this idea was made for me and me alone. I don't think I can say this with complete certainty, but I believe a superpower of shyness is the ability to write an excellent letter. Shy people are filled with things they never say. Words dance around in our minds all the time—all the witty remarks, correct answers and good advice we would say if we weren't so shy. If I could get away with writing letters for everything, life would be so easy. In letters, I can sound amusing and smart. In letters, shyness can't come through as easily. Miss Lotti walks around the class, handing out index cards like the ones we made about ourselves. My legs are actually bouncing as I wait for her to come to me. "Excited, Jenny?" Miss Lotti says and smiles. "Here you go."

I look at the card. A girl with long, wavy light brown hair practically jumps out of the picture toward me. She has brown eyes and is wearing a baseball shirt. I'm not sure how to describe it exactly, but it looks like she has a lot of energy. She has one older brother, two dogs, likes the color green, and loves horses. Her name is Lizzie Cray. Lizzie is a good name. I haven't met a Lizzie yet. Miss Lotti instructs us to tear out a piece of writing paper from our journals and write a letter to our pen pals. I start right away. I've already thought all about what to say back to her.

Dear Lizzie,

My name is Jenny. I love horses, too. My mom won't let us get a dog because she says she'll have to clean up after it all of the time. I live in Apple Hill with my mom, dad, and sister. My dad says if my sister and I behave, we might get an Atari 2600 for Christmas. For Halloween, I wanted to go as E.T., but my mom said she doesn't know how to make that. Then she found a pattern. I hope I don't have to wear a coat over my costume. Do you like school? What's your favorite thing to do in the summer?

My birthday is in the summer which makes me younger than most of the kids in my class. Have you ever been to the Plaster Funhouse? It's this place where you can pick out something ceramic to paint and then they glaze it for you. My mom took me there for my birthday. I found this little ceramic basket with two dogs. I painted it as realistic as I could. Sometimes I paint things to be unrealistic like a pink horse or something. I just felt like making these dogs look real. Maybe they look like your two dogs if you put them in a basket. We can't go to the Plaster Funhouse that much since my mom says it's too much money. What will you be for Halloween?

Love,
Your pen pal,
Jenny Watts

I want to write more, but I figure I need to wait until I see her note back to me to make sure she likes me first. I love everything about this idea. I've always wanted a pen pal. Sometimes I write to my cousin Terry but she's a teenager. Usually I write her once, she writes back, then I write and then I won't hear from her. She says she's not much for writing but always tries when it comes to me. To have a pen pal that has to write you back and is your age and just a town over is much better. Plus, when we get in middle school, Lizzie and I will be in the same school. I'll have a best friend by sixth grade, which will be really helpful. Maybe once Jennifer sees that I'm good friends with a girl like Lizzie, she'll like me more. Then all three of us will be best friends. I feel myself beaming. I walk over to Miss Lotti to hand in my note.

"Miss Lotti?"

"Yes, Jenny?"

"Are we allowed to take the postcards home?"

"Sure.

I walk back to my desk and carefully slide Lizzie's postcard into my desk. When I get home, I find two pieces of blue construction paper and tape three sides together and with a black marker, I write, *Notes from my Pen Pal.* As the weeks go by, I compile more cards from Lizzie and keep them in my folder. I can tell she's not much of a letter writer, which could mean she's not very shy which is good.

Dear Jenny,

Too bad about the dog. We had to leave our dogs when we moved here over the summer. I miss them so much. Hopefully we'll get them back soon once we're settled. I haven't seen E.T. I hope I can soon. Maybe we can see it together. For Halloween, I'm going as a ghost. Write back as soon as you can.

Love,
Lizzie

Dear Lizzie,

What is it like having an older brother? A ghost costume is perfect. I won't spoil it, but in E.T., they pretend to dress Elliott's sister up as a ghost but it's really E.T. He's an extra-terrestrial, which means alien, which is why the movie is called E.T. for short. He needs to get back to his planet but he also becomes best friends with this boy Elliott. I hope I didn't ruin the movie for you. Maybe my mom can take us to see it one day.

What is it like living in Chestnut Hill? Where did you live before moving there? Is your teacher nice? I love Miss Lotti. Since she's best friends with your teacher, I bet your teacher is nice and pretty, too. Is your name short for Elizabeth or is it just Lizzie? My name is short for Jennifer.

When I grow up, I think I want to be a teacher or a farmer. I think being a librarian might be fun, too.

Love,
Jenny

P.S. Do you think freckles are ugly?

Dear Jenny,

We moved here from Oregon. It's very different here. I like Chestnut Hill so far I guess. Having a brother is okay. He's busy with school and sports but he's always nice to me and takes care of me a lot. I didn't understand much about what you were saying about E.T., but now I want to see it even more. Do you go to lots of movies? I think I'll tell people I'm E.T. dressed as a ghost then. Then people will think I have seen the movie. What is it like having an older sister? My name is just Lizzie. My mom named me after a character in a book. She tried reading it to me once, but it was written a long time ago and hard to follow.

Love,
Lizzie

P.S. I wish I had freckles. I do not think they're ugly at all. Here's a picture of my mom. See her freckles? I love freckles. I don't have any but if I did I wouldn't think they were ugly.

P.P.S. Please return the picture.

Dear Lizzie,

Having an older sister was more fun when we were younger. Do you have a lot of friends? What do you do at recess? I play four-square with my friends and sometimes swing. We have a swing set in my backyard. It's a little rusty but it still works great. If you swing too high though, the whole thing bops up and down. It's kind of scary but fun. Have you ever had a mean boy bother you? Your mom is so pretty. I like her freckles. I made sure I didn't bend the picture at all.

Love,
Jenny

Dear Jenny,

At recess, I chase the boys around the blacktop. I'm faster than they are. So, I guess I like to run. I've never played four-square. Mean boys don't bother me. I'm tougher than they are, too. Let me know if you need help. My brother taught me these things called pressure points. You get someone there, and then they can't move. No more mean boys. Mean people are the worst. Oh, headlocks are good, too. I'll show you when we meet.

Love,
Lizzie

SUPERPOWER #3: INVISIBILITY CLOAKS

As a shy girl, I have the power to be invisible. I often hear, "Oh, I didn't see you there." Last year, I had the job of messenger for my class. Every morning, I had to go down to the office to pick up any messages they had for my teacher and deliver the absentee list. I loved the job for the fact that I could leave my class and walk in the hallway by myself. It's really peaceful when it's not full of kids. I would take my time getting to the office, looking at the artwork outside each class, taking a drink from the water fountain or skipping between classroom doors so they wouldn't get mad that I wasn't walking. I hated the office part though. Two women work in the front section of the office: Mrs. Leinowitz and Mrs. Kramer. They're who my mom calls whenever I'm sick and not coming to school. They keep her on the phone for ridiculously long lengths of time when she's just telling them I have a stomachache.

No matter what I do, at least once a week, I would scare them. They wouldn't hear me open the door to the office and walk back to the mailboxes so on days when they hadn't seen me come in, they would jump in the air when I would go to leave the office. "Jesus, Mary and Joseph! We need to put a bell on you or something. I've known ants louder than you!" they say. I tried clearing my throat, opening the office door as loud as I could, shuffling the mail about. I would even say hello, but they would be busy and not hear me. At first I felt embarrassed as if I was doing something wrong, but after the fifth time, I was irritated. Stop comparing me to ghosts and ants. At least, compare me to a spy or something cool. I kind of liked the spy idea and would consider it further as a career choice. Instead of trying to make myself known, I went the other way and tried to get in and out of the office without any of them seeing me just as a spy would. It became a game for me. Could I get in and out without them seeing me and could I gather any interesting information? Throughout the year, I learned more and more about Mrs. Leinowitz's bad back and lazy husband and Mrs. Kramer's four-year-old granddaughter than I ever wanted to know. I don't think anyone would pay for this intel, but all spies need to start somewhere. Plus, it's where I figured out the invisibility superpower and its many uses.

I can create invisibility whenever necessary. For the most part, it works. I can't figure out the Frankie Myers breach yet. In other areas of life, my invisibility works pretty well. Let's say a teacher asks a question that I don't know the answer to. The trick isn't to simply look down or away from the teacher. No, the trick is to make yourself invisible. I do that by pretending I'm writing down something very important that they just said. You can't just look down at your paper. That makes you a sitting target. You can't make eye contact with the teacher either. It's too easy for them to call on you then. Writing what the teacher just said, no matter what they just said, gives the impression to the teacher that what they said was so important that I needed to write it down. It's my re-direction invisibility tactic. Everyone likes to think what they say is important. When a teacher sees you writing, they no longer see you, they see their worth. Their wisdom is scratched into my notebook forever.

Halloween is somewhat a problem. I know it seems like Halloween is the perfect opportunity to be invisible with all of the costumes and whatnot, but it's actually tricky. To be invisible on Halloween takes some thought. Costumes by their very nature, draw attention to the wearer. You have to make sure it's the right attention, which is really no attention. We're allowed to wear our costumes to school. If you don't wear one, everyone will think you're making a statement. You'll still have to walk in the costume parade through the school, but you stand out as someone who either thinks they are too cool so you really better be that cool, or you're lazy, or you are too insecure with yourself to dress up and have fun. I need to strike the right balance for a costume. I don't want to be the same thing as everyone else, which creates comparisons. I don't want to be anything too fancy or too unusual nor too drab, babyish, uncool, or stupid.

However, I forgot to communicate any of this to my mom. So, the night before Halloween, she's sitting down, ready to put her feet up for the night with visions that I can just wear my E.T. costume to school the next day. When I come downstairs to remind her that we can't wear masks to school, she curses. She quickly apologizes. Up until last year, we could wear masks but then some kid tripped in the parade causing the girl in front of him to fall down as well. She chipped two teeth. Her parents are lawyers so when they petitioned to ban masks, my dad called it the beginning of the Bubble Wrap Kids. The stories of his childhood are all told with a purpose of reminding us how wimpy kids are nowadays. Apparently, back in his day, he walked ten miles to school, all uphill in pelting sleet with no coat and wolves chasing him as he carried twenty pound bags of sand just because. And on Halloween, they wore masks, gosh darn it. My dad didn't care enough about the fight to save Halloween at school though. Neither did the principal. He just agreed with the lawyers, banning masks forever.

With lots of effort, my mom drags herself from the couch and I follow her upstairs. My closet doors don't really close anymore since I have so much stuff packed in there, but they don't really open all the way either since I have so much piled in front of them. My mom yanks the doors open and I can tell it's all she can do not to yell at me about how I need to clean. She exhales deeply. "Here we go," she says and bends down, digging through stuffed animals, old craft projects, construction paper, shoes that don't fit, etc. "How about this?" She holds her arm out with my butterfly costume from two years ago.

"Um." I really don't want to put her through anymore, but that thing just won't fit nor will it pass my costume tests. It's way too babyish.

"You could wear those and all green clothes and go as a grasshopper or the Grinch or a leprechaun."

Why is she on this green thought? I see nothing green around her. "No," I say.

"You don't have much choice at this point." She sits on top

of the new pile she's just made of all my stuff.

"Here," April says, throwing her witch costume from two years ago on my bed.

"Oh, I forgot about this one. Perfect. How is that, Jenny?"

Yes! If April wore it, it must be cool. I try it on. The black baggy dress is a little big, but I don't care. Classic Halloween outfits are the perfect way to blend in and remain invisible. My mom kisses my forehead and tells me goodnight as she heads back downstairs.

In the morning, my mom pins the dress and instructs me how to arrange it when I need to use the bathroom at school so I won't prick myself. I put on my coat and gloves and witch's hat and walk to the bus stop behind April. The middle schoolers don't wear costumes to school anymore. April was allowed to trick-or-treat with her friends last year, with no parents. I didn't realize that that happened when you got older; that you could outgrow certain things, like trick-or-treating with your family. I like going around the neighborhood with my dad. He plays tennis so he has shiny tracksuits in yellow and blue. When he was in a meeting all the way in Arizona last year, he was the only person who wasn't a smoker, so the smokers gave him a gas mask to wear during the meetings as a joke. Now he wears the gas mask and depending on the color of the tracksuit he wears, he's either Darth Banana or Darth Blueberry for Halloween each year.

Today, since some of the costumes are too difficult to move down the aisle, the front seats of the bus are packed with princesses, monsters, and animals. I take the first seat I see in the middle of the bus. Before the bus leaves my stop, a plastic skeleton mask jumps out at me. I shriek. It's him. Of course he wouldn't follow the rules of no masks. "Ha, got you." He pushes me over in my seat to sit next to me. "Why didn't you dress up?" he asks.

I know I'm walking into something bad here, but I take his question to heart. "I'm a witch."

"I know, but why didn't you dress up?" He laughs a fake laugh where he slaps his knees and holds his stomach all designed to make people around us hear him. "I get it. You knew you didn't need a costume to look scary. It's good to go as yourself but you could tell people you're going as something like, like, Little Miss Ugly Freckle Face or something. Are you going to cry?" I'm trying my best not to. "Look, guys. I'm making a witch cry. *She's melting. She's melting.* I don't want any melted witch on me. See you later, Freckle Face." He laughs and then moves to the back of the bus. I lean my head against the window and take some deep breaths. I won't cry. I won't cry.

I walk into school, focusing on not crying. When I see Miss Lotti dressed like a butterfly, the tears just start pouring out. She doesn't ask why I'm crying. She just hugs me and lets me cry for a few moments. Her perfume smells like roses. Some of my classmates walk past us into the room. Miss Lotti kneels down and holds my face in her hands. "Are you okay, Jenny?" I nod, knowing I need to move past the sadness now. She wipes the tears from my face. "What happened? Did you fall? Did you forget something?"

"Someone called me ugly," I say.

"Oh no." She hugs me again. "Well, whoever said that doesn't know what they're talking about. You're beautiful inside and out. Come into class. I have a surprise for you." We walk in together.

She helps me hang up my coat and hands me a tissue. "I have a surprise for you but you need to keep it a secret, okay? Follow me." She keeps her arm around me as we navigate through a minefield of questions from my classmates. She stays steady answering each one with: "*just a minute,*" "*not now, no,*" and "*yes, you may go to the bathroom.*" She sits in her chair with a big sigh of relief. "Okay, now, where is it?" She looks through a pile of papers on her desk. "Oh yes. So, your pen pal received special permission to send you another note this week. The other kids don't have one, so please don't tell them or else I'll have to hear about the injustice of it all." She smiles at me as she hands me a note.

I wait until I'm at my desk to look at it without anyone noticing.

Dear Jenny,

Happy Halloween! What do you call a tired skeleton? Lazy bones.

Love,
Your pen pal,
Lizzie

It's the best letter ever because it wasn't an assignment. She wanted to send me another note. This time, the sadness really leaves me. I imagine us being best friends forever. I pull out a piece of paper and write, *Lizzie and Jenny, Friends Forever.* It feels good to write it. I've seen other girls stick these papers on notes to each other. Now I feel included in the friend club—the club where girls have best friends. With the sadness gone, my mind can think clearly. The best way to be invisible on the bus is to not take the bus ever again. Or at least until next year when Frankie fails fifth grade again and remains on the elementary school bus.

The doorbell begins ringing before my dad and I are ready to go trick-or-treating. We normally don't get too many trick-or-treaters up here since people don't want to climb up the hill just to hit two houses, ours and Robbie's. Our two other neighbors are older and they keep their lights off during Halloween. Mrs. Echelon lives in the first house on our street. Since she likes to go to bed early, she usually drops off some butterscotch candy for my sister and me during the day. Mr. Brechlman who lives right next door to us just doesn't like Halloween or kids very much. Word gets out quickly in a neighborhood about what streets are the best or who is giving out full-size candy bars or who is handing out raisins. With the first two houses on our street not participating, most people decide it's a waste of time and head back down to the normal neighborhood streets. This year, however, Robbie put a sign down at the bottom of the hill with an arrow. The sign says, *Come up for treats if you dare.* Then he made tombstones and skeleton bones out of cardboard and placed them along the way. Once my mom saw the sign, she quickly ran to the store to get more candy. She actually came home with the good stuff, too. I think she likes the idea of stepping things up like Robbie. April left without getting ready here. She's going to get ready at Cammy's house. She brought two pillowcases with her to fill with candy.

Darth Blueberry and I go to Robbie's house first to check out the creepy sounds of a woman's scream and creaking doors coming from there. My dad signals for me to be quiet and points toward the bushes. Instead of going to the door, he starts walking over the lawn making his way to the side of the house. When he gets closer to the front bushes, he starts to run. "Boo!"

"Oh my God!" Robbie falls out of the bushes with a gorilla mask on his face. "Mr. Watts. You almost gave me a heart attack." My dad is laughing in his gas mask, which makes for a funny wheezing noise.

"Terrorizing the neighborhood, Robbie?" my dad asks.

"Always." Robbie takes his mask off. "Want some candy? We've got lots this year." He jumps over the bushes, opens the door to his house and grabs a large skull filled with candy. He dumps fistfuls into my bag. "You guys should come back later. My dad is out buying some dry ice. It's going to look really spooky."

"Oh, hi Steve," Mrs. Kred said, coming to the door. Mrs. Kred looks ridiculously tiny in her house full of huge boys. "Jenny, let me see you. You look great! What is that anyway?"

"I'm E.T.," I say through the mask. It's already starting to itch.

"Lovely. Well, next year, you'd make such a beautiful ballerina." Mrs. Kred has four boys so whenever she sees April or me, she seems in awe of us. Like if she saw us playing on our swing set, she would come by and compliment us on how nice and quiet we were. I get the feeling she wants to play with us like we're dolls. My mom didn't see much of her, but when she would invite Mrs. Kred over for coffee, Mrs. Kred would enter the house and exhale deeply. She always remarked about how quiet the house was and how the walls didn't have any holes or bang marks anywhere. Mr. and Mrs. Kred seemed a lot older than my parents and they didn't really seem like parents, more like exhausted adults. It was as if the older boys got all the parenting and now they just didn't have any more left. Robbie gets in trouble in school every year, and they have to leave work to go down to meet with the principal and everything. I don't think they have the energy to do much about it. In fact, Robbie told us that they usually take him out for ice cream after these meetings.

"Did Robbie get you some candy, sweetie?" Mrs. Kred reaches over Robbie's shoulder and grabs another handful of candy out of the skull and put it in my bag.

"More kids are coming, I have to hide." Robbie pushes the skull to his mom and ushers her inside as she sent us a wave goodbye. "Mom, flip over the tape, fast!" He moves past us back into the bushes. "No more sneaking up on me, Mr. Watts."

My dad and I hear screams from the trick-or-treaters at Robbie's house as we make our way down the hill to the rest of the neighborhood. The best thing about trick-or-treating with my dad is how much he loves it. Each year we try to go to more houses than the year before which is difficult because my dad loves talking with everyone. Last year we stopped at Evergreen Mills Drive so this year we at least want to go a few houses past that one. We have one rule: when we get our favorite candy, we're allowed to eat it right away. My mom has one rule for us, too: when we get her favorite candy, Twix bars, we need to leave it for her. Twix are a rare Halloween treat. His favorite is Snickers and mine is a plain Hershey bar. When we reach the house of his tennis friend, Mr. Freeley, the high school music teacher, I know we'll be there a while. I stand behind my dad, looking through my candy bag as they talk and talk.

"You hear I'm directing the community play again this year?" Mr. Freeley asks my dad. "*Bye, Bye Birdie*. I did it about three years ago for *Annie Get Your Gun* and now they've asked me back."

"I didn't know you were so talented," my dad says. "Certainly can't tell from your tennis game."

"My tennis game is going to look even worse since I'll spend all my time creating this masterpiece," Mr. Freeley says. "Hey, we need lots of townspeople including elementary age kids." He shrinks down to my level and speaks to me as if I'm about three years old. "It's a play about how a small-town girl wins a chance give a famous singer one last kiss on the *Ed Sullivan Show* before he leaves for the army. It's based on Elvis Presley. How about it, Jenny? Want to be one of the townspeople and then we can convince your dad to audition, too?"

Before I answer, which to be honest was just going to be a shrug, my dad answers for me. "She's my shy one. I don't think she's seeking any limelight." He laughs. I cringe. However, I am more relieved at not having be in a play than mad at my dad. I always hear those stories about how these famous actors are really shy and then they got into acting. Like Lucille Ball. She has red hair and is apparently really shy. I don't buy it though. Just because you say you're shy because maybe you aren't very talkative or get slightly nervous in front of people, doesn't make you truly shy. A truly shy person would never even think of getting up on stage in the first place. I would love it though. Secretly, I would love it if I were a famous actress or singer. I suppose everyone dreams that though. What if my dad did say yes? What if I had to do it and it turns out I was good at it?

The candy is really getting to me. I feel jittery but tired. We drag ourselves to five more promising houses past our goal. By the time we trek back to our house, my feet feel heavy and my eyes are closing. The hill to our house feels never-ending. My dad carries my bag. My mom quickly changes me out of my costume, shoves my toothbrush in my mouth and puts me to bed. I dream that night that Lucille Ball sits me down and tells me she really is shy, then we have to stop the conveyer belt of chocolates.

If my invisibility fails when needed, avoidance works. I decide the best way for me not to have to see Frankie Myers on the bus is to avoid the bus. I'm not exactly sure how to do this. I can't walk to school or ride my bike since it's too far and I'd have to cross a major road. Faking a stomachache is my only option. Elliot in E.T. held a thermometer to a light bulb so his mom thought he had a fever, but I don't need to stay home all day; I just need to miss the bus. When my mom calls for me to wake up, I stay in bed. The day after Halloween is an easy one. Everyone has a stomachache but my plan could backfire as my mom may insist I ate too much candy. I'll have to take it up a notch. I pull the covers up over my face and rub my cheeks so I'll look flushed. After a few more calls to me, she comes up the stairs.

"Jenny, what are you doing still in bed?"

"I don't feel good." Commence the shivers. Most fevers make you shiver.

She feels my head and hands. "You're a little warm. What's wrong?"

"My stomach," I say in a weak voice. "And, I feel so tired, like my arms won't move." I lift my arms and let them flop back to bed and return to shivering. Should I add chattering teeth? Probably overkill.

"It's probably all the candy you ate. Why don't you try getting dressed and see if you feel better." She says it as if it's a question, but it's not. I sit up slowly, holding my stomach as she watches. Whenever I fake a stomachache, a strange thing happens: my stomach will start to hurt. I'm not sure why, but at that moment, my stomach does hurt. My mom pulls out some clothes for me. I can tell she's not sure how sick I am and this is always her test. Unless we have fevers or are throwing up, April and I have to get up and get dressed, then we have to "see how we feel." I swear my ear could come detached from my head and my parents would still tell me to get up and see how I felt. The thought of having to see Frankie makes my stomach hurt a little more. I put on my clothes and then sit back on my bed, acting like it's taken all of my energy. My parents never believe me about stomachaches now anyway. I faked too many in first grade when I didn't want to go to school. I don't exactly remember why except that school felt like it was too much for me.

"You really don't feel good?" my mom asks, looking closely at me.

"Maybe if I can just rest a few more minutes and then you can take me to school later?" I've never played this card beforehand. It sounds really reasonable to my mom, I can tell.

"Okay. Well, lie back down then. I'll check on you in a few

minutes."

I crawl back under my covers and instantly fall back asleep. When I hear my mom coming up the stairs later, I wake up. I've definitely missed the bus at this point.

"Oh, you're awake," she says when she pokes her head into my room. "How are you feeling?"

"Much better. I can go to school now." Truthfully, once I miss the bus, I'd rather just call it a day and not go to school but then my parents will worry.

"Oh." My mom looks at me, feels my hands and forehead. "Okay. Well, come down and I'll make you some breakfast then."

I'm not sure how many days I can fake a stomachache to get a ride to school but I must say it feels great to sleep in and have my mom drive me. When I try it again the next day, it doesn't work as well. When I start crying though, my mom believes me again that my stomach must hurt and she lets me go back to bed. After sleeping longer, I wake up and get dressed again and announce that I'm ready for school.

"Sit down, sweetie," my mom says and starts making my breakfast. "Is something bothering you at school?"

"No."

"Sometimes when I'm nervous about something, my stomach hurts. Are you nervous about anything?"

"No." I don't know why I don't tell her. I guess I think she'll tell me to tell the principal and I don't want to do that because then it will be a big deal. "I just like you driving me to school."

"You don't like the bus anymore?"

"No. Maybe you can drive me to school every day and then pick me up, too."

"Hmm. Is there anyone being mean to you on the bus?"
I can't help it, I just start crying.
"Who is it?"
"No one."
"If you tell me if someone is bothering you, I can help."
I shake my head. I want to be the kid that rides the bus and everything is normal, but I'm not. I faked stomachaches in first grade, I don't make friends easily and I'm shy. I hear it in my head all day long. No matter how much I try to change it, it doesn't change. I think at least going to school even if it's not on the bus should just be seen as an accomplishment. I mean, does anything good ever come out of riding the school bus? Usually, the bus ride is where friendships break down over who sits with who or kids get yelled at for standing up. Favorite action figures get lost, rolling around on the floor forever. A glove or hat gets left, never to be seen of again. The bus is really not that great, nor useful as a growing experience. My parents didn't take the bus and they turned out fine. I know my parents aren't going to see it that way for long. I'll take what I can get for now though. When I'm older, I think this invisibility thing will work more in my favor. As for now, I have too many people expecting me to do too many expected things. When I'm a super spy, I'll ride school buses and turn bullies in to the principal before they can bother anyone.

SUPERPOWER #4: HOPEFULNESS

I think most shy people are full of hopefulness. I don't think we're a glass-half-empty sort of tribe. We live in hopefulness. I live in hope of those small moments where someone may say something nice about me or that I will be recognized for being intelligent or beautiful or something cool. This hopefulness often throws off my ability to read situations though. My mom takes me to and from school and I love it. I hum in my seat and look out the window. I think this situation is perfect. Though I was hopeful, I knew this arrangement would not last. Moms don't like when their kids act differently one day. After two weeks of this arrangement, she picks me up from school during math class and we go see a friend of hers, Dr. Sedac. I was actually excited to meet this friend after she and my dad told me about him. They acted as if they were jealous of my appointment. Plus, what kid didn't like to get out of school during the middle of the day? When I handed Miss Lotti my mother's note about my early dismissal, she told me to just remind her when the time came. I felt so official.

I watched the clock most of the day. When it was finally 1:30, I raised my hand right as Miss Lotti was talking. She looked at the clock and nodded to me. As I packed up, I felt everyone looking at me, wishing they could pack up, too. Now, my parents didn't exactly prepare me for this "friend" of theirs. I thought my mom and I would go to his house and maybe he lived on one of the old farms and had horses. He would be like my old kindergarten teacher, Mr. Heschel who I loved but he left in the middle of the school year for some reason. Mr. Heschel used to ride a magic bubble to school and danced around the classroom and played the guitar at music time. Dr. Sedac would give me ice cream sandwiches and let me brush the horses. I have no idea why I built up the visit to Dr. Sedac's so much when all my parents had told me was along the lines of, "You'll just love him. He's really good to talk to." I should have studied their faces a bit more. They had that look they used when they're hoping I'll like something, like spinach. "This spinach is fantastic, you just have to try it. It tastes like candy." Then they put it on my plate and watch me with their mouths in a huge smile, but their eyes look stern, warning me to just say I like the spinach.

I walk down the hallways to the school office. I hear teachers in their classrooms talking to their students. I don't want to be late, so I jog in between classroom doors and then walk in front of each door so I won't get in trouble for running. When I walk into the office, my mom is already there. "Here's my girl," she says.

"I didn't even see her come in!" Mrs. Kramer remarks.

Dr. Sedac did not live on a farm. Well, if he did, we didn't go there. We see him in a two-story office building off the main road. His office is on the bottom floor. The building smells musty. When we push open the door to his office, the door creaks open to reveal a worn-out carpet, a bubbling fish aquarium in need of a cleaning and hard seats shaped in a U.

"I guess we just sit here." There is a reception desk but no one is there. My mom and I sit next to each other and I feel the specialness of the day wear away. As if my mom can sense this, she pats my knee and smiles at me but I can tell she's nervous. "I just thought maybe we could speak to someone to figure out how to make you happier at school and with the bus." I don't say anything. While my baseless hopes about spending today riding horses didn't pan out, at least I feel a new hope—that this Dr. Sedac will have answers for me. We wait for ten minutes listening to the bubbling of the aquarium. The door on the other side of the room squeaks open and a man with a super curly perm peeks at us. He motions with his hand to come in. My mom stands up to come, but he stops her. "Let's start with Jennifer first," he says. "Then you and I will talk."

My mom turns and bends down to look me in the eye. "That sound okay?"

I nod, not sure what any of this means but I feel as if I've done something wrong. Dr. Sedac's office has a huge desk facing two chairs. His chair is faded leather on wheels. He sits down with a sigh and knocks the chair backward a bit, reclining. "Please, sit," he says.

I sit on the edge of the chair near the door. "So, Jennifer, do you know why you are here today?"

I shrug—a move April would do.

"Do you see a doctor for check-ups?" he asks.

I nod.

"Okay, well, that doctor helps to keep your body healthy. I'm a doctor to keep your mind healthy." He picks some lint off of his black pants, which I soon discover is his favorite hobby during my time here. "So, is there any reason you can think of that your mom may want you to be here talking to me?"

"No," I say barely above a whisper.

"Have you been having any problems at school?"

I shake my head.

"Your parents tell me you are pretty quiet in school. Do you not feel comfortable speaking?"

"I guess not," I say. I look down at my fingers.

"Your parents believe you need to gain some confidence. Do you know what confidence is?"

I nod.

"How would you describe it?"

"What?"

"Confidence?"

"Um, it's speaking in school," I mutter.

"Sort of. It's believing you have something important to share. And believing in yourself."

"Okay."

"Would that sound good?"

"Sure." Yes! Tell me how to do that!

"So we'll just talk here each week and figure out a way that you can gain more confidence. I think we'll meet at least twice a week initially. Anything you want to talk about?"

"No." The way he said my case required twice a week is turning over in my head. Am I a really serious case? What does that mean? Am I worse than other kids who only require seeing him once a week?

And then we just sit there, minutes ticking by. Why won't he just tell me what to do? Does he have a pamphlet of how to be cool or something for me to read? He keeps picking lint off of his pants and I stare at my fingers. I notice the carpet is a scene of pinecones and trees. I didn't know they made carpets like that. I start daydreaming. The wall behind him turns into a giant tree with long branches. It wraps itself around Dr. Sedac and grabs him, pulling him away from his comfortable chair and lint extraction. After the tree takes him away, it disappears, leaving me alone in the room. A bell rings. I smile a little.

"Your homework for this week is to raise your hand during class to answer one of your teacher's questions tomorrow. Got it? Okay, go out and send your mom in. It was nice meeting you, Jennifer," he says as he brushes off his pants.

I jump up and leave. My mom gives me a thumbs up as she goes into his office and they shut the door leaving me in the waiting room with the fish by myself. A yellow triangle fish swims through the green water. I watch him. How lucky that they never have to worry about being anything else besides fish. I doubt they see doctors who work with them to stop being shy. Lots of fish in aquariums seem shy. They always swim away and hide if you tap at the tank. No one thinks there's anything wrong with that. It's merely survival instincts. It's strange to know my mom and Dr. Sedac are in there talking about me and how my case requires lots of meetings. Or maybe, they're sitting in silence, too. The main door opens with a push and a short, plump woman comes in with grocery bags in each hand.

"Oh, hello dear," she says as she struggles to get herself and the bags through the door. The break in the quietness feels jarring. And this woman is all noise and movement. "Is your mom in with Dr. Sedac?" she asks as she sits behind the reception desk. "That's right. You must be Jennifer, our 2:00 appointment. Tell me, is it Jennifer or Jen or Jenny?"

"Jenny."

"Well, hello Jenny. I'm Mrs. Sims. Want to help me fill the candy jar here?"

"Okay." I walk over and she hands me one grocery bag filled with candy corn and another filled with Hershey's kisses.

"We can use this dish for the kisses and this one for the candy corn. They had a sale on all of the Halloween candy so I just had to get some. Of course, we should probably check it to make sure it's still good." She winks at me.

I open the bag of candy corn and pour it into the jar. Then I fill the dish with Hershey's Kisses.

"Go ahead and take some, dear. Need to make sure it's fresh after all." She reaches in a drawer and takes out a puzzle box with a small .25 cents sticker attached to it. "Any good at these things?"

I take the box. It's a 500-piece puzzle of the state of Connecticut. "I'm okay," I say. These are the people I love. The ones who don't let you be shy and aren't judging you. And they give you candy.

"Let's set it up over at the coffee table." She brings the box and the jar of candy over to the table and lowers herself on to the floor without groaning like adults normally do. Maybe it's not a farm with horses, but a parentless room with what is probably a trustworthy adult telling you to eat candy is pretty good.

"What school do you attend?" she asks as she pours pieces from the box, searching for ends.

"Howard."

"Oh lovely. I know Principal Jackman. She's wonderful, isn't she?"

I nod.

"Were you nervous to see Dr. Sedac today?"

"A little," I say as I find two corner pieces.

"Well, I always tell him to be less intimidating to the children but he doesn't listen. Men never do." She laughs.

I smile. I never know what to do when adults let you in on news as if you are an adult, too. It's refreshing but really unfamiliar. We spend the next twenty minutes trying to put together the puzzle which neither of us is any good at and eating chocolate which we both excel at.

When we hear Dr. Sedac's voice, Mrs. Sims winks at me, stands up and returns to behind her desk and opens a file.

Technically, Dr. Sedac said I needed to raise my hand tomorrow. Tomorrow is the field trip to meet our pen pals though. So, I really won't have much of a chance anyway. We're going to the Old Cider Mill. There's not much to do there now but it's free and they have picnic tables. Right after Halloween, they stop making cider and they move the few animals from the petting zoo to somewhere else. I'm not even sure if we can tour the cider mill. I went a few times with my mom just to get the cider donuts they make. We buy a dozen at a time and have to stop ourselves at eating two each in the car on the way home. Field trips are strange. The teachers dress in jeans and sweatshirts.

Everyone packs a lunch and has to wear the same colors. Miss Lotti decided on our school's color: purple. So in our classroom before we leave, we are a sea of dark purples, light purples, dark blues, tan shirts with purple lettering or just plain white shirts. It doesn't matter since we're going to be outside all day and unless you already have a purple winter coat, no one will see our shirts. I am the first person to get on the bus, which means I'm sitting by myself. Every girl walks right past me. It's okay though, my legs are shaking with excitement. This is the moment. I'll have a best friend soon. I have those worries of her not liking me once she sees I'm not popular, but overall, my hopefulness is completely winning. My letters were really good.

Our bus pulls into a parking spot next to another bus. "They're here," Miss Lotti says. She jumps up and claps. "This is going to be so fun. Here we go."

We file off the bus, unsure of what to make of this blind-date field trip. I'm pretty sure we all feel we are being marched to an awkward encounter. Over by the cider mill, a class of students is sitting in a circle. I hear a few of them call out that we are here. We follow Miss Lotti who is practically skipping down the sidewalk to where the other class is sitting. When the other teacher, Miss Hanson, sees her, she waves one of those huge waves that feels like a hug. Miss Hanson and Miss Lotti talk for a moment and then look at all of us like proud parents. They look around the area, deciding where to move all of us. My class is still in line, unsure of what to do, while Miss Hanson's class searches us over to find their pen pals.

"Okay, kids, let's move over where there's more space and we'll form one huge circle and call out names. Then we have a scavenger hunt for you to do with your pen pal."

We take a seat in the field. No matter how many times we've been instructed to sit in a huge circle over our elementary school careers, it still doesn't come easily with a few kids always either left out or sitting in the center. The grass is so cold it almost feels wet which prompts some arguments through the boys. "It's wet." "No, it's just cold." "Just stop being a sissy and sit down." My class stays on one side of the circle while Miss Hanson's makes up the other. Miss Lotti starts calling out one student's name at a time, and then they go into the middle of the circle and wait for their pen pal to come. Some of the pen pals already recognized the name and person from the pictures. They jump up before hand. Others have their names called to find their match. I keep scanning the crowd, but I'm not sure which one is Lizzie. I see a few girls who look perfect, just like Jennifer and Susie. They're wearing pea coats with corduroy skirts and tights. I'm hoping I get one of them. "Jenny," Miss Lotti called.

As I stand up and walk to the center of the circle, Miss Hanson calls for Lizzie. No one comes forward though. I feel my face flush. One of the perfect girls raises her hand.

"Yes," Miss Hanson says.

"Remember, you made Lizzie and Jacob stay on the bus until they were ready to behave?"

"Right," Miss Hanson says and walks back over to the bus, leaving me front and center by myself.

Then Lizzie springs off the bus and yells, "Woohoo!" I hear her class snicker but she doesn't seem to notice. She grabs my hand and leads me to a spot to sit together. "I didn't realize your hair was so red from the picture," she says.

I always feel someone calling attention to my red hair is an insult. It seems as if the only people who like my red hair are women my mom's age, and they always remark at how I must hate it now. I'm not sure with Lizzie though if she's insulting me or just stating a fact. "I love being out of school for the morning, don't you?" she says. "I was so excited, so of course it felt as if it took forever to get here though. Have you been here before? I wonder what the scavenger hunt is."

I'm not sure if it matters that I'm shy with Lizzie since she speaks enough for both of us.

Miss Hanson comes over and hands us a clipboard with a pencil and a checklist. Does anything feel more official than a clipboard? "Okay, you need to find all of the items on your list by working together. When you find the last item, you'll find the prize. Then come back here and sit in the circle again."

"Let's go," Lizzie says and grabs my hand, pulling me up. We run hand-in-hand for a minute. I've never done that with a friend. It feels odd. I want to like it, to be one of those people that hugs and holds hands easily, but I'm just not. Lizzie stops abruptly. "What are we looking for anyway?" She looks at the paper on the clipboard. A boy from her class runs up behind her and pulls the ball on the top of her hat. "Hey!" She runs after the boy, hooks her foot around his and trips him, sending him flying forward.

"Miss Hanson, Lizzie tripped me," the boy says. He's pen pals with Nick from my class. Nick and I don't know what to do with this situation.

"He grabbed my hat. Don't worry, I took care of it," Lizzie yells back to Miss Hanson who is coming up to us.

"Lizzie, please come here," Miss Hanson says and stands not too far from me as the boy and Nick scamper off. "We're going to have a good day, okay? If there are any problems, you let me know. Just enjoy yourself and get to know Jenny." She then looks at me. "Miss Lotti told me such nice things about you, Jenny. We thought you and Lizzie would get along so well and really bring out the best in each other." She says this to me in a voice normally reserved for kindergartners, leaving me to understand that Lizzie is meant to bring me out of my shell that everyone is so eager to do while I'm to put Lizzie back into hers. I feel betrayed by Miss Lotti. I didn't think she was one of the ones who thought I needed to change. I'm embarrassed. I see Jennifer with her pen pal. She's paired with one of the perfect girls. There they are, both perfect with perfectly feathered hair swinging in unison over their perfect pea coats as they walk together. They'll probably be friends forever. Lizzie wears a coat that is obviously a hand-me-down from her brother and I'm not sure she's met a hairbrush yet. After agreeing with Miss Hanson, Lizzie doesn't notice my unhappiness. She grabs my hand and we're off once again.

"First thing on our list: find a squirrel. Easy. Over there." She points up a tree. "Check. What's next?" I can't shake the sadness. I thought Miss Lotti saw more in me than shyness. "Earth to Jenny. We need to find a smooth acorn and bring it to the end."

"Hmm?"

"A smooth acorn. We should probably look over there." She points to trees near the gravel road.

"I don't think they want us near a road."

"Right," she says. "I knew you were a smart one. Probably

paired me with you to keep me out of trouble. Where should we look, captain?"

"How about over there?" I point to the tree where I see all of the other kids picking up acorns.

"Yes! Let's go." As we run over there, she does a cartwheel at full speed. "Can you do that?"

I shake my head. When we get to the tree, I start looking right away, distancing myself from Lizzie. I pick up a few contenders and put them in my pocket. I love acorns. I love how they have little hats. Is there anything cuter in nature? "Jenny! Any luck?" Lizzie calls from the other side of the road. Kids from my class look over to me. I feel Jennifer's eyebrow-lifted glance. I don't want to yell back so I just nod.

"What?" Lizzie yells again and comes over to me. "I can't find any."

"I found these ones. They might work."

"Let's see. Nope." She throws one over her shoulder. "Nope." Another one goes flying. "This one." She throws the rest away. She spits on the acorn and smooths it down. "Perfect, here." She hands it to me and I try not to act disgusted that she basically just handed me her spit on an acorn. I place it in my pocket and wipe my hand down my jacket. "What's next?"

"Next, we need to find an apple."

"They are really challenging us, huh?" Lizzie says. "Find an apple at the Old Cider Mill next to the apple orchard. I mean really. Give us something a little harder."

We walk, well, I walk, and Lizzie skips, runs, and jumps toward the apple orchard. I had come here with my family just last month and the trees were full of leaves and apples on every branch. Now the apples are all on the ground, smashed and rotting and the leaves were falling around them. A few trees had an apple or two clinging on for dear life. I rooted for them. When I got home, I thought I would write a story about an apple hanging onto a tree all through winter, waiting to be picked by a family the following fall. I'd have to figure out if the ending was happy, with the apple being put in a pie or disgusting, with the family cutting into the apple to find worms. I like stories with happy endings, but it's important to acknowledge basic science that a year-old apple might not be that fresh anymore. Maybe the worms could come to life like *James and the Giant Peach*.

"You're a daydreamer." Lizzic is eyeing me closely. "I'd offer you a penny for your thoughts but daydreams are just for the dreamer. Or something poetic like that. Let's see, here's an apple, there's an apple, over there is an apple." She keeps checking off the apple box on the sheet. I know she's making a mess of it. I also know it shouldn't matter but it's a clipboard and a checklist. People should have more respect. "I love seeing one apple left on a tree, don't you? Wonder how long it will stay."

We both look up at one red apple on a middle branch of the tree. "Maybe all year," I say. "Then some family will pick it next year and it will be full of worms."

"Or they make it into apple cobbler a la mode! My favorite."

"Have you ever read *James and the Giant Peach*?"

"I love it! Have you read *Charlie and the Chocolate Factory*?"

"Yes, I love Roald Dahl."

"Me, too! Have you read *Vile Versus*? It's awesome and weird."

"No, I haven't."

"I'll get you a copy from the library. Maybe we can read it together."

Just then two boys from her class run up to our tree, jump up and swipe at the apple. It falls to the ground. The boys run to another tree.

"Well, I guess that answers the question of how long the apple will stay. It will stay all year or until two nitwits come along."

"Boys," I say. I want to say how angry I am at them. Why can't they ever leave anything alone ever? From the time I was in kindergarten and Billy Maloney swiped my Hello Kitty eraser from my desk and stuck it up his nose I've always wondered just exactly what their problem was. Why are they not capable of just sitting still or leaving things alone? I hold it in for now though and remind myself, it's just an apple in a tree, not a favorite eraser in a nose.

We search for our next scavenger hunt item—a leaf turning colors. I have to agree with Lizzie here. It's fall in Connecticut at an apple orchard. As my sister April would say, "This isn't a Scavenger Hunt, it's a 'Duh, That's Everywhere Hunt.'"

Lizzie starts reading down the checklist for something less obvious to focus on. A bird, an acorn, mud (stay out though), a tractor, a barn. We accomplish all of those just by standing where we are and pointing to each item. Finally, we see one that sounds intriguing.

"Next we need to find a clue at the silo."

"What's a silo?" Lizzie asks.

"I have no idea," I say.

None of the kids appear to know except for one boy in Lizzie's class. "It's that thing," he shouts and we all run after him to the small tower-looking thing.

"Let's beat the boys," Lizzie calls to me and takes off. I was beginning to like Lizzie when she was calm, but now she's at full speed again.

I watch her weave through the crowd of students like a football player and make her way into a running race with a few boys from her class and mine. She reaches the silo first and grabs one of the scrolls that are laid around the bottom of it. "Yes! First one. Ha!"

I'm walking just in front of Jennifer, making my way to Lizzie.

"She's so strange," I hear Jennifer's pen pal say. "She moved here over the summer. I tried being friends with her for a little while. You know, just to be nice, but she's too strange. Too crazy." Jennifer's pen pal is one of the perfect girls. Why do teachers do that? Can't they spread around the popular people?

"Totally," Jennifer says. "It's hard trying to be nice to everyone when not everyone is worth the effort. I guess she's Jenny's pen pal. That's probably good. Jenny never talks. I think she has some sort of mental problem or something. I try to play with her sometimes to be nice, too. It's exhausting."

I'm torn between wanting to curl up into a ball and die and feeling slightly happy that someone was talking about me. Usually I feel pretty invisible so it's interesting to hear my name being discussed. I think the wanting to die feeling is winning though. I need to show Jennifer that I know Lizzie isn't cool. At least I wouldn't be associated as having such a strange friend.

"Here's our clue," Lizzie says as she runs toward me waving the scroll high in the air. When she reaches me, she falls to the ground, out of breath. "Whew. Had to beat the boys, you know?"

"It, like, wasn't a race," Jennifer's pen pal says. The girls giggle and walk away.

I roll my eyes, hoping Jennifer sees me do it so she'll know I agree with her and her pen pal.

Lizzie doesn't seem to care. "So, what's it say?"

I unroll the scroll, and I have to admit, I love scrolls. It makes me happy to open one. I know it's fake, but they always look so cool and official. Clipboards and scrolls should be used everyday. Why did scrolls ever go out of fashion? I've asked my parents for our family seal so that I can burn wax on a scroll and press it. They gave me an inkpad and a stamper with a picture of a dog on it.

"It says, the end of the hunt is near, but first you need to find the home of the bear." Most of us have been to the Cider Mill for field trips, donuts and the annual apple festival. We know about the small cave near the picnic area. From all around us, we hear kids say the word *cave*; it sounds like seagulls squawking. Lizzie takes off running again. When she reaches some boys from her class, one of them knocks into her, sending her to the ground. She scrambles up and grabs his foot, bringing him down as she climbs over him. "Ha, ha," she calls over her shoulder. He jumps up and races after her and grabs her hat. They race to the cave. They're the first ones there. I'm nervous they're going to start fighting, but they both focus on the task and look for the final clue. By the time I reach the cave, Lizzie is standing in a corner by herself. "Don't look suspicious," she whispers. "I found it. Act natural so no one else will see." She opens her hand a small amount for me to peek inside. She has two shiny stones in a small bag—one purple and one blue.

"I think one is for you and one is for me," she says. "That way, we'll always remember the first time we met. Which one do you want?"

"I guess the purple," I answer casually, but I love rocks and can't wait to have mine. I see Jennifer, Susie, and their pen pals eyeing us. They walk over.

"Where did you find those?" Susie is ask-accusing Lizzie. She has that way of talking so that the person she speaks to always thinks they've done something wrong.

I cross my fingers that Lizzie tells her and doesn't act weird about it. "Really want to know or do you want to try finding it on your own?" she asks.

"We wouldn't, like, ask if I didn't want to know." Jennifer laughs. I laugh, too.

"Okay," Lizzie says. "Follow me." She leads them to where she found ours and picks up two sets for them. "Here you go." They take them and walk away. Lizzie comes back to me. "Some people miss out on the fun."

When we turn in our scavenger hunt forms, we're handed questionnaires and told to find a quiet spot to interview one another. Lizzie searches for a spot for us and luckily, she chooses a one not near everyone else. She sits on a pointy rock leaving me the obviously more comfortable rock next to it. We spend the next ten minutes interviewing one another.

All About: Lizzie Cray
Favorite Ice Cream: Bubble Gum

Favorite Book: Charlie and the Chocolate Factory
Favorite Flower: Daisies
Future Career: Reporter
Favorite Movie: Star Wars
Favorite Place: Beach in Oregon
Favorite School Subject: Gym
Favorite Memory of Fifth Grade So Far: Today

The teachers call us into a circle again which I wish they wouldn't. When no one is around and she's not acting like a goof, Lizzie is really nice to talk with. We walk back as we are told. Some of the girls are holding hands with their pen pals as if they are new best friends. Even some boys have their arms around each other. I look at Lizzie and see that she is picking at a scab on her elbow. Miss Hanson stands in the center.

"Wasn't this fun?" she asks in that same sing-song voice. "I see a lot of great friendships have been made today. We'll continue our pen pal writing and have another get together in the spring. Now, I wanted to read this poem about friendship for all of you. It's by Robert Frost." She clears her throat:

A Time to Talk

When a friend calls to me from the road
And slows his horse to a meaning walk,
I don't stand still and look around
On all the hills I haven't hoed,
And shout from where I am, What is it?
No, not as there is a time to talk.

I thrust my hoe in the mellow ground,
Blade-end up and five feet tall,
And plod: I go up to the stonewall
For a friendly visit.

"What do you think this poem says about friendship?"

A boy from her class raises his hand. "I think it means you should stop working and have fun with friends."

Good answer. Then, another boy raises his hand. "I think it's about farming." Not so good.

Lizzie joins in: "I think he's talking about a ghost." And worse.

"Well, it's not about a ghost," Miss Hanson says. "The poet is saying how time with a friend is time well spent. Today, we had time with new friends instead of having a regular recess. Our lesson this time was how to meet a new person and invite them into your life." However, once the subject of ghosts begins, you can't just walk away from it. Where we are in Connecticut, even in the summer, it kind of looks like fall—prime ghost season. Abandoned one-classroom school buildings are boarded up not far from boarded up farmhouses and crumbling colonial rock walls. We have super old cemeteries all over the place, not to mention the few odd tombstones that you just stumble over occasionally. Add to that the fact that a company actually runs a ghost tour through our town (waste of money in my dad's opinion) but still, ghosts are pretty much never far from our minds around here. Kids from both classes start questioning her.

"Are there any ghosts around here?"

"My brother once saw a ghost."

"I think maybe the man he saw in the poem was actually a ghost and he should bring his blade."

"Did you know about the ghost that haunts the cider mill?"

I see Miss Hanson's face as she moves from kindergarten-sweet to fifth-grade fed up. "Nowhere in any of what we spoke about were we talking about ghosts. We are talking about friendship."

"I think ghosts can be friends," Lizzie says.

Miss Lotti stands up to help. "That's enough ghost talk today. Okay everyone, we have to get back to school. We'll keep on writing to each other. Say goodbye to your new friends."

Lizzie tackles me with a hug. She moves me from side-to-side saying, "Goodbye, goodbye. I'll miss you!" I'm sure everyone must be staring at us. I try to squirm free. She lets me go and smiles at me. "Bye, Jenny!" she calls from the first step of the bus. "You're my best friend!"

I actually smile until I see Susie and Jennifer looking at me as if I was made of mold. I make that cuckoo sign with my index finger swirling around the side of my face so they'll know I know my pen pal is crazy. Their faces remain blank though. I look away and walk to my bus. It would feel nice to hear that I was someone's best friend if that person wasn't seen as really strange. Lizzie isn't the best friend I had hoped for.

SUPERPOWER #5:
FREEDOM OF FAMILY

At home, I can be myself. Since I know this statement is true of most people, I often wonder what everyone's true self is. Do popular kids have truer selves that are actually uncool? Like, do they go home, take off their preppy outfits and sit on the couch, eating Doritos and playing *Pac Man* all afternoon? As a shy kid, once I head off that bus, I feel like a great burden has been lifted. I can't wait to go on my swing set or talk with my mom. Though lately, my home life is becoming slightly prickly. I need to be on guard for April moping about. As long as I hear her coming, I can either stop whatever childish thing I was doing or simply hide until she leaves. I suppose you can't always be yourself at home, like if you have visitors or guests. Then you have to be a more formal version of yourself.

Today, though, my aunt, uncle and cousin, Terry, are coming for Thanksgiving. With them, you don't have to be formal. They are very easy to be yourself with. If I could be someone else, I would choose Terry. Terry is my older cousin who lives in New York City. Well, I wouldn't actually want to be her. I just wish I could be like her. If I were her, I would have to live away from my parents and not in Connecticut, which is the most beautiful place. Terry is not shy at all. When she enters a room, it feels as if someone switched on a warm, bright light. She speaks in this deep, raspy New York voice.

Terry's mom and my mom are sisters; they are complete opposites. Aunt Joanie reads tarot cards, drinks wine, and loves gossip. She dragged my mom to the town ghost tour, though secretly I think my mom really just wanted an excuse to go. Whenever she is here, she and my mom will go to the cemetery forty minutes away where their grandparents are buried. Aunt Joanie will walk around reading the tombstones and telling any gossip she remembers about any of the names she knows—and she knows lots of them. "This one," she'll say pointing to one tombstone. "Remember how nasty she was? She thought I stole her lawn ornament and would give me evil stares."

"You did steal it," my mom reminds her.

"That's right. What was it?"

"A plastic baby deer."

"Well, I wouldn't have stolen it if she hadn't gotten Mr. Lawson fired from the bakery for burning her hot cross buns. Here he is. Mr. Lawson. Right near her. What a nice old man. Died 1975. I hope he's haunting her every night in here. *Hot Cross Buns!*"

My mom never gossips and seems to be constantly thinking of ways to be nice to everyone, like some sort of obsession. At times, she seems exhausted. My dad is always telling her to stop trying to please everyone. I overheard him kind of yelling at her one night about that when she was staying up making forty cupcakes for a class party and sewing costumes for the school play and making flyers for a school fundraiser. Anyway, it's fun when Aunt Joanie visits because she lets mom off the hook. My mom looks relaxed, like she doesn't need to care about being perfect. She doesn't gossip, but she'll sit with a glass of wine and laugh and laugh at all of the crazy soap opera stories Aunt Joanie tells her.

Now that Terry is sixteen, she's allowed to babysit my older sister April and me. All day I've been looking forward to it. Terry and I helped my mom get ready. Terry did her makeup for her and I picked out a necklace. She looks beautiful but nervous as she grabs her coat to go. Terry nudges her out the door as my Aunt Joanie holds my mom's hand. "The number to the restaurant is on the fridge and if there's any problem, there are numbers for our neighbors."

"They'll be fine," my dad says.

"Yeah, Terry has only lost one kid she babysat," my uncle said and winks at me.

"In my defense, the parents paid me to lose the brat," Terry says. "Now go. We're fine." She shuts the door behind them. "Okay, you're all mine, ha ha ha. First, chocolate chip cookies." She rummages through the cabinets. "Do you have any music down here?"

"I'll grab my record player," April says, coming downstairs as soon as she heard the front door close. "We can plug it in on the kitchen table. Have you heard *Freeze-Frame*? Jenny only owns one record: Kenny Rogers." She rolls her eyes. My dad is charging her a nickel every time he catches her rolling her eyes. He's saving up to buy a boat with the money and says at this rate, he should have enough in a few weeks.

Terry pauses, holding the flour bag and Nestlé's Tollhouse Chips. "I love Kenny. You have his greatest hits record?"

I nod. April used to like Kenny Rogers. I actually got the record to be like her. She started collecting records and listening to music in her room all of the time. I wanted to do that, too, though I knew nothing about music and couldn't ask April because she hates being copied. Last year, I stayed home sick from school one day with a real stomachache which then became a fake stomachache. I can't help it. School is tough when you are shy. Plus, my mom makes being home during the day so cozy with cookies and extra blankets. When it became obvious I was faking, my parents made me a deal. If I would go to school for the whole rest of the year without faking an illness, they would buy me any item $20 or less. From all of my days at home, I kept seeing this long commercial for *Kenny Rogers' Greatest Hits*. And it was $19.99. Perfect. So that's what I got after not faking. April liked it for a little while since we had seen Kenny on *The Muppets*, but now she hated it.

"Oh fine," April says. "We'll listen to it one time only." She goes upstairs to get her record player.

"I'll get my record," I say following her.

April lugs down the record player with the cord trailing behind her and runs back upstairs to bring down her records. "Quick, put on Kenny before we are stuck listening to 'Centerfold' over and over," Terry says.

We eat raw cookie dough by the spoonful while listening to "The Gambler." The song would end and Terry would yell, "Again! *You gotta know when to hold 'em. Know when to fold 'em.*" We all sing at the top of our lungs, including April. She almost looks like the old April I knew before she entered the Aqua Net Phase of her life known as junior high. As far as I can tell, this is the phase where nothing and no one is cool and you need lots of hairspray. But now we are covered with flour and shaky with sugar and she looks like the girl I used to play on the swings with everyday.

"Wait, what's that noise?" Terry says, lowering the record player.

We hear the sounds of car doors being shut and voices.

"Boys!" Terry says and looks out the kitchen window. To the side, she can see the shadows of our neighbor Robbie's older brothers going into their house. "That's right. You have all those cute boys next door."

"Yuck. They're not cute," April says.

"She only thinks Jeffrey is cute," I say. April punches my arm. I feel my face flush because I know I've said something funny.

"Who is Jeffrey?" Terry asks, sticking the spoon under April's mouth like a microphone.

April grabs the spoon and starts stirring the cookie dough absently. "Well. Okay. He's super cute. He's a friend of mine. He's in high school and he's always one of the leads in the community play."

"April wants to try out for the play just because of him," I offer. I thought I was offering usual information, but the way April glares at me, I can see she does not agree.

"It's so cute your town does that. What play is it this year?"

"*Bye Bye Birdie*," April says. "It's about this town in the 1960s where a girl named Kim is chosen to kiss this really famous rock star named Conrad Birdie goodbye on national television before he leaves for war. But she has a boyfriend named Hugo so it gets a little awkward. Jeffrey is either going to play Conrad Birdie or Hugo."

"That's right, I saw that movie. But, what are you doing with a high school boy though?" Terry asks. "He's your boyfriend?"

"No! He's just really cool. And I'm fourteen so I'm a year older practically for my grade because of my birthday. My friends think maybe he likes me. I don't know if he has a girlfriend."

"Hmm," Terry says. "What's his number?"

"No!" April's eyes go wide.

"Just a little call to see if he's home. We should get to the bottom of his dating life. It's a service to the community."

I can tell April is in between complete embarrassment and curiosity. We both believe Terry is capable of anything. Everyone always loves her and good things seem to follow her. When she was in fifth grade, she won a trip to Italy for an essay contest. So as embarrassed as April may be, you can't help but wonder if something good will happen if Terry calls.

"Okay. His number is in the phone book." April jumps up, grabs the book and flips quickly to a page with the corner turned down.

"You have the page marked?" I ask.

"Shut up," April says. Aqua Net Phase is completely back.

"All right, read it off to me," Terry said as she picks up our kitchen phone and spins, wrapping its long cord around her waist. "Go."

April slowly tells her the numbers and Terry dials. With each turn of the dial, April's face gets redder. "Oh my gosh. Maybe we shouldn't do this," she says and covers her face with her hands.

"Too late," Terry says and laughs her wonderful throaty laugh. "It's ringing. Ringing. That's three rings."

Terry's face erupts into a huge smile. "Hello, is Jeffrey home?"

"Oh, hello Jeffrey." She mouths "it's Jeffrey" to us. April comes over to listen on the other side of the phone.

"I'm with Teenagers for Drama Survey Team. Tell me, Jeffrey, what are you doing at home this fine evening . . . ? Hmm. Interesting. Do you play guitar most evenings . . . ? Mmm. Right. Good. And do you participate in any plays . . . ? Wow. That's a lot of interesting parts you've played . . . Mmm. Hmm. Mmm. Hmm. That one, too? More? Wow. Very good. You're quite the actor. Tell me, do you have a lot of fans . . . ? Interesting. And do you have a girlfriend?"

April gasps.

Terry mouths, "No!"

"Tell me, what do you look for in a girlfriend?" Terry moves the base of the phone away from her mouth so she can eat chocolate chips. "Well, thank you for your time, Jeffrey. Oh, you have more? Go ahead. Yes, right. You have been quite informative." She hangs up. "He's very chatty, huh?"

"He's really talented." April acts as if he's super famous.

"Well, he has quite a list of what he likes for a girlfriend. I think he mostly just described all men's version of the perfect girl."

"What was it?" April looks as if she is ready to become whatever Terry tells her.

"The blond hair surfer-type," Terry says and looks at April with a compassionate smile. "Not to worry. I don't think there are many of those in Connecticut."

"Okay, Jenny, anyone I should call for you?" Terry asks. "Any first crushes?"

"Gross," April and I say.

"She barely has any friends yet, forget about boys," April says.

Terry looks at me seriously. "I'm sure she has lots of friends. She's a sweetheart."

I feel my heart swell. I don't get many compliments.

"She really doesn't," April says, eating more batter and crushing me.

"I do. I have Anna from my class last year."

"Anna doesn't count. She never speaks and she's not allowed to do anything after school, like ever," April says with her mouth full of chocolate.

"I have my school pen pal," I offer in desperation not to look like a friendless idiot in front of Terry.

"I thought you didn't like her," April says.

"Well, she likes me," I mumble.

"Why don't you like her?" Terry asks.

"She's cuckoo," I say swirling my finger around my ear, hopefully sounding like April and her friends when they talk about a girl they don't like. "She tackles boys and likes picking scabs and is loud and gets in trouble with the teachers."

Terry laughs. "She sounds like me," Terry says.

"No, she's nothing like you," I say.

"See, so Jenny has no friends."

"I guess," I say. I hold my hands under the table and make my fist at April. I always do that when she makes me mad. I never let her see it, but it makes me feel better. I'll do it behind my back or under my leg or under the table.

"Well, I'm your friend. And, I say give the pen pal another chance," Terry says. "Tomboys need friends like you. And it's always fun to be friends with someone completely different than you. You should try out for the play, too."

"No!" April says.

"Oh stop." Terry lightly hits April's arm with a dishtowel. "I think Jenny would be great in a play. She's so creative."

"Maybe," I whisper.

"Social suicide for me," April says. She says that often.

We take the cookies out of the oven.

"Now what to do?" Terry looks around. "Let's spy on those boys next door."

"Why?" April asks.

"Why not? We need flashlights, coats and chocolate."

"I still have my Halloween candy," I say and run for my room.

When I come downstairs, April and Terry are waiting on the back porch giggling. I throw on my coat and meet them. It's a cold and dark night with lots of stars.

"Synchronize watches," Terry says, looking at her bare wrist. "Well pretend to anyway." April and I push imaginary buttons on our wrists. "Flashlights on." We push the switches, sending up light into the sky. A breeze makes me shudder. "Zip up coats all the way." Terry takes off her striped scarf and wraps it around my neck. "Let's go."

We heave open the porch gate and walk down the flight of stairs into our backyard. Our porch is the best part of our house. It extends the full width of it, making it perfect for riding Big Wheels when we were younger. Big Wheel riding was the first inkling I had that April was starting to drift away from me. We used to ride together for hours. Then she started telling me she had a great plan for an obstacle course to surprise me with. I would wait down at the swing set for her to finish planning the course for me. I would wait and wait and watch her zoom around the porch and then eventually she'd just go inside the house. I'm ashamed to admit I fell for this obstacle course close to ten times before I realized she wanted to play without me. Beyond the swing set is a path leading to Bloody Rock. I'm not allowed there. It's a cliff that goes down a few feet. I follow the two bobbing flashlights down the stairs. At the bottom, we walk into the trees separating our house from Robbie's. Branches snap under our feet. Through the trees, we can see the lights on at their house.

"They're home," April says.

Terry stops, putting her hand up into a fist by her head. I bump into April. "Watch it."

"Okay. Candy," Terry says, reaching her hand behind her. I pass up some Milky Ways to April. She takes one and passes the other to Terry. We stand there in a line, unwrapping and eating chocolates. "Trash," Terry says and passes her wrapper to April.

"Trash," April says and passes me both of their wrappers.

I fold them up and put them in my pocket. My mouth is too full of caramel to protest. Terry looks back at us and motions to us with wild hand gestures that I have no idea what they mean. With two fingers, she points to her eyes, then over her head, then to the right and left. Then she gives us each our own serious nod before laughing hysterically, and moving forward, tripping on a tree root. She rolls around on the ground. "Man down, man down. Save yourselves."

April and I laugh.

86

"Okay, okay. Let's get serious," Terry says and makes a very stern face. April and I square our shoulders. "Forward." We trample through the leaves and trees until we're at the side of Robbie's house.

When we get there, we crouch down and look to Terry for our next plan. I've never been involved in something as non-important but important-feeling at this operation. "Okay, I'm going to go behind the house and see what I can see. You two keep lookout." She runs behind the house. April and I look at each other. She sits down on the ground and puts her legs out in front of her and leans back on her hands. It's as if she remembered she needed to look cool even though no one was here to see us.

"Why don't you sit?" she asks.

"The ground looks pretty damp," I say and remain hunching on my feet.

"You're so strange," she says. "The ground is fine."

I pull my coat underneath me as much as it will go and sit. We wait. I can feel the wind chapping my face but it feels nice to be outside in the dark. Everything looks different. I can see the side of our house and my bedroom window.

"This is stupid," April says. "I don't think she's coming back. I'll go get her."

"I'll come with you."

"Suit yourself."

We find Terry on her way back to us from the back of Robbie's house.

"I've been compromised," Terry says and she falls to the ground like she's dead.

"What on earth are you talking about?" April says, pulling

Terry back up.

"The boys are coming out. They saw me when I knocked on their screen door. They were just watching *Dukes of Hazzard*."

We hear their front door open and out tumble all four boys. They don't really look at us, they just walk past us and we follow their energy into the woods. "Mind if we cut through your yard?" the oldest boy asks Terry.

"You do know I don't live here, correct?" she asks.

He turns and looks at her face. "You're not April or Jenny?"

"No, I'm Terry. Their cousin. I'm sixteen and live in New York. April is fourteen and Jenny is ten and have lived next to you for practically their whole lives so I can see how you may have me confused with them."

He nods and starts walking again. It feels good to know that he knows our names but I also don't think he's joking that he doesn't know who we actually are or the fact that there are three girls following him, not just two.

"Ouch!" April yells when a tree branch snaps back on her.

"Sorry," Robbie calls.

"Robbie always knows how to treat the ladies," one of the brothers who is not the oldest calls back.

"Where are we going?" April asks, clearly annoyed to have to hang out with Robbie.

"Bloody Rock."

I stop and reach for April's arm. "We're not supposed to go there."

She shrugs her arm away. "Don't be such a baby. I go there all the time."

She continues. I stand still. Their shadowy figures are beginning to disappear and I know I need to make up my mind quickly or else I'll be alone in the dark. I look up at my house and I'm not even sure I would be able to get inside. I don't know if Terry locked it. When I look back, I don't see any of them. My heart starts beating faster. This is my own backyard. My swing set creaks a few feet away. It's my place but it feels so unfamiliar in the dark. I can't even make out the path to get to Bloody Rock now. I start running home, figuring I will wait on the porch if the door is locked.

"Hey," I hear someone say behind me. A figure runs toward me. It's Terry. "Aren't 'cha coming?"

"I'm not supposed to go to Bloody Rock."

"Oh, oops," Terry says. "Why not?"

"Because it's on a cliff and I could fall and get hurt."

"Oh. Well, we can't leave April with these idiots. They sure are cute, but my God, do they share one brain cell between the three of them? Just come with me and we'll get April and come home and listen to more Kenny Rogers." She puts her arm around me. "Sound okay?"

I nod. Though she's sixteen, she's not much bigger than me, but I think she likes babying me a bit. And I don't mind. She's so easy with her love of everyone. She keeps her arm around me as we make our way to the path again.

"Now where is the path?" We shine our flashlights toward the trees where we think the path begins. "Here it is." The path is narrow so I walk in back of her. It's not long before we hear voices. At the clearing, we see the boys and April sitting on rocks. In the distance, I can see houses down below. We're not up as high as I thought we would be. From the way my mom scares us about this place, I thought it would be much higher with jagged edges and knives pointing out from the ground and monsters hiding behind trees ready to push us off the cliff to our deaths. Still, I stay away from the edge.

"Where were you guys?" April asks, in her annoyed voice. The boys are busy throwing rocks down, trying to hit some target. At least that's what I think they are doing. One of them will throw a rock and the others will try to throw their rock farther.

"Hey, have you guys ever seen the blood?" Robbie asks Terry and me.

We shake our heads.

"Seriously?" The boys stop throwing rocks. "You live right here and you've never seen the blood that makes this Bloody Rock?"

"I don't live here . . . never mind, yes, I live here and have never seen it," Terry says.

"Well, I have," April pipes in, looking not bored finally. "Jenny leads a sheltered life."

"So let's see it," Terry says.

"Over here." The oldest boy leads her to the edge of the cliff. "You have to bend down to see it."

Terry walks to where he is and leans over the cliff, shining her flashlight. "That?" she asks.

"Yep. See the red spots?"

"Barely. I hardly think that warrants calling this Bloody Rock. It's probably paint splatter."

"How can you say that? It's not paint." The boys laugh, seeming offended by Terry's disbelief. "Why would someone bring paint out here?" one of the middle boys questions.

"Yes, honey, I'm going to paint the rock with a little bit of red paint," the other boy says. "Be home soon. That makes a lot of sense."

"She's not from here," the oldest boy says. "She doesn't know the story. Do you know it?" He's looking right at April now. I'm not sure we've ever made eye contact with one of the older Kred boys. April seems flustered for a moment. I can see what Terry means; he is cute. And he speaks slowly and when he actually looks at you instead of goofing off with his brothers, it feels intense.

"Of course I know the story, but it's stupid," April finally answers.

"It's not stupid, it happened," Robbie says.

"So, someone tell me the story," Terry says. She walks over to me and pulls me down to sit with her. She whispers, "One story and we'll head back home."

The oldest brother comes and sits right in front of us. He puts his flashlight in his lap so we can just make out the outline of his face. "So, way back during the time of the Pilgrims or something, a young couple built their house pretty close to where your house now sits," he says and looks at me. I feel my face flush and am thankful that it's dark. Terry puts her arm around me. "It was pretty tough living. The winters were cold. The nearest town was hundreds of miles away. So, like, this couple was completely on their own. They saw no one for months and months. Even though the husband was kind to her, the wife was getting really sad. She couldn't take the isolation.

"Then one night, they heard someone calling to them. It was a small voice, but they heard it. It said, 'Help me. Please help me.'

The husband and wife took a lantern and walked out to where they heard the voice. They saw a shadowy figure in the distance. 'Please, I tripped over one of your rabbit traps and am too weak to stand.' The husband walked toward the figure and was surprised to find an old woman. He looked around and couldn't see any horse or carriage or even footprints in the snow. He didn't know how she could have gotten here by herself. She looked too frail. He bent down and took the woman's arm. She wobbled up and put all of her weight on him. 'Oh thank you, young man. I surely would have died out here without you.' The wife told her to come inside for the night and offered some hot coffee. The husband felt nervous about letting her into their house but his wife insisted. He relented, figuring what could this old woman do to him?

"The old woman was too weak to leave their house so she stayed with them for weeks. She would make delicious soups and stews for them and the wife grew to love her but the husband remained uneasy. Then one night, when they went to bed, the husband heard chanting. He looked over to his wife who had been sleeping next to him but she was no longer there. When he looked down from his loft, he could see the old woman and his wife sitting side by side, holding hands and chanting as if in some kind of trance. He called to his wife. She looked up at him and her eyes were black. The old woman cackled. She said, 'Do not step in our circle of fire or you will surely meet your death.' He looked and saw that around them was a ring of fire. He ran toward them and as he reached for his wife, she became a devil. He backed away and ran out of the house but the women followed him. He ran right here, to this rock. He had nowhere else to run so he hid. As they ran toward the cliff, he held a branch out, tripping the old woman over the edge of the cliff. Before she fell though, she grabbed his wife's hand. The old woman's head hit the rock, dying instantly and leaving a splattering of blood that rain could never clean. He watched as his wife fell back. As she did, her eyes turned back to brown and she was herself again but it was too late. She fell to her death. When the husband went to get her body, he only found hers but not that of the old woman. The husband was really upset, believing he killed his wife for no reason. Had he imagined the witch? Was it all a trick of his mind? He never recovered and lived out his days in madness all alone. It's said that during the night sometimes around Halloween, you can hear a witch cackling in the wind. In fact, I think I can hear it right now."

On cue, Robbie jumps out behind Terry and me. We scream.

"Robbie!" I say.

"Wow, I never heard you talk actually," he says and smiles.

Terry is laughing. April punches Robbie's arm before one of his brothers tackles him.

"You were so scared," Robbie says.

The oldest brother hasn't moved from his spot. He's looking at Terry, smiling. "It's a true story," he says.

"Well, we need to get going. I'm being a bad babysitter by being here."

"You're not my babysitter," April says.

"I know. But I think we should get back anyway."

April shrugs her shoulders and starts walking back toward home.

"Thanks for the story, guys," Terry calls back.

"Anytime," the oldest one says.

"Did you see how scared they were?" we hear Robbie asking as we walk through the path.

When we got up to our house, I feel completely scared. I can't believe all of that happened right here. Terry though, starts cracking up and falls to the living room floor. "Have you ever heard anything so stupid? And they believe it completely. I didn't want to make fun of their little ghost story, but my goodness it was hard not to laugh in his face. I had to bite my lip to keep from laughing. They wouldn't last a second in New York. They're way too gullible."

"I told you it was stupid," April offers and starts laughing too.

I'm glad they thought the story wasn't true and that it was ridiculous, but I knew I wouldn't be able to sleep that night. I needed to add the old woman to my list of things that scared me. I wasn't sure how I would fend off the witch from entering my room as I slept. I thought something at the foot of my bed would work best since that's the part that faces Bloody Rock.

When Terry throws her sleeping bag down on my floor that night, I ease up a bit. Scary stories can only scare you if you think about them. Of course the first night you hear them is the worst. With Terry in my room, everything would be fine.

"I've been thinking," Terry says, as I'm about to sleep. "You should try out for that play, too. I think you would be really good at it."

"You do?"

"I do."

"But what about my shyness?"

"What do you mean?"

"I don't think I could be up on stage."

"Shyness shouldn't hold you back from something you want to do," Terry says. "Besides, I've never thought of you as shy. I think that the play might be fun for you. And you're beautiful so you could totally be a movie star." She puts her hand to her forehead and acts as if she's Carol Barnett being Scarlett O'Hara.

"No I couldn't." I laugh.

"Sure you can. Anything you want." Terry yawns. "Goodnight Goose." My dad always calls April and me goose. I don't know why. We'll go to school and if he's here, he'll say, "Knock 'em dead, goose." Really, I suppose it should be, "Knock 'em dead, geese," but I think he means the statement to us both individually. Anyway, Terry loves it so now she calls me that as well.

The night of the play auditions arrives and I wish Terry was still here. She would have remembered to tell me to go. I want that push. I want someone to drag me there. However, my dad is running late from work and April is pacing in front of the house. My mom is busy ironing curtains for her friend's curtain store where she started working a few times a week. If I want to try out for the play, I'm going to have to get ready and stand out there with her to hop in my dad's car when he gets here. You can be un-shy with your family, but sometimes family can make you even shyer. Your family has you pigeonholed into your role so they already expect certain actions from you. If you want to break out of what's expected, you need to be heard. Telling them I want to be in the play sounds so embarrassing though.

I hear our Monte Carlo pushing down the road as the head-lights appear. April starts walking down the driveway to meet him. *That's it*, I tell myself. *That is it. You are doing this.* I grab my boots and my coat and yell a quick goodbye to my mom before she can ask me what I'm doing. April turns to me. "Where are you going?"

I stop. She doesn't wait for an answer though. Instead she walks over to the passenger door and I hear her groan about how late they are. I walk closer. My dad waves for me to come closer. He rolls down his window.

"Hey, Goose," he says. "Can you please take my coffee cup inside? Forgot to wash it out at work and it stinks to high heaven."

"Sure," I say. I grab his travel mug.

"Off to the theater," he says in a British accent. With that, he begins backing out of the driveway. I feel disappointed and relieved. I try to enter the house quietly so my mom doesn't hear me, but she's the only one that always hears me.

"I thought you were going with them," she says.

"Nope." I put my dad's coffee cup in the sink. "I think I'll go swing for a bit."

"Okay. Isn't it cold though?"

"It's fine." My swing is where I do my best thinking. Plus, it's the only thing I can think of doing right now that explains why I have my coat and boots on so my mom won't think I'm even stranger than she already suspects. I don't exactly have any answers though. I know I should want to do more, but it also scares me too much to do more. Being Lucille Ball would be great, but I don't know how she did it. How do you get over the fear to do the things you think would be fun? People say all the time to just be yourself, but myself isn't what I want to be nor is it what anyone else wants me to be. Be yourself, but not shy and strange and say and do the right thing all of the time. I don't know how it all works but you can't swing and be sad. It's physically impossible unless you were like swinging while you watch something incredibly sad, like a fire in your house. But even then, you would probably stop swinging so you could get help. With this knowledge, I pump my feet harder and swing higher so I can feel the tickle in my belly and shake away all the other thoughts.

I'm brushing my teeth and getting ready for bed when I hear my dad's car coming up the driveway. I finish and meet my dad and April as they come to the door. My dad grabs me up into a big hug. "How was your day?"

April scoots past us and into the kitchen. "You will not believe what dad just did," she tells my mom. "Dad asked for a part in the play. My life is ruined."

All of her friends were signing up to be in the play solely based on Jeffrey Greeson. None of them would admit that though. My parents were just so happy that she wanted to join something instead of sulk in her bedroom and make life miserable for us. I know they hoped their old April would be coming out of this nightmare cocoon soon. She used to love to do every activity from plays to ballet to gymnastics. I didn't say anything, but I heard her practicing lines from the play for the audition all week.

My dad puts me down. "Gotta go defend myself." He walks into the kitchen with his hands up in the air as if calling peace with the enemy. "In my defense, I jokingly said to Bob Freeley that I would play Conrad Birdie. I sang the only line I remember from the movie which is, '*Kids, what's the matter with kids these days,*' and he was so impressed by my singing, he signed me up to play the father."

"You're failing to mention that no one else wanted to play the father in the first place," April says.

"Details, what are they good for?" he says. "Anyway, it'll be fun. My first step to becoming the next Robert Redford."

My mom looks at April and then at my dad as if trying to figure out if this story is true or not. "You really have a part?"

"Yes, one of the leads. Don't worry, I won't forget you all when I'm rich and famous."

"I don't understand," my mom says. "You can't sing or act. You're terrible at remembering things. How will you learn all your lines?"

My dad grabs an apple from our fruit bowl, wipes it on his shirt, and takes a bite. "Thanks for the vote of confidence," he says with his mouth full. He wipes the apple juice from his chin with his sleeve.

"Oh, April, I'm so sorry," my mom says. "I would never have let him take you there if I knew he was going to do this."

"What?" he asks. He really has no clue what is so wrong here socially for April. "This will be fun. Ape and I never get to spend time together anymore. Now we'll be at practice together two to three times a week."

"Oh my God," April says. "My life is ruined." She sits down at the table and covers her face with her hands. Once kids enter middle school, it seems it's not cool to have anyone know you have parents. They certainly aren't not supposed to be seen anywhere near you.

"What part did you get, April?" I ask.

"I'm just one of the stupid townspeople."

"What does that mean?"

"I don't know," she says in an eye-rolling tone. "I'm in parts where they need lots of people. We have to learn some dances and songs. No one will even notice me."

"Do you get to wear a costume?"

"I think so," she says. "Ugh, what does it matter? My life is ruined." She grabs her hair and pushes it out of her face. "Dad, can you pretend you don't know me?"

"Remember how we ran that race together last year? That was fun, right?"

"Dad, that was like three years ago." April's face is in complete shock that my dad can be so clueless in so many ways.

"Okay," he says. "I will pretend I don't know you but I think once your friends see how good I am, you'll be bragging about me."

Later that night, I hear my mom talking to my dad. I shouldn't do it, but I eavesdrop a lot at night. She's telling him that she thinks I wanted to go join the play with them. He doesn't believe it though. "If she wants to, she'll ask. Plain and simple."

I've learned some bits about genetics like where you get your eye or hair color from based on your parents. I wonder if after my dad, there just wasn't any genes left for self-confidence and that's why I have none. I mean really. He can talk his way into a part in the play and not even care that he has no acting or experience at all while I can't even ask my own parents if I can try out for the play.

SUPERPOWER #6: PEOPLE WATCHING

Invisibility allows you to people watch without looking too strange. People watching is a skill. Some people like to watch random people at airports or in restaurants and make up stories about them. I don't. I like to watch for all of the hidden clues that hint at who they really are and what they're really doing. I'm always looking for the playbook about life—that book that tells you how to act in every situation. By watching people without them seeing me, I pick up slang that I'm never cool enough to use, like, "That's so rad." I also pick up the way they stand or sit. Sure, one could think that standing or sitting doesn't require any thought, but if you watch closely, you can tell a lot about a person by the way they sit at a desk in school. Super smart kids sit tall and straight. Creative kids sit farther back in their seat and are always holding a pen or pencil that they move absently. Kids who hate school either slouch or sit close to their desk with their knees bouncing as if ready to leave at any minute. The cool girls sit with one bent elbow allowing a hand holding a pen near their face while the other arm rests folded in front of them on the desk. Once you think too hard about how to sit or stand, your arms become these strange tentacles attached to your body that you don't know what to do with. Not only do I pick up tips from people watching, it also helps me see moments when other people are scared or shy. I see the way they swallow deeply or their eyes look down or the little bit of sweat that forms on their forehead. No one else sees it, but I see it and it makes me like that person more each time. I like knowing I'm not the only one who ever gets nervous.

At recess, I use my superpower to hear Jennifer talking about the play. She was cast as a townsperson, too. Unlike April though, Jennifer is acting as if being a townsperson is equal to being one of the leads in the play. The girls are all excited for her and asking if they can join to. Jennifer says she thinks there aren't any parts left. I'm right there, almost ready to take my spot at the swings when it hits me that I should mention my dad and sister. The play would give Jennifer and me something in common since I'll be there for lots of the practices anyway. She's telling Susie she should join as well though she's not sure they need more towns-people. She offers a chance to paint scenery to Susie. I feel my skin prickling as I start to speak.

"My dad knows the director," I say. "I could ask if they have more parts if you like. My dad is playing the father in the play."

They don't hear me since my voice came out kind of squeaky. I try again, but am uncertain if they didn't hear me or do not care. I decide to just leave it for now. When she sees me at play practices, maybe we can become friends then. This play is just what I needed. Since she won't be around Susie, Jennifer will probably want to get to know me. Plus, she'll see that my dad and older sister are cool, so maybe she'll see me in a new light.

My mom wanted to work a few more hours at the curtain store so I told her I didn't mind going to the practices on those days. Plays are the perfect setting for people watching after all. I run out to the swings and stay there until the whistle, daydreaming about Jennifer and me wearing matching sweaters and exchanging friendship pins that we wear on our sneakers.

Once inside, Miss Lotti hands out our notes from our pen pals again. I can't help viewing the whole pen pal program as a huge disappointment.

Dear Jenny,

I had fun meeting you. I hope you don't think I'm too crazy. My dad says we can get together again soon. He says we can meet any day after school. Where do you think we should meet? I can come to you.

Love,
Lizzie

I know it will probably never happen. Plus, I'm not sure we're supposed to see our pen pals on our own. It may be breaking pen pal rules. Still, I feel I need to make sure Lizzie knows that we won't see each other outside of school for now. I write quickly and don't fill up my paper as I did before meeting her.

Dear Lizzie,

How are you? I have to go to the community play practice with my dad and sister most days after school while my mom works so I don't think I can meet you after school.

Love,
Jenny

As the day continues, my hopefulness of Jennifer and I becoming friends has changed to me reliving the scene of them ignoring me. I keep focusing on what I said to Jennifer and Susie. Had they really not heard me? I really think they did. Why couldn't Miss Lotti have put me with a cooler pen pal so maybe I would have a popular friend for once? Add to all of this the fact that I need to see Dr. Sedac today and my mood is completely slipping low. I dread the days I need to go to Dr. Sedac. I have to give Miss Lotti a note each time and the class wonders why I get to leave early. I feel like they know it is not for a good reason like I'm a talented gymnast leaving for the Olympics. Maybe they all think what Jennifer thinks: that I have a mental problem. And now, I'm going for treatment. I don't have much faith in Dr. Sedac. I'm not sure my mom does either. Each week, she quizzes me about our sessions. I heard her telling my dad the other night when they thought I was asleep that she doesn't think he has enough personality to help me. My dad tells her, very practically, either stay with Dr. Sedac and see it through or find someone else. I can tell my mom isn't sure how to leave from Dr. Sedac though. Whenever she picks me up, she seems as nervous as I am.

"We'll just try it through December, okay?" It's a question that's not really a question.

We enter the drab office building. Mrs. Sims welcomes us with her usual smile and promise to work on the puzzle afterward. I'm prepared to walk into his office and sit the way the creative kids sit at school. I'm even holding a pen as a prop. I walk into his office. He doesn't look up from his papers. I close the door quietly so I don't disturb him. He motions to my chair. I sit, leaning back ever so slightly and crossing one ankle over the other knee. It immediately feels wrong though so I put it back and then sit forward with both hands holding the chair at the side, one with the pen as well. I hear his wall clock ticking. This time I imagine the pinecones on the floor coming to life like a little army and attacking the lint on his pants. I smile. He looks up and frowns.

"What should we say when we enter a room?"

I feel as if I'm in trouble so my face flushes. I shrug.

"We say, *hello*."

I nod.

He laughs. Not a nice laugh. A laugh like the ones April gives me when I say something stupid.

"Please stand up and walk back to the door and try again." So much for walking in and giving an air of creative confidence.

I want to run from his office so badly. Does he mean for me to go back out the door and start completely over or to just start from the door, but already in his office? I hesitate at the door, unsure of what to do. I open it. I hear him laugh that laugh again.

"No need to go out and back in," he says. "This isn't a stage. Just turn around and show me you know how to enter a room."

I do as I'm told and whisper "*hello*" from the door.

"Yes, yes, fine." He motions for me to sit again. "The point is getting you confident enough to handle normal social situations. Do you understand that?"

I nod.

"Yes, sir."

"Yes, sir."

"Often, shyness can come across as rudeness. When you enter without saying hello or only nod instead of speaking, I take offense, believing you are being disrespectful to me. For this reason, even if you say nothing else, you must remember your *hello*, *thank you*, and *pleases* just as other children do. Shyness is not a free pass to never speak."

I nod, ashamed.

"Perhaps what you could try is holding your face a different way while learning to overcome your shyness so people will not infer that you are rude. It seems your face's natural tendency is to hold a downward position so that you look as if you are frowning. Try keeping a smile on your face instead. Like this." He gives a very creepy mouth-only smile. His eyes remain stern. I never knew my face looked rude on its own. I try to mimic what he does, curling the corners of my mouth up. "No, it's more like this." His face doesn't change. I feel mortified. "See how my lips aren't sneering, they just look pleasant, as if I'm happy to talk with you. You don't want to look fake at the same time."

He looks anything but pleasant, more like the tiger in *The Jungle Book* right before he wants to eat someone. Still, I try again. We sit there fake smiling at each other for what feels like hours. I pray for a giant lint ball to appear on his pants so we can stop. Finally, he sighs and begins reviewing his notes on me. He flips pages, scribbles here and there, and then closes the file.

"How many times did you raise your hand in class last week?" he asks.

"Ten."

"Mmm hmm. Really?" He leans forward and doesn't blink while he watches me—with his mouth turned down by the way. One, two, three, four, five, six, seven, eight, . . . it's as if he turned the thermostat up on my face. I feel beads of sweat on my forehead. I curl my lips up, hoping that's what he wants. Is he a mind reader? Is he searching my brain for the truth? Technically, I didn't lie. I did raise my hand ten times; I just timed it in a way that makes it feel like a lie. If you raise your hand near your face the second the teacher is about to call on someone else doesn't that still count as raising your hand? Well, if he can see into my brain, he can decide if I lied or not. But if he can see, then he'll also know what I'm thinking right now, and now, and now. He'll see that I'm not sure that I may have lied. That could be good if he sees I didn't mean to. I'll sit here and wait. I look down and feel him studying me until I hear his chair squeak backward. He picks lint off his pants. Phew. I stare at my hands. How can he think telling me I have a rude-looking face would be helpful in building my self-confidence? *Hey Dr. Sedac, you're no prize yourself.* That's what Terry would tell him. *And you should invest in a lint roller.* Are there any shy people living in New York City? It seems like they all just state the truth and don't put up with any insults.

As the time dwindles down, he grabs his yellow notebook pad like the one my dad uses. He scribbles something, tears it off quickly and holds it up, waving it toward me. "Well take it," he says. "It's your homework. Remember, I can only help you if you do the assignments I give you and come in ready to talk the truth. Send your mother in."

I walk out of his office. My mom looks up from talking with Mrs. Sims. She has a smile on her face until she sees mine. Her shoulders straighten and she smoothed her hair. "I suppose I'm up now," she says and gives a parting smile to Mrs. Sims.

"Good luck, dear," Mrs. Sims whispers before my mom opens the door.

Once she's in his office, I ignore Mrs. Sims, sit down, and read my homework:

> *Take the bus every day this week. Hand the bottom of this note to your teacher: Please keep track of how many times Jennifer raises her hand in class and record it on this paper.*
> *—Dr. Sedac*

"How did it go, dear?" Mrs. Sims asks as she walks her candy bowl over to me. I shrug my shoulders. "That good, huh?"

"I don't know what I'm supposed to do in there."

"Oh, well, you can talk to him. He went to this really fancy school and they told him how to solve people's problems. So, if you have any problems, he can help."

"Oh," I say. "I think the problem is just me. Who I am. No one likes that I'm quiet." Mrs. Sims nods, as if she understands what I mean. "And, there's someone on the bus who is mean to me." It feels good to say it to someone.

"I see."

"And now, he wants to embarrass me in front of Miss Lotti."

"The boy from the bus?" Mrs. Sims asks. I know she means to help, but when I'm upset and grown-ups can't follow along, it makes me more upset.

"No, Dr. Sedac. See?" I hand her the homework.

"Ah. I never liked raising my hand either. Ruthie Anne. That girl was in my class all through grade school. She raised her hand constantly. As annoying as it was that she knew every answer to every question, it kept the pressure off the rest of us. Last I heard, she was married to some politician." She chuckles. "Well, I don't think people don't like you because you're quiet. I think they love you and want to make sure you feel comfortable speaking your mind. You've got lots of good things to say after all. And that person on the bus needs to leave you be. I hate mean kids. Nothing worse. Well except mean adults. Here's what you do: when you get on the bus, sit as close to the front as you can and resist the temptation to slide toward the window. Place your bag near the window so he has nowhere to sit near you. The troublemakers always go to the back. And don't worry about being quiet; I think it makes you nice to be around. Everyone else is just babbling on and on. It's nice to have someone who doesn't need to do that. But if you want to speak up, everyone is happy to listen because they know what you say is important."

I can't wait to be Mrs. Sims's age. All of these matters just won't matter. At some point, I won't have to fix myself, and instead can be one of those old women who walk around the grocery store with their plastic hair curlers and bathrobes. No one is hauling them off to talk to Dr. Sedac. Instead, they can choose if they want to ever speak to anyone or even take the curlers out of their hair in public.

My mom comes out. Her shoulders are hunched and her face is red. She smiles weakly at Mrs. Sims. "See you next week," she says.

I watch my mom closely in the car. She keeps tapping the steering wheel with her fingers like she's thinking. We left the meeting with Dr. Sedac and went for pizza, just the two of us. She seemed far away, thinking. Normally, I don't mind, but today I feel like maybe I've done something wrong. If she knows I sort of lied to Dr. Sedac, maybe she's too mad at me to speak. Yet, she did smile over dinner, hold my hand to the car, and help with my homework as if she was in a fine mood. I can just tell something is wrong though.

That night, I listen hard to my parents downstairs to see if they say my name again. Since I can't hear what they're saying exactly, I take my blanket and pillow and sneak to the top of the stairs. First, they talk about the boring stuff that I often don't listen to—my dad's work, errands that need to be done. Then it happens. "I don't know that Dr. Sedac is helpful."

"Why?"

"I'm just not sure he is compassionate enough to help Jenny. He's kind of mean."

"Well, this was your idea. I thought you heard good things about him."

My mom stays quiet for a while.

"Maybe we'll try for a few more weeks and then I'll decide."

"Sure."

"It felt as if he was scolding me. He said I need to make an effort to encourage friendships for her. I tried that one, remember? With the woman from my cake class? Well, that was a disaster. I just . . . I want her to be happy, but maybe this is making things worse. I don't know what to do."

"I know," my dad said in a serious voice. "I really think she'll just grow out of it when she's ready. Wonder what made her so shy."

"Well, I wasn't the most outgoing child."

"There you go, it's because of you." My dad laughs. "I suppose you turned out okay. If she's happy, I'm happy. Maybe she just wants to be left alone. Not everyone can be the class clown or most popular, you know? And, people do grow up and grow out of things. You keep telling me how quiet you were but I've never seen it. Now I can't get you to be quiet so I can watch *Cheers*."

"What is this show?"

"Guys at work were saying it was funny. Shh."

I drag my stuff back to my room. I can't decide if what they said was good or bad. I like the idea of never going back to Dr. Sedac, though I would miss Mrs. Sims. I would like a new friend. I always imagine a best friend would be beneficial. I fall asleep, imaging again that Jennifer and I are best friends and I'm confident and perfect, just like her and all the other kids look at us with envy.

At school, I hand Dr. Sedac's crumpled note to Miss Lotti. She reads it and nods. "Well then, I get to hear more of your beautiful voice today?"

"I guess so."

"Wonderful. Don't be nervous. I'll go easy on you." She smiles at me. "Oh, I saw Miss Hanson yesterday." She grabs her purse from under her desk and starts searching it. "Here it is. Your pen pal actually wrote another note to you. I guess she really likes you. Miss Hanson and I were hoping the two of you would hit it off."

"Why?"

She raises her eyebrows at me, either surprised that I asked a question or at the question itself, I can't tell. "We thought the two of you would bring out the best in each other, I guess." Miss Lotti looks at Dr. Sedac's note again before answering me. "Miss Hanson told me Lizzie needed a friend who was a good listener. Someone understanding as well. I thought of you."

I'm slightly suspicious since her answer avoids the real question about me and the big shell everyone wants me out of, but I'm not sure I want that answer. I like this one better. I walk to my desk but Jennifer stops me. "Is that a pen pal letter?"

I nod.

"Why do you get one? Do we all get one today?"

"I don't . . . " Before I can finish, she sticks her hand straight up in the air and asks Miss Lotti about her pen pal letter. When Miss Lotti tells her I'm the only one to get one today, Jennifer's face leads the class in how they should respond. Her open mouth and accusing eyes let everyone see the great injustice I have caused.

"She wrote to me," I whisper to Jennifer.

"Still not fair if we don't all get one," she says.

Miss Lotti ignores her and begins writing our spelling words on the chalkboard.

"Must be because your pen pal is so weird, she gets special treatment. So not fair." I know she is saying this to me, but she looks at everyone around her instead.

I sit at my desk, embarrassed. I feel as if everyone thinks I've done something wrong, but Miss Lotti snaps into strict teacher mode. Her tone tells everyone to stop it. I slide the note in my desk to read at lunch when no one is looking.

Dear Jenny,

The community play is at the high school right behind my house. Well, pretty much right behind my house. There's an old cemetery I have to walk through and then a path, then the parking lot, then the school. My brother is a student there. I guess when we're in high school, you and I will go there, too. I'll meet you there and sign up. That way, we can become actual friends instead of just pen pals. See you there.

Love,
Lizzie

No! This news is not good. Not good at all. I just want to watch the play from my little spot. I write back immediately, but I don't think she'll get it in time.

Dear Lizzie,

That's okay. The play is boring. You do not need to come. Thank you. It must be creepy to have a cemetery behind your house. So, I will just see you at our next pen pal field trip then. And maybe wait to write me again because it was not fair that I got a letter and no one else in my class did.

Your pen pal,
Jenny

I ask Miss Lotti how quickly she can get the letter to Miss Hanson, but she doesn't seem to sense my urgency, telling me she'll see her over the weekend. She smiles at me. She totally doesn't get it. I think she thinks I am just so excited to send back a note, not that I'm trying to stop my life from being ruined. I hand her the note in defeat. I just hope that Lizzie forgets or finds something else to do.

I went to the first two play practices so my mom could work at the curtain store. I have to say, watching a play come together is like a play in itself, though slightly less boring and you can get out of your seat at any time, not just intermission. Our county has been putting on plays every year since the sixties. Usually, we just go when people my parents know or one of their kids are in it. *We've seen Annie Get Your Gun, Oklahoma, The Sound of Music,* and *The Music Man.* To be honest, I find myself sleeping after the first twenty minutes each time, until my dad nudges me to point out some person he thinks I know or should know. The play practices give me a great chance to people watch. Plus, I love spending time in the auditorium. The seats all have flip-up desks to use so I bring my homework. I find my usual spot in the auditorium. It's far enough from everyone that I can watch them without looking strange. I brought my homework and *Charlotte's Web* to read. Usually I just watch everyone around me without opening my books. It's just too interesting. In the few play practices, I've seen April's group move closer and closer to Jeffrey's group. The groups are somewhat together as in Jeffrey's group knows April's group is watching them and April's group flip flops between watching them and giggling to being cool and acting as if they don't care.

For now, the kids my age who are in the play stay near their parents until they are called into action. At some point, Susie decided to join the play. Before the first play practice, I spent ten minutes trying the feather my hair just like Jennifer's and wore a sweater with a collared shirt underneath. I imagined myself walking confidently into the auditorium and calling over to her. When I got there though, she and Susie were next to each other in deep conversation so I walked past without saying a word. I still think this play could be a good thing for my social life. Sometimes my mom tells April to sleep with her books under her pillow so she'll learn by osmosis—with the knowledge seeping into her head. Maybe, like the book under April's pillow, I'll osmosis myself into a friendship with them.

I hear the older teenage girls talking about how cute someone is and look over to see Lizzie standing in the middle of them. I shrink down in my seat. She's asking the older girls something. They point over to the director and she walks over to him. He's on the stage in the middle of talking to the adults, but she steps right up there, excuses herself and asks him something. I see him look on his clipboard and hand her a piece of paper. She takes the paper, looks around the auditorium and then squints her eyes looking right at me. She bounces down from the stage and runs toward me.

"Jenny!" She's waving the paper over her head as she makes her way to me. I glance in the direction of Susie and Jennifer, without letting them know I'm glancing. It's my empty-eye stare that I learned from Terry. If you ever walk into the wrong classroom, she says you just do this stare that makes you look like you are looking at something else very important, without noticing anyone else near you. Then you just back out of the room and hope you don't trip. Jennifer and Susie watch as Lizzie runs down the aisle toward me. She sits next to me. "I just joined the play. Well, I need to fill out this paperwork but then I'll be in the play with you. Isn't that great? Do you have a pencil?"

My hands are shaking but I find a pencil in my pencil box for her. She sits next to me filling out paperwork. "What part are you? Are you one of the townspeople? Or one of the stage hands?"

"Well, I'm not actually in the play," I whisper. "My dad and sister are."

"What did you say?" she asks in her loud voice. "You have a quiet voice."

My face flushes. I hate when new people call attention to the fact that I'm quiet. How do they realize it so quickly? It feels as if someone has just told me I'm ugly. "I said my dad and sister are in the play."

"Cool. Where are they?"

"My sister is over there. She's the tall one with the long brown hair. And my dad is over there with the director. He's playing the dad in the play."

"Wow. He's famous. So, why don't you have a part?"

116

"The director wanted me to be in it but I'm just not."

"Why not?"

"I'm just not."

"Stage fright?" she asks in a silly deep voice while raising her eyebrows like a doctor.

I actually laugh. "Kind of."

"So, what do you do instead?"

"I watch, or I read. My mom works on Tuesday and Thursday nights so I come here and sometimes she picks me up early."

"What are you reading?" She flips over my book. "Oh, this one is sad. I like happier books. If you have paper, we could write our own book? I love doing that." I hand her my notebook. "Great. What should our book be about?" I shrug. "Yeah, I got nothing either. How about a ghost story? I love those. Or a mystery like *Encyclopedia Brown*. Can you spell *encyclopedia*? I memorized that and *Mississippi*. Well, let's see, a ghost story."

"I live near where that one ghost story happened."

"Really? What's the story, maybe we can use it?"

I tell her all about the ghost story from behind my house, stealing glances toward Susie and Jennifer, who keep looking back at us and whispering.

"Do you ever hear the ghost cries?" Lizzie asks. I shake my head. "That's good. I wouldn't like to hear a crazy ghost when I'm trying to sleep." She's puts the notebook down and jumps up. "Sign up for the play with me! We can do everything together then you won't be scared and we can have fun. I'll go get you the form." Before I can say anything, she runs back up on stage and interrupts Mr. Freeley again. He hands her another form without really looking at her. She runs toward me again, this time waving two sheets of paper at me. When she reaches me, she's out of breath. "Here ya go. We can be townspeople together. I think they need plenty of townspeople. Oh hey, isn't that girl in your class? I think she's pen pals with Charlotte." She motions over toward Jennifer. I nod. Lizzie waves over toward her but Jennifer rolls her eyes and looks away. I move over in my seat, trying to make it seem like I am not really next to Lizzie. Lizzie just shrugs. "What's her problem? She's kind of a snot, huh? Fill out your form and I'll hand it in. That way we can be in the play together and see each other at all of the practices."

I'm in awe that she shrugs off Jennifer and her lack of acceptance so quickly. I fill out the form because I'm not sure what to do. Part of me is excited to actually join the play. Another part of me longs to sit in my spot and watch. The director did ask my dad if I wanted to join after all. *It's just a form*, I tell myself. I know I can back out if I want to. I've gotten out of lots of things in my life. My parents used to sign me up for all sorts of things and the day of it, I decided I just couldn't do it. It's a terrible feeling really. I want to do it, but then I just feel scared. Sometimes my parents understand and other times they yell. For years, they've studied my interests. Any time I showed any sort of talent for anything, they've helped me pursue it until last year. Last year, since I'm a fast runner, they signed me up for a kids race. What happened was slightly my fault as I pretended to be excited for it. I went with my dad the morning of the race, trying to convince myself that I could do it, but as soon as we pulled up to the school, I started crying. My dad hit his steering wheel with the palm of his hand. He's never angry or frustrated so when he is and you've caused it, you feel your soul break a little. "Come on Jenny," he said. "You can do this. You said you wanted to do this. You're going to miss out on your life if you are too shy to even do what you want to do." The next part was really awful. I refused to get out of the car. My dad came around to my side of the station wagon and opened the door. First he tried to be inspirational. "You can do this. You're the fastest runner I've ever seen." Then he tried bribery. "Do this and then we'll go celebrate at Baskin Robbins."

When I started crying harder, he dropped inspiration and bribery and went to trial lawyer. "Why do you keep doing this? You say you want to do something so mom and I arrange it so that you can and then you won't do it. Now what are we doing? Staying or going?"

I wiped my nose on my sleeves. "We'll stay," I said.

"That's the spirit," he said, and for a moment, he looked proud. I'm not sure if he was proud of himself or me though. Once I got out of the car and saw all of the people around the track, I froze. My dad tried to nudge me a bit over to the track. "You'll see, it will be over before you even know it. You just run once around that track with lots of kids your age and then we go home."

He kept patting me on my shoulder as he led me through the crowd. "Okay, you line up here with the other runners and I'll watch you from right there." I felt blood thumping in my ears. As my dad walked away, I grabbed for his hand, but he was gone.

I stood in a group of kids. Near me were kids who didn't seem very sure of what we were doing here but they didn't look terrified. In the front were the super confident kids, ready to win the race. When the gun shot, my legs didn't move. "Move!" I felt a push. The kids from the back pushed forward and I went down, scraping my knee. Other kids fell, too, but they got up and began the race. I stood up and looked around for my dad. Everyone was watching the racers. I walked off the track and blended in with the spectators. No one seemed to notice. My dad found me before the race finished. He hugged me. "Well, you stood at the starting line. That's something."

I hated myself. I hated that my dad was proud that I stood at the starting line. "Why aren't I normal?"

"You are, honey," he said.

"No, I'm not. All of those other kids are normal. They ran the race. They weren't scared."

"I'm sure there are other things that are hard for them."

"April doesn't think I'm normal."

"Well, no older child ever thinks the younger child is normal. You're shy. Mom and I push you on these things because it seems like you want to do it. We don't want you to miss out on things you want to do."

We sat on the cold damp grass and watched the race finish and the awards ceremony. We sat there as everyone left. Then this strange emotion takes over me—it's confidence that comes way after the fact, which is basically useless confidence. I stood up and ran around the track, one lap. In my mind, all of the kids were there with me. As I rounded the corners, I was in the lead. My dad high-fived me when I finished.

"You could have won that one," he said.

After that, my parents stopped trying with me. We no longer discussed activities I might want to try. I knew if I ever wanted to pursue anything, it would be up to me now. It's strange when you realize people have given up on you. I don't blame them. I know I'm a complete pain, but if no one pushes me, I will miss out, and have to go see Dr. Sedac pick lint from his pants forever.

With a rush of energy, I fill out my form and will myself to act normal. "I guess we need a parent signature," Lizzie says, with the pen clicking against her lip. "Hmm. I know my dad won't mind, so I'll just sign it. No problem."

She comes with me to get the signature from my dad. He's busy on stage learning what all the play terms mean. I've been reading some of his script each night and now understand most of the directions like, *stage right, stage left, downstage*. I tried teaching my dad but sometimes he acts just like one of the boys in my class. He acts like he knows everything and what he doesn't, it won't matter. Basically, we're the exact opposite of one another. I wait for him to see me before interrupting. He comes downstage and squats. "What's up, doc?"

"I need you to sign this," I say, handing him the form and a pen.

He looks at it. "Really? You want to be in the play?" I nod. "You realize that means being up on stage in front of people?" I nod again. He looks me over and then looks at Lizzie. "Who's this?"

"Hi," Lizzie steps forward. "I'm Lizzie. I'm Jenny's pen pal from school. Nice to meet you, Mr. Watts." She sticks her hand out to my dad. He shakes it.

"Do I have you to thank for getting Jenny to join the play?"

"I think she wanted to," Lizzie says, which is truly a great answer.

My dad looks at me again, then smiles and *chews the scenery* (a new term he learned) when signing it by pretending to lick the top of the pen and then make grand strokes as if it's the Declaration of Independence. "April is going to be so happy." He winks at me. "Proud of you, kid."

I blush and take the form back. Truth is, I'm proud of myself, too. I'm doing something to empty the Fear basket and take a step past the starting line. It's something an Emily would do. Lizzie runs back up to the director and hands her forms to him. "Congratulations, you are in the play."

"My friend, too," I hear her say. The director looks at the two papers quickly.

Lizzie cartwheels up the aisle back to me. I notice Jennifer's eyes follow her all the way over to me. I give her a little smile and shrug when Lizzie sits next to me. Jennifer's face doesn't change. She looks at me and then flips her hair when she moves her face and whispers to Susie sitting next to her. Susie glances over to us next. And then, the worst thing, they giggle. That can't be good.

"We're all set," Lizzie says. "We're townspeople. We just wait until they call us. What should we do? I know, I can braid your hair. Turn around."

"Um, okay," I say. I've seen other friends do this with each other and of course, I always wanted that kind of friendship. I just didn't imagine it would be with someone I have nothing in common with like Lizzie.

"So, I'm not the best at braids, but I've been working on a new one." She tugs at my hair, trying a number of times to get it right, but when she finally finishes, I can feel the braid lopsided and clumpy. "Well, good thing you have beautiful hair. I can't mess it up too badly."

I wait for her to say something else to take away such a nice comment, but she doesn't. It's something Terry would say. Something with no motive except for me to feel good about myself. I don't think people do that enough. I know I should say thank you, but my throat feels tight. Plus, I don't think she cares to hear it or not.

"Townspeople. Townspeople." A small athletic woman is walking around the auditorium yelling in a bullhorn with a whistle around her neck. Coach Jay is the assistant director of the play and the middle school girls' basketball coach. People who do not need bullhorns should be banned from using them. Coach Jay doesn't need a bullhorn and seems slightly delighted at the number of people plugging the ears to avoid the noise she's making. "C'mon Townspeople. Gotta get used to this lovely voice. Townspeople, meet me out in the hall. Townspeople to the hall now. Hut two, three, four. Hut." She takes her whistle and blows one long whistle into the bullhorn and then laughs.

Lizzie and I follow grandparents, teenagers, middle-schoolers, and a handful of kids our age out the double doors into the hallway. Do all schools smell the same? No one is exactly sure where we belong as Coach Jay is still terrorizing the auditorium. I see April and her friends sitting on the floor in their own circle off to the side. One of the grandfathers has opened a closed door and rifled through the brooms, mops, and buckets to pull out a few chairs and a step stool for the grandmothers and moms to sit while we wait. Coach Jay pushes through the doors and jumps into the middle of the circle we had naturally formed. She's quiet for a moment as she walks around and looks at us while checking things off on her clipboard. My stomach drops as

I begin to wonder if she's planning on calling out our names or making us act in front of her. Or maybe she's going to look at us and decide to cut some of us from the play. As she approaches Lizzie and me, Lizzie stands up straight, clicks her heels together and salutes Coach Jay. That ends the silence as Coach Jay laughs. "At ease, soldier," she says and gives Lizzie a wink.

"Best looking group of townspeople I have ever had the pleasure of meeting today," Coach Jay announces. The double doors open and the director comes out and stands next to Coach Jay.

"I see you have all met my assistant director, Miss Josephine Crow, or as she's known in these parts, *The Unstoppable Coach Jay*." He places one had on her shoulder and the other snatches the bullhorn from her hand. "She will not be needing this again. You are in great hands here. I realized I have no idea what I'm doing so I've brought her in to help out with no doubt that she will eventually take over. What I can tell you is that you are involved in one of the finest traditions our town has to offer. Since 1945, our community has come together with kids ages one to ninety-two to put on a play. It's truly a special event when you think about it. Year after year, members of the community come to the auditions to be a part of something bigger than themselves. For that, we should be proud of our efforts." He looks down at a paper he's holding. Then he flips it over and over again. "I had some other magical words but I can't remember them. So, in summary: a great tradition made possible by people like you. We'll have a great time working together for the next few months. That is all. Carry on."

The grown-ups chuckle. I'm not sure what's happening, but

Coach Jay and the director look like a cute couple. She pushes him away and scoots him back toward the auditorium, making a playful move of grabbing the bullhorn back. "Okay, now that he's gone, let's talk, townspeople. All of you are integral pieces of this puzzle. Without the townspeople, the show just wouldn't come alive. In this play, the townspeople have a number of scenes where we'll require dancing and singing and even fainting. It's okay if you don't have the best voice or aren't the best dancer. You're meant to create the audio and visual backdrop to our main characters. As long as you don't fall over or get a hold of a microphone, no one will notice if you are off key or out of step. That said, don't be off key or out of step!" The grown-ups laugh again. "Now, time to pick some fainters. Anyone looking for a few moments of fame, we need some girls who can faint and boys who can catch them. You sir," she points to a man dressed in a button-down shirt with the collar up underneath a V-neck sweater with the standard tan grandparent pants. "Yes, you. Shall we demonstrate?"

He moves forward, looking confidently nervous like the people who get pulled up on stage to participate in magic shows. "I'm going to faint and you are going to catch me. It's the ultimate game of trust. Ready?" He moves behind her, pretending he's a quarterback.

"One, two three," he says, "Hut."

Coach Jay puts one hand on her forehead, her knees give way, she sighs and falls like a rag doll into his arms. The townspeople clap. Coach Jay and the man stand up and take a bow.

"Thank you, sir. Nice cologne. Now, if you think you have what it takes to be a fainter, I'll hold auditions over here. We need a very young girl, a number of teenage girls and one of you beautiful, older, wiser women. All takers, come over here and line up by age group if you will. Anyone not interested in fainting, please grab a copy of the script on the table there and a schedule and I'll see you next week.'"

Lizzie jumps in line, trying to pull me with her, but I back away quickly. Jennifer and Susie float past me, obviously trying out as fainters. No one from April's group stands from their circle. No one stands at least until the auditorium doors open, bringing a flash of light and the sounds of clapping from inside that fits the person walking outside—Jeffrey. Or shall I say it the way the girls say it *J-e-f-f-r-e-y*. April's group pops up at once as if they could smell him coming. "So this is where all the pretty ladies are," he says.

"Ah, has everyone met the star of our little theater group here?" Coach Jay asks. "Jeffrey, meet your adoring townspeople. Jeffrey is playing the part of Hugo. Now, can you do some good out here and convince some teenage girls to volunteer to faint?"

"Making girls faint is my specialty," he says and winks. Coach Jay smacks him on the shoulder.

He flips his brown hair from his face. Flip hair, wait, wait, flip hair, wait, wait. I've been watching him trying to figure out why all the girls love him. Personally, I think the boy playing Birdie is much cuter. He looks like C. Thomas Howell and he's not full of himself. "Ladies," Jeffrey says as he walks toward my sister's group and the older group of high school girls near them. "For me." He places his hand on his heart and makes puppy-dog eyes. Yuck. The girls laugh. A few of them grab hands and run toward Coach Jay. The ones that don't, get the honor of Jeffrey sitting with them—confusing the ones who are now in the fainting line. I see them look at each other, conferring over whether it's cooler to stay in the line or go back so they can talk with him. They all stay where they are though.

Surprisingly, I see April walking toward the line. "Are you going to try out?" I ask her.

"I guess so," she says. "What are you doing here?"

"I'm in the play now." I brace for the eye roll.

"That's cool," she says. She walks past me. That was it. Cool. Interesting. "Just great," I hear her say under her breath. That's more like it. I make my way toward the table, excited to have my own copy of the script. I've been reading my dad's copy. I love the feel of all that copied paper in my hands. At night, I try singing Kim's songs. She's the main character and a red head, at least in the movie version. The fact that Ann Margaret is considered pretty by everyone gives me a glimmering hope that maybe one day I won't be asked if I eat too much ketchup. In our play, Kim is played by Annabeth Higgins. She doesn't have red hair, or freckles. She has smooth pale skin and dark hair with blue eyes. I haven't seen her perform at all yet. For now, she, Jeffrey and the boy playing Birdie sit with the director a lot and read lines.

"Jenny," Lizzie yells to me just as I grab the script. Everyone turns to look at me. "Jenny, over here." Lizzie is standing with Susie and Jennifer and Coach Jay. Coach Jay motions with her hand for me to join them.

"I think it will look cute if one of you girls faints and three of you catch her since we don't have any boys your age here. So, one of you on the left, one on the right and one in the center." She positions me behind Jennifer with Lizzie to my left and Susie to my right. "Ready, set, faint." Jennifer falls limply into our hands, but most of her weight falls on my arms. I'm not the strongest person. Had it not been for Lizzie and Susie grabbing Jennifer's arms at the last minute, Jennifer's head would have hit the floor.

"Earth to Emily," Jennifer says as she stands back up. "You have to catch me."

Coach Jay pulls me toward the left and Lizzie to the middle as if we are pieces of a chess game. "That looks better. Ready, set, faint."

Jennifer faints again, this time with even more drama. Lizzie catches her with no problem as I meekly pretend to help. "Gotcha," Lizzie says.

"That will do," Coach Jay says. "Remember your spots for next time." We're dismissed and I can't help but notice Susie pretend to spray Jennifer with cootie killer. Is that because of Lizzie or me? I will obsess over this question forever and already feel tired thinking of the sleep I will lose. Lizzie saw it, too, but I have a feeling she will not give it another thought, mostly because she tells me to spray her with some. I look at her, shocked. There's no way I would let Susie and Jennifer see me spray cootie killer on Lizzie to be interpreted that Jennifer has cooties. No way. "Fine," Lizzie says and makes her finger look like she's spraying it herself as she flips her hair like they do. Susie sees and grabs Jennifer's arm for her to look. Jennifer's face gets red. She marches over straight toward Lizzie, who I am trying to distance myself from now. Right before she reaches Lizzie, she turns sharply and walks to me.

"Why is your friend doing that?" I can't speak. I want to

tell her Lizzie isn't my friend so she'll know I'm cool enough to know that Lizzie isn't cool. Instead, I shrug and feel ready to cry.

"Why are you asking her?" Lizzie says. "I'm doing it because I saw you doing it. I figured it was something us *thespians* do after a scene. Is it not?"

"Us what?" Susie challenges.

"Thespians," Lizzie says and places the back of her hand on her forehead as if she's about to faint. Then she stands up straight and smiles. "You know, actresses."

Susie and Jennifer look at each other as if trying to read each other's minds for how to handle this situation. "Yes," Jennifer nods slowly to Susie. "Of course that's what it means." She grabs Susie arm and they run away laughing.

"Yikes," Lizzie says. "What crawled up their . . . sorry. Older brother talk I'm not meant to say in public." She covers her hand with her mouth. "Does your teacher say that to you all the time? Well, *older sister* talk I suppose in your place."

"No." I'm still thinking about what just happened. Had I made an enemy of Jennifer? Did she now think I was Lizzie's friend? Did she believe Lizzie wasn't making fun of her? More sleepless nights lay ahead of me. I felt my stomach start to ache.

"Are you okay?" Lizzie asks.

"No," I say. "I don't think you should be mean to them."

"Oh." She looks sad. "Sorry. Sometimes I don't know what I'm doing. See you next week, okay?" She gives me a quick hug and walks away. I feel as if I've deflated a balloon, but she has to know you should try to be friends with Jennifer and Susie, not make them mad at you.

On the way home, I sit in the car thinking, thinking. *How*

could I be so stupid? Why did Lizzie have to show up? Why couldn't Lizzie be like Susie and Jennifer and then we would all be friends? April is silent, too. I wonder if she's thinking things like I do. I wonder why some people always think and think even when they want their brain to just shut up and others don't. I don't think Lizzie is home thinking about any of this. While I don't want to be her, I wish my mind were like hers. April didn't make the cut to be a fainting girl so she's just a townsperson like me. I don't think April should take any offense to that though. The fainting auditions weren't very scientific. Coach Jay just walked through afterward randomly assigning people. My dad doesn't seem to notice neither of us is talking. He's whistling his songs from the play, happy to be in the car with his girls. He always says that with a goofy grin. "Spending time with my girls." We could be sick with chicken pox and he would sit next to us, watching cartoons and eating pancakes, saying, "Spending time with my girls." His mind wouldn't be bad to have either.

SUPERPOWER #7: SWING SETS, MOVIES, CHOCOLATE AND MOMS

Let's say you're not a shy person. When you're not a shy person, that may mean you're a people person. You just love people. Then, you would need people in a way that I don't. As much as I would love to be a people person, I usually leave people feeling as if I've said something wrong or made a strange face or didn't say enough. I am therefore not a people person. Instead, I have other loves. I love my swing set. I can think about *E.T.* or *Star Wars* all day. And when I do feel bad from an encounter with people, there's always chocolate. When all else fails, I have things to retreat back to, just like in *Star Wars*.

I think of these things as I sit in Dr. Sedac's office once again, I'm jealous that he gets a swivel chair and I don't. I would love a swivel chair if I have to sit here in silence for twenty minutes. My chair has lots of lint sticking to the fabric so Dr. Sedac may even enjoy this one better and let me take some spins on his chair. I pick at the chair lint, hoping he'll want to trade. It's the same tactic April used to use on me if she chose the wrong candy. She always tries to be adventurous instead of sticking to the basics. "Yum, this tastes like cotton candy, I swear," she would say knowing my weakness for cotton candy. I'd fall for it and end up with some disgusting sour thing and she would claim no backsies so I couldn't even get my chocolate back.

Dr. Sedac isn't falling for it though. Maybe I should lick the chair and tell him it tastes like cotton candy. Instead, he slowly swivels, rubbing it in with each turn that his chair is way cooler than mine. He keeps his fingertips touching as if he's some sort of Jedi and his gaze directed at the gray skies outside his office. I swear the skies are always gray when I'm here and I no longer think that's just a coincidence. I handed him the note from Miss Lotti. She exaggerated a bit about how often I raised my hand in class and she put in some comments about what a delightful student I am and how she's happy to have me in her class. Dr. Sedac read it for what seemed like forever. Then he placed it in a folder marked Jennifer Watts. It was a rather thick folder filled with what I don't know. I've barely spoken to him other than to apologize for my rudeness each time. We say hello in the beginning, then we sit, not talking through the middle and then he gives me an assignment and I leave while remembering my manners. Oh no. Is the folder filled with what other people think of me? Did they ask neighbors and teachers and kids in my class to explain how strange and quiet I am? My stomach sinks. Does everyone know I need professional help? Great. That will just confirm how strange and unfit I am. I need to know what is in that folder. Maybe I can use my spy tactics here. If Terry comes to visit, forget spying on the neighbors, I think we need to stage a break-in. Unless she's in on it too. Please not Terry.

I know I'm probably supposed to use this time to think about things I want to discuss with him, but usually I just think about this whole process in general. If you want a shy kid to spill all of their deepest thoughts, maybe you should start the conversation by asking questions and being nice. I'm in fifth grade, I'm shy around kids my own age let alone adults so why would he think I could come in here and open up to him when all he does is scold me on my rudeness for being so shy? I've decided I don't like him and I won't talk with him. And, I'll take all of his lint away from his chairs. Had he been kind, maybe I would tell him about how terrible school has been lately.

Ever since the play, Jennifer and Susie have gone from acting like I didn't exist to acting like I'm the stupidest person they've ever met. They call me Emily all the time now and not in a good way. They say it and smirk and it's only at recess or lunch when Miss Lotti isn't around to hear them. "Emily, where's your friend?" They ask me that and though it doesn't seem like a bad question, they say it in that sing-song way that lets you know they want to crush you. "Make sure your friend washes her hands before the practice," Jennifer says. "I don't want her cooties all over me." Then Susie chimes in with, "Yours either." Boom. My heart crumbles. After that, I decided I was done with school. I've had stomachaches every morning. I can't face it. I can't face a teacher who doesn't like me, popular girls who make fun of me, a mean boy calling me ugly. Why go to a place like that when I can stay home with my mom and make cookies? Tell me, what sane adult would put up with any of that? My stomachache worked the first day, but only then. Now I spend the morning trying really hard to convince my mom that I can't go to school. She practically has to drag me to the car and then I cry the whole way there. So, that would answer why I'm having added sessions with Dr. Sedac.

The play was my first try at doing something to get out of my dreaded shell and it completely backfired. I wish I could go back in time and not even mention the play to Lizzie. This whole year is not going as I wanted it to and I don't think any year will go as I wish it would because I'm not who I want to be. I want to be liked. I want to be loud and funny. I don't want to be a weirdo that never speaks. All of this talking in my head would probably be great for a psychiatrist to hear and fill up my folder with, but I just don't think Dr. Sedac is the one who will understand me. I'm not sure it makes sense even to me. Just talk. If you want to talk more, just do it. That's what I tell myself all of the time. My parents are always telling me how special I am and if I could just let the world see that, life would be great for me. I know they mean well, but I don't know how to let the world know and I don't know why it's so easy for everyone else to be themselves all the time. Everyone else speaks their minds even when no one wants to hear them. Frankie Myers is a terrible person who isn't afraid to be terrible. No one wants to hear him. I'm not even taking the bus because of what he has to say. Yet there he is, being himself—letting the world see his specialness of being awful. Why can't he be the shy one and keep all of his awful thoughts to himself? Then he could sit in this chair and bully Dr. Sedac into getting the swivel chair.

I'm feeling pretty angry by the time this session is over. My fists are clenched as Dr. Sedac hands me my instructions. "You are to take the bus to school this week," he says without looking at me. "Have your bus driver sign this form at the end of it." I look at it. It has an explanation that I'm fearful of the bus and under psychiatric care. No! I crumple the paper. I didn't even think, my hand just took it and crumpled it. Dr. Sedac snatches it back, smoothed it down and places it back in my hand. He points to the door. I don't say goodbye or thank you. I leave, closing the door slightly louder than normal.

My mom and Mrs. Sims stop talking. I want them to see that I'm not crying over sadness or some big breakthrough. I'm crying because I'm mad. I'm mad that I have to come to these sessions that make me feel awful for no good reason. I'm mad that my parents think I need this help. I know I need it, but I wish they didn't know I need it. I'm mad that Frankie Myers exists. I'm mad that Lizzie has ruined my life. I'm mad that people are mean and shy people can't just be left alone. I push past my mom and sit in the farthest away chair from her and cross my arms. "He wants to see you now," I tell her and turn away from them. I look at the gray wall in front of me. I hear my mom walk into his office. Mrs. Sims comes over and sits next to me. She doesn't question me, she just pats my back. Time makes all outbursts feel stupid. Ten, nine, eight, seven, six, five, four, three, two, one. Yep, I go from angry to feeling ridiculous. "Sorry," I mumble to Mrs. Sims.

"For what?"

"For being angry."

"A little anger is good sometimes. Plus, you didn't hurt my feelings at all. No apologies needed to me. I am sorry that you don't seem to be having a good time here." We sit quietly while my breathing gets slower and my fists unclench.

My mom comes out and slightly slams the door as well. "Jenny," she says sternly. "Put your coat on. Mrs. Sims, I'm afraid we need to cancel the rest of our appointments. This arrangement isn't working."

Mrs. Sims nods and pops up. "No, I don't think it is. I will miss you both though. Drop by sometimes, okay?"

Could this be real? Are we really leaving here forever? I put my coat on quickly before my mom changes her mind. I walk out the door behind her. Mrs. Sims runs out after us. She hands me a full bag of Hershey's Kisses and gives me a quick hug. If Dr. Sedac had been like Mrs. Sims, maybe this arrangement would have worked.

I get in the car and my whole body feels relaxed. I have a bag of chocolate, a note to the bus driver that I no longer need to deliver, and no more appointments with Dr. Sedac. I feel free. I start to unwrap a Kiss when I notice my mom hasn't started the car. Her hands are covering her face. I stop unwrapping, waiting for her to speak. My mouth is already salivating over the promise of chocolate. I unwrap it quietly and quickly pop it in my mouth. Then I wait while it melts in my mouth. She's not crying, at least I don't hear crying sounds. When she takes her hands off her face, she smooths her hair and turns around to look at me. I swallow the Kiss.

"Why won't you take the bus?"

I don't answer.

"Why are you fighting me about going to school?"

I don't answer again. I really want another Hershey's Kiss.

"Look, if you tell me why you don't want to do these things, I can help you. Did Dr. Sedac help you at all?"

"No," I say. "He was mean. I don't like him."

"He is mean, isn't he? He said you have a strong attachment

to me that keeps you from wanting to branch out and live your life. And that I coddle you too much. Do you think that's true?"

"Um." I'm not sure what coddle means.

"Right. And then he went on and on about my parenting style and all my shortcomings. Like he's some prize, you know?" She sounds like April. She grabs a Kiss, holding it in her hand while continuing to talk. "Well, he's not. I don't care what he says, if you never want to talk again, that's up to you. You're not the first child who has ever been shy or didn't like school. It's fine that you're shy. I'm not going to keep thinking I need to help you. Maybe you're happy being shy and I should just butt out."

"Please don't say that," I say. I let the bag of Hershey's Kisses drop from my lap. "I don't like it when you and dad give up on me."

"I didn't mean it like that. I'll never ever give up on you. I just don't want you feeling bad about yourself."

"Maybe I need to be pushed. I don't know how to be. I don't know how everyone else knows just how to be themselves and be so comfortable that way. I don't know how to do that. Did they all read some book? Is there a book I can read? I don't like being who I am. I don't like everyone all the time telling me how shy I am like there's something really strange about me and how I need to change. I don't like that everyone thinks that they should have a say in how I am. It just makes me feel like I'm wrong. Like everything about me is wrong." I'm rambling now and can't seem to stop. "I hate Dr. Sedac. I hate coming here. I hate Frankie Myers. I hate that he bullies me on the bus. I hate that I don't have lots of friends. I thought Miss Lotti liked me how I was but it turns out she only sees me as shy, too. She paired me with Lizzie just so Lizzie's craziness would wear off on me. So, if you don't mind, I just want to stay home, watch television, dream about *E.T.*, listen to Kenny Rogers and be left alone by a world that thinks I'm not right anyway."

My mom looks me over, not saying anything. I sniffle. A few raindrops hit the roof of the car. We listen to it without talking. "Okay," my mom says finally. She nods to herself and then looks in the rear-view mirror right at me. "We got this. We can do this, Jenny. I can help you." She still doesn't start the car. I hand her a few unwrapped Hershey's Kisses, which she pops in her mouth one by one and chews with purpose. I can tell she's thinking in that very determined way she does sometimes. Usually, it's the face she makes when filling out paperwork, hemming pants, or decorating a cake.

"So, are we going?" I ask, slightly nervous that Dr. Sedac will ride his swivel chair out here and command us back inside.

"Right," she says and starts the car. A man talks loudly about watching the news at 11:00 from over the car radio, which reminds me how optimistic we had been on our way here. We listened to "Eye of the Tiger" on full blast, pumped up with silent hopes that this time Dr. Sedac would be helpful. She turns it off and we drive home in silence. I watch the rain drip down the sides of the windows. I find one droplet to watch each time swirl its way down until it gets stopped. I make up stories about each raindrop as it falls. Do other kids do that? Is that normal? I make pencils talk to each other in my head and raindrops speak. That can't be normal, right? I can't see Jennifer having one raindrop say to the other, "Race you to the bottom!" I know it's not normal, but I love that no one can see inside my mind. At least in here, I can be abnormal with no one calling attention to it. It felt good to tell my mom everything. I didn't name Jennifer and Susie because I know my mom is a solver. I don't want her running to Jennifer's mom saying Jennifer needs to be nice to me. But it feels good to give some of my grief away. My mind is quiet. I can watch the droplets, make them speak in my head and think of nothing else.

I sleep that night better than I have in a while. When I wake up, the sun is up. My mom didn't wake me up for school. I'm unsure of what this means. I'm afraid to move because the thought of a pretend sick-day where I don't have to pretend to be sick is intriguing. I know it's not the weekend. I glance at my *E.T.* wall calendar to be sure. Nope, it's Thursday. I sneak out of my bed and look outside. No snow or ice. My curiosity gets the better of me. I throw my robe on and head downstairs.

"Oh good, you're up," my mom says. She puts pancakes on the table.

"Where's April? Do we not have school today?"

"We have what I am going to call Regrouping Day. April is at school. She was pretty annoyed to hear you get another day off, but this isn't necessarily a day off. It wouldn't hurt if you acted a little sick in front of her tonight though. We need to make some plans today. Also, this is your last day staying home from school unless you are truly sick. Deal? Finish your breakfast and we'll get started."

Regrouping Day starts with a legal pad. It has my dad's scratchy handwriting all over it with lines and arrows. "So, your dad went to this training seminar last year called *Getting What You Want Out of Life* and he thought it could help you. It helps you make lists of what's important to you, what makes you happy, what you wish for, and then it gives you a plan to get that. Sound good?"

I nod. I love lists.

"Now, some of what needs to be done is adult stuff. You may not like it, but some of the things you told me yesterday are beyond you handling them. I realize learning how to diffuse bullies is a wonderful life skill, but I made some calls last night and learned this Frankie Myers is basically a psychopath so your father and I will handle that one. As for Miss Lotti, my first instinct was to call her but you're a big girl now. You should talk with her yourself. I'll help you with tips from dad's other training, *The Art of Speaking to Change Your Life.* Seriously, he goes to so many of these, I think he needs to attend one called *Stop Going to Seminars and Get to Work.* However, I think it can help us. What do you think?"

I can see what my dad sees in these seminars. The titles sound so powerful. Of course I'm excited and hopeful about Regrouping Day. Maybe my mom and I can figure out how to have a better year here—hopefully by the afternoon. Then I really want to watch television and eat cookies. We write out what to say to Miss Lotti. She has me write out lists about what makes me most shy (school, organized activities, adults) and what I love (swinging, *E.T.*, *Star Wars*, chocolate, running, being outside, hikes with my family). She writes what she most loves about me on a small piece of paper and folds it up. "Keep this in your book bag whenever you're feeling low, just think of it and smile," she tells me. I write out times I felt proud of myself, which is really difficult. My mom has to keep reminding me of things. She has so many memories she thinks I should be proud of, but I just don't. "Remember when you drew that beautiful picture of the apple tree?" "What about the time you helped Mrs. Kred weed her garden?" "How about when you rode your bike around the entire neighborhood without stopping?" I wouldn't exactly say I felt proud of myself those times, but that exercise just makes me feel like a loser so we move quickly from it. My mom looks at me in slight astonishment that I can't see what she sees. Luckily, she doesn't push me on it though. We role play what to say to Miss Lotti. Eventually, I start feeling full of confidence and support. Then we get to spend the afternoon together. We make cookies, rake the garden, and paint rocks.

Armed with my plans to speak with Miss Lotti, I'm ready for the first step from Regrouping Day. My parents are ready, too. They're walking April and me to the bus stop which would feel tenser if it wasn't so funny to see my dad pretend he's April. "No one walk with me, okay? I'm going to like die, if my friends see me with all of you at the bus stop." He flips his pretend long hair and grabs her bag and walks down the driveway. April is fuming. She catches up to him and grabs her bag, flips her hair, and walks away quickly, muttering to herself. In our defense, we do stay away from her when she walks up to Cammy and Robbie, but they both love my parents.

"What brings all the Watts family out this fine morning?" Cammy asks.

"Don't ask," April says.

"We just need to talk to Jenny's bus driver," my dad says.

Robbie walks over to us. He bends down to look right in my eyes. "Haven't seen you here in a while. Bus bully?" I nod. He shakes his head. My bus pulls up, my dad goes to walk over to it, but Robbie stops him. "If I may, Mr. Watts." He steps up the bus stairs.

"Hello Ruth," he says to the bus driver.

"What are you up to, Robbie? No good, I bet," the bus driver replies but she laughs, obviously entertained by him.

"Looking for a bus bully."

"Robbie, I can handle . . ." my dad starts to say.

"Mr. Watts, I have a sixth sense about these things. Allow me."

"It's probably Fr . . . " the bus driver starts to say Frankie's name.

"Shhh. I'm telling you people, I can pick out a bully by sight. Seriously, it's one of my many gifts. Ruth, do you mind if I do a ride along and then you can swing me by the middle school? Mr. Watts will get you some Lotto scratchers for your trouble, right?"

My dad looks confused but he nods.

"Robbie, you're too much. No problem, come along little one," the bus driver says to me in the sweetest voice. Normally, she's just yelling at us so it's strange to see her face smile. My parents aren't sure about this arrangement, but it's out of their hands.

I scramble up and glance back to the rear of the bus. Frankie is back there. I sit in the front seat. Robbie stands across the aisle from me, looking over the students behind him. "Start it up, Ruth," Robbie says. The bus moves forward. Everyone is silent as they stare at Robbie. He looks huge in here in a way that he never looks outside of the bus. I think we're so used to seeing certain sizes from tiny kindergartners to fifth graders. He walks down the aisle with his hands out in front of him as if he's holding a metal detector. "Beep, beep, beep," he says, pretending his hands are leading him. Frankie is the only kid looking up at Robbie with a smirk on his face. Robbie walks past him at first and just as Frankie is about to laugh, Robbie backs up. "Beepbeepbeepbeep." He's standing in front of Frankie with his hands pointing directly at Frankie's face and his arms shaking. "Hello, Frankie. Haven't seen you since you decided to make a career out of elementary school." He pushes Frankie toward the window while he sits down practically on top of him. He places his arm around Frankie and talks with him the whole way to school. None of us can hear what he's saying, but Frankie's face is ghostly white as he keeps nodding.

When we arrive at school, Robbie announces to all of us, "My friend Frankie here apologizes to anyone and everyone he has bullied on this bus. It won't happen again. Right Frankie? Classic Frankie—so quiet. Frankie, I can't hear you. There we go. Let's show our gratitude to our new friend here by letting him off the bus first." Frankie walks down the aisle. It's so quiet, we can hear his sneakered footsteps. I watch to make sure he's not waiting for me but he doesn't. He runs into the school. Robbie puts his feet up on the chair in front of him and crosses his arms behind his head. He sighs. "That felt good." I give him a little wave and he salutes me.

Next up from our Regrouping Day, I need to talk with Miss Lotti. This step isn't easy but my mom and I went through it. She played the part of Miss Lotti. We figured out what I would say. Then, my mom gave me the pin my dad received from one of his seminars. It said *Yes I Can*. We pinned it on the front of my shirt in the morning. As I was eating breakfast, my mom and I heard April coming down the stairs and realized the pin wasn't such a good idea. Quickly, she reached over and took it off my shirt. Instead, she told me to put it in my pocket so I could touch it and remember that I could do this step.

I wait until the afternoon to talk with Miss Lotti. All morning I kept going over what my mom and I had planned for me to say, but I was losing the courage. As we are lining up for lunch, I put myself in the last place and force myself. When Miss Lotti is about to leave us to the cafeteria, I stop to ask her if I could talk with her. She leads me back to the classroom where she pulls out her peanut butter and jelly sandwich. I bring my lunch to her desk. "What's new Jenny?"

"I'm in the community play."

"Really? I think that's wonderful. It's *Bye Bye Birdie* this year, right? I love that this town still does that. I was in one once when I was around twelve. I loved it. So, what do you want to talk with me about?"

"I want to know why you paired me with my pen pal. Is it because you don't like me the way I am?"

"What? Why do you think pairing you with Lizzie would mean that?"

"Well, she's crazy and wild and loud, everything I'm not. So I figured you wanted me to be more like her so that's why you paired me with someone so different than me. You don't like that I'm shy." Phew. Said it. It's out there. I want to take it all back now and run away. Miss Lotti looks heartbroken. She puts her sandwich down and looks at me. There's a slight chance I've put too much thought into this one. I do that sometimes—build something up in my mind that really doesn't exist. I want to cry because I think I hurt Miss Lotti. Our relationship will never be the same. She'll see me as the ultra-sensitive kid.

"I'm sorry that's the way it seemed to you," she says. "I suppose in some ways that may have been in the back of my mind."

I nod, wishing I never asked to have this conversation. "It's okay," I whisper and take a bite of my sandwich.

"However," she says and holds my hand, which immediately makes me want to cry. "It's not because I want you to change. Different people bring out different aspects of ourselves. Take Miss Hanson and me. We've been friends for ten years but we have different interests and personalities. In fact, we're a little like you and Lizzie. I'm definitely more reserved like you and she's always going full speed ahead."

"But she's not beating up boys and doing cartwheels all over the place." I say it trying to be funny, but I think I end up sounding mean.

"Well, not anymore at least," Miss Lotti said and eats more of her lunch. "Tell me, what do you look for in a friend?"

I love how Miss Lotti can ask a question like that but make you feel comfortable while she waits for an answer. She doesn't stare you down, instead, she keeps eating and smiling, not picking lint. The hard part is I don't know what to look for in a friend. Truthfully, I do want a friend that brings me out of my shell but in a way that also makes everyone love us. We wouldn't be mean like Jennifer and Susie can be sometimes. With this friend, I would know what to say, wear, and do at all times. Maybe we would even have our own language. So, I'm not sure how to answer Miss Lotti without basically saying, I want a perfect person to be a sidekick to.

"I don't really know how to explain it," I finally say.

"I get it. It's hard to put it into words, huh?"

I nod.

"Someone like you," I say.

"See, that right there is why I paired you with Lizzie." She squeezes my hand. "Miss Hanson said Lizzie needed a good friend. She needed someone kind but brave. Lizzie has had a lot of difficulties over the past year. You know they moved to the area recently, right? Well, things haven't been so great for her and I wanted to pair her with someone I think is great. Someone who wouldn't be so quick to judge her and could listen to her. I wanted someone with a huge heart and I thought of you right away. If you could find it in your big heart to be a good friend to her, it would really help. I don't think she's had the easiest transition making new friends here. Miss Hanson told me how much Lizzie talks about you. I thought the friendship was going so well. Is she too crazy or do you think you could help Lizzie feel a bit more at home here? It would be a huge favor to Miss Hanson. However, I also don't want you to feel obligated."

"Yes," I say, very adult-like. "She is in the play with me actually." I didn't like the idea of being Lizzie's friend, but I love the idea that I was chosen to be her friend because I can help her. I like being helpful. Now it seems like a secret plan between Miss Lotti and me.

"That's great, Jenny. I think you are just what she needs. I was shy, too, you know," she says. Lots of adults tell me that. I'm not sure I believe them. Maybe they were slightly shy at some point, but I don't know many shy adults. "I never want for you to change who you are because I like you just as you are. Are you still seeing that Dr. Sedac?"

"I don't think so." We're eating as if we're friends and I'm feeling pretty confident at the moment, so I tell her, "He was a jerk."

She laughs. Her eyes are wide. "Really?"

"Totally. He wasn't helpful at all and I couldn't really talk to him without him being mad at me. My mom didn't like him either though. His secretary, Mrs. Sims, she was really nice. She let me eat Hershey's Kisses and we did puzzles. I'll miss her, but I don't want to go back to that place."

"That's too bad he didn't make you feel comfortable. Maybe he should have had the Hershey Kisses." I agree. We eat quietly for a few moments. "Jenny, would you like to eat lunch with me every Friday in here?" I nod. Yes! I really want to prove to her that I truly like her and wasn't mad at her for pairing me with Lizzie. "Perfect. It's a date."

When I get home, my mom is waiting at the top of the hill for me with her arms wide. I run to her like I haven't done since I was a first grader. Though I'm nearly as tall as her now, she manages to lift me up into a hug.

SUPERPOWER #8: HELPFULNESS

once heard this story from my priest about an elephant walking in a parade. The parade organizers thought it would be wonderful to have this elephant lead all of the floats, dancers, bands, and waving people down the street in front of lots of people cheering. What they didn't know is that the elephant would walk a few steps, then stop. Or walk a few steps forward, then turn around and walk in the opposite direction, running into the band marching behind him. The parade was a disaster as the elephant zigzagged through the crowd, unsure of what to do. Then, someone gave the elephant a stick to hold in his trunk. When holding the stick, the elephant was able to walk forward and lead the parade. The stick gave the elephant purpose. The elephant had a focus—not dropping the stick so he no longer was distracted by all of the cheering people. The priest was using the story to remind us of how to snap back into focus our faith and not get distracted by unimportant things in life.

I think about that elephant often. It's like when teachers give the worst-behaved kids in the class the job of line leader or door holder. Having that job gives them order in their minds. They have to hold the door so there's no time to goof around. Plus, they feel important because they have a responsibility now. Lizzie is my stick. Shyness always takes a backseat to helpfulness. If someone has seen past my shyness and given me a job, I always welcome it eagerly—except for like chores at home, that's totally different.

I come to the play rehearsal with a new perspective. I'm actually excited to see Lizzie. If Jennifer and Susie ask why I'm her friend, I can tell them I'm just helping as Miss Lotti asked me to do. In order to help her, I've brought some exercises we can do that my mom and I did from Regrouping Day. I've created a notebook for her. On the front, I wrote her name in bubble letters. On the first five pages, I've put these headings: *My Favorite Things, My Least Favorite Things, Things I Hope to Do, Things I Hate to Do, Things I Wish Could Change.* I wrote the headings in my best handwriting. Actually, my handwriting is one of the things I like best about myself. When I want it to be, it's pretty with swirly letters. Last year, a substitute teacher pulled me aside to ask me how I learned to write in such a manner. Then she showed the class my paper to look at the penmanship. Of course, it was slightly embarrassing but mostly it was fantastic. I'm not shy about my handwriting. It was one of those times where the class found me interesting. They passed around the paper as if it was a fragile, ancient scroll and everyone said how nice the letters were.

With my new sense of helpfulness, I have a new confidence. I walk past Jennifer and Susie on my way to find Lizzie and actually say hello to them. I'm not sure they hear me though. I look around for Lizzie but don't see her anywhere. She's more of a

finder though—one of those people you never have to find because they always find you first. I expect her to come bounding
over to me soon so I sit and wait with the notebook on my lap.
She doesn't show though. I look at my watch. Coach Jay should
be calling the townspeople soon. I don't want Lizzie to be late.
What if Coach Jay gets here and has to wait for Lizzie? What if
I have to catch Jennifer faint without her help? It would just be
Jennifer, Susie and me. As much as I hoped I would like that, the
thought makes my skin feel prickly—like heading into a briar
patch willingly. We have a briar patch across from the end of
our driveway which I've headed into plenty of times unwillingly
when my bike or Big Wheel has gone out of control.

Just as I thought, Coach Jay calls the townspeople out into
the hallway. Into the briar patch by myself. I wonder if I should
just pull out my homework and pretend I can't be a townsperson anymore, but since Jennifer and Susie are in my class, that
wouldn't work. I follow the smiling group out into the hallway.
To my surprise, Lizzie is already there. She waves when she sees
me. It's not one of her normal crazy waves, just a slight one. I
walk over to her, now unsure about the whole situation. Is it possible she no longer likes me?

She greets me nicely enough, but she's not herself. No cartwheels, no splits, no quick hugs. "Are you okay?" I ask her.

"Yes, of course," she says.

"I didn't think you were coming tonight when I didn't see
you."

"Oh, I saw you, but you looked busy." She looks away for a
moment, then quietly says, "I know I can be a lot to take. I wasn't
sure you wanted me hanging around you."

"Oh," I say. I think of how Miss Lotti thought I would be a kind friend for Lizzie. I guess I haven't really been that yet though. "I made you something." I show her the notebook, and I feel grateful that I have it, like it's proof that I did want her as a friend, even if that's not necessarily true. She flips through it.

"I love it," she says and hugs it close to her. The old Lizzie seems to be coming to life. I can see it in her eyes.

"It's a Regrouping notebook where you can fill out all sorts of things. I can help you with it if you like."

"Sure! I'd like that." She looks toward Jennifer and Susie. "I'm sorry I embarrassed you in front of your friends. I didn't mean to."

I know my response should be the truth: Jennifer and Susie are not my friends. Really, even I can see that with or without Lizzie, those girls would have found some other reason not to like me. However, I don't want to say that they're not my friends. Saying it is just proving I'm not popular. Instead I nod and thankfully, Coach Jay begins speaking. She herds all the townspeople around to the stage. The stage floor is dark and kind of dusty with footprints, but I have to admit, it's pretty cool to be on the stage when there's no audience seated below. We play a game called Stage Simon Says. After she's run through all of the stage terms we need to know, she shouts them out in the megaphone. When it comes to Simon Says, my system is to always go out near the end after a respectable time playing. Preferably, I like to go out in a group situation so as not to call attention or seem like a fool. I'm actually quite good at Simon Says but I never want to be Simon and stand in front of everyone. Sometimes when you're Simon, it's impossible to get anyone out and so you're stuck doing silly things in front of people as they grow tired of your ineptitude at calling out new tasks quickly. There's only so many times you can tell people to touch their head and nose.

Coach Jay yells, "Simon Says, 'Stage Right.'" We all scramble to stage right.

"Simon Says, 'Stage Left.'" We run there. Well, the younger people run. The older people pretend they're moving quickly, pumping their arms, but their legs go slowly.

"Simon Says, 'Head's Up.'" We all cover our heads and crouch down.

"Good." Coach Jay grins. "Stage Right."

A few people go which is ridiculous because she even paused before saying Stage Right. It was really obvious the next one wouldn't be Simon Says. However it was a group of April's friends so either they decided the game wasn't cool or wanted to look like they weren't paying attention. They giggle away and slowly other middle schoolers trickle away, too.

"Simon Says, 'Fourth Wall.'" We all head to the front of the stage and shake our heads no. She told us we are never to break the fourth wall. Breaking the fourth wall is when you talk directly to the audience.

We go on and on and it starts to seem that Coach Jay doesn't really see this as a winners and losers game. I think she just wants us to know the stage. She calls everything so painfully slow, that it could go on for hours. I'm actually happy when Jeffrey hops on to the stage and grabs the megaphone.

"This is seriously the lamest game of Simon Says ever," Jeffrey says. "Are you people ready for the lightening round?"

The older girls suddenly come back to the game.

"I said, are you ready for the lightening round?" The girls and the retired people shout yes.

"Who is this guy?" Lizzie asks.

"Jeffrey Greeson," I answer.

"He seems like a total GGTTU, you know?"

I don't know.

"Sorry, we used that in my old school. It means God's Gift to the Universe."

I giggle. That's completely what Jeffrey thinks he is.

"I don't know, I don't know if you are all ready for the lightening round," he says and flips his hair. He's walking in front of us with a John Travolta strut. Coach Jay playfully tries to take back the megaphone. Is she under his spell, too?

"Let's crush this lightening round," Lizzie says.

"I'm not sure you all are ready," Jeffrey says. "Ladies, do you feel ready?" he asks April's group. They're just about ready to faint as if he's Conrad Birdie.

Before they answer, Lizzie yells, "Just get it over with already!" He looks over in our direction, confused. His face turns quickly back to smug though.

"Be patient, be patient," he says. "I want to make sure you're all ready."

"We're asking you to be Simon Says, not paint the Sistine Chapel," Lizzie calls again. I can tell he doesn't know what that is. I'm not sure I know either. I stand behind Lizzie, not wanting to be singled out, but kind of loving that she's giving him a hard time. "Can we play now before moss starts growing on our backs?"

Jeffrey glares at her quickly, not enough that anyone else would see. She glares back.

"Simon Says, 'Stage Right.'"

I'll hand it to him: he is better at it than Coach Jay. He calls the instructions quickly, causing lots of the older people to stop playing. I leave when I see a large group of people get tripped up. Soon, it's just Lizzie and an older girl. It's obvious the older girl believes the winner of this game gets a date with Jeffrey. Lizzie stands her ground through call after call. After he finishes four rapid-fire calls, Lizzie looks at me. On his next call without saying Simon Says, she walks purposefully over to what he called, getting herself out. It looked like that moment in *Star Wars* where Obi-Wan Kenobi decides to let Darth Vader defeat him. Just like in the movie as it is now, I don't understand why. Lizzie skips over to me as Jeffrey congratulates the middle school girl who won, giving her a hug as his fans come toward them.

"Why did you lose?"

"I was getting bored," she says, shrugging her shoulders. "Plus, that girl really wanted to win. Are you going home now?"

"No, it looks like my dad isn't finished yet."

"I'll stay with you then. I don't need to go home yet. We can work on the notebook."

We walk back into the auditorium. "Hey," we hear Annabeth Higgin's unmistakable raspy voice. She and Birdie are sitting in the unlit section of the auditorium. "Good game up there. Are you Scott Cray's sister?"

"Yes, I'm Lizzie and this is my friend Jenny."

"Hey, I'm Annabeth and this is Charlie." He nods. I'm star struck. They're basically the leads in the play, along with Jeffrey. I've been watching them interact and they're really so cute together. They seem much older than Jeffrey though Jeffrey is cast as Annabeth's boyfriend, Hugo. I was kind of hoping not to learn the boy playing Birdie's name since I like to think he really is Conrad Birdie. He seems cooler than everyone else in the play, except for Annabeth. They're kind of like Han Solo and Princess Leia.

Annabeth pops up to come closer. "I remember when I was as young as you two. It seems so long ago now. I bet you still get to play dress-up and get muddy. I miss those days." She has that same sparkle in her eyes that Lizzie has. Normally, I would think someone basically saying we get to do baby-stuff would be making fun of us, but Annabeth looks sincere.

"A play is kind of like playing dress-up," Lizzie offers.

"That's true," Annabeth says, but seems still to be wishing she was our age. "Want to sit with us? We're just waiting for our scene but they're working with the grownups first."

"It's seriously taking the parents forever to understand their parts," Charlie says and laughs. "I'm beginning to wonder if they just don't want to go back to their real lives."

I look to the stage and see my dad along with his pretend wife, Mrs. Craig, my crazy art teacher.

"Jenny's dad plays your dad," Lizzie tells Annabeth.

Annabeth grabs me into a giant hug and swings me around, with my feet lifted off the ground. "I've always wanted a sister."

"Annabeth, put the poor girl down," Charlie says. "I apologize for my friend. Boredom makes her crazy which is why she forced me into the play with her."

"Oh stop, you needed something to do now that your soccer career is over," she says over her shoulder. "Your dad is so cool," Annabeth says when she returns me to the ground. "I wish my dad would do plays and stuff. He's always traveling for work."

"Thanks," I say.

"Sit with us, really. I'm so bored and I love kids. Tell me everything. How do you like living here so far?" We sit with Annabeth. She and Lizzie talk away while Charlie and I sit mostly silently. His silence seems cool though. Lizzie then shows Annabeth the notebook I made for her. She flips through it. "I love this. Let's do it." Much of their conversation hasn't interested Charlie, but he looks at the notebook over Annabeth's shoulder and gives a slight nod. A nod that I think means he likes the idea. Or, he is just acknowledging the idea. I'm not sure, but I think he likes it.

"Annabeth and Charlie and Jeffrey, we're ready for you." I see the director straining to see us from the stage. "You up there?"

"Coming," Annabeth yells down. Charlie jumps up and grabs her hands, pulling her along. "So great talking with you." Then she pulls back from Charlie slightly but keeps holding his hand as she whispers in Lizzie's ear. I can't hear what she's saying but I am dying to know. She gives Lizzie a one-handed hug before Charlie tugs her up to the stage. Annabeth and Charlie are on stage while the director calls out for Jeffrey again. He's sitting in the aisle with his fans, including my sister. Throughout the night before and after Simon Says, he has sat there with a guitar in his lap. I don't think he ever played it. He slowly stands up, flips his hair, and bends down to ask April something which I'm guessing is to hold his guitar. Sauntering up to the stage, he doesn't use the stairs on the side, but instead in one motion places his right hand on the stage and throws his legs up and somehow lands on his feet. He gives Annabeth a hug and Charlie gives him a handshake.

I look back at Lizzie; she's looking at the notebook.

"We should get started, huh?" I ask.

The light seems to have gone out on her. "I'd like that," she says, "but I think maybe I should go home."

"Oh, okay." I'm not sure if I've done something to upset her.

"I really love the book, Jenny. It's the nicest thing anyone has ever given me." She gives me a quick hug and walks out of the auditorium. I'm not used to all the hugs, but I want to be. I turn to see my mom calling to me. I leave the auditorium as well and as my mom and I head to the car, I see Lizzie crossing through the parking lot. I point her out to my mom.

"She doesn't have a coat on," my mom notices immediately as moms do. "Is her mom picking her up?"

"No, she just walks here by herself usually."

"Hop in, we'll see if she wants a ride."

We pull up alongside Lizzie. My mom tries to crank her window down but it always sticks when it's cold. She puts up one finger to Lizzie, telling her to wait a minute as she uses all her might with her other hand to finally inch the window down. "Hi, I'm Jenny's mom. Hop in. We'll give you a ride home."

Lizzie hesitates but my mom gives her one of her goofy, I'm-a-nice-mom, not a serial killer smiles. Lizzie opens the door and joins me in the backseat.

"Thank you," she says. It's dark, but the parking lights reflect a tear on her cheek.

"You'd freeze out there."

"I don't mind the cold, but thank you," Lizzie says. "I don't live too far, just up MacIntosh Way next to the old cemetery."

Lizzie sits quietly as my mom hums to her music. We reach

her house. It looks lonely. No other houses are nearby. I can just make out the crumbling tombstones serving as her neighbors. No lights are on in her house. My mom pulls up and in the darkness, I can see her thinking face.

"I'll walk you up," she says. I sit in the car and watch and try not to think of the Bloody Rock story. It's creepy up here. Though I can see the high school lights through the trees, I feel a world away from anyone except the tombstones. I reach over and lock the door Lizzie used, in case of any ghosts. Do ghosts use door handles though? Shoot. I don't think they do but I climb forward and lock all of the doors in the front. I scan all around me. The wind blows—I'm positive it wasn't windy before now. How can Lizzie be so happy and full of energy living here? C'mon already. Finish talking, Mom. You don't need to find out everyone's life story in the first two seconds of knowing them. As I'm checking behind me again for any ghosts, I hear someone try to open the door.

"For goodness sakes, Jenny, unlock the doors, it's freezing out here." My mom is back. I unlock her door and climb back to my seat when a shadow raps the window.

"Ghosts!" I huddle into fetal position.

"What has gotten into you? Open the door for Lizzie. She's coming out with us for dinner."

Through the window, I see Lizzie laughing. I let her in the car. We start driving, then she turns to me and says, "Boo!"

I jump. "Not funny."

"I don't think there are any ghosts out there. I've sat outside at night a few times to check, but never saw any. Plus, I've read all the tombstones. I think they were nice people."

I expect my mom to stop this conversation. She's always skittish about letting April and me know about death. Our goldfish has now been alive for eight years but changes size, color, and fin shape. Whenever my dad watches the news, she has us leave the room. April thinks the news is boring, but it bothers her when my mom won't let her watch it. She thinks she's old enough to handle it but my mom argues that there's plenty of time to see how awful the world can be when we grow up. So, I figure she would steer the conversation away from a graveyard, but she seems lost in thought.

"When we moved here over the summer, at first I wouldn't go near there, but I was also so curious. Ever get like that? Like you want to know something so badly but you're scared at the same time? Well, that's how I felt. Then I thought if I take a notebook and paper and made it like I was a scientist or something, I wouldn't be as scared. There are ten people there. Six of the graves are one family. The oldest date was 1804. Then the rest were born in 1818 and so on up until 1845. The saddest are the two little kids, a girl and a boy. They only lived to be five and four. They have the same year of death so something must have happened. Their mom died the next year so I think if you can die from sadness, that's probably what happened. The rest of that family were men. I think one, the oldest, was the grandfather, and then the other two were brothers, maybe one was married to the mom. The other four had different names. I did some research at the library when we moved here. I guess right where my house is now, there used to be an old church but it burned down in 1865. Anyway, I don't think any of them are ghosts, I think they're all up in heaven or reincarnated, but all were happy. What do you think?"

I had been listening, finding all that she was saying fascinating if not super fast. First, I didn't know you could look up things like that in the library. Maybe I could find out about Bloody Rock there to see if that story is true. Second, Lizzie is brave. I would never hang around a graveyard by myself. Third, I wonder what happened to those little kids. I'm still processing all of it when I realize Lizzie is waiting for me to respond. I look at her and see her eyeing me closely. I don't think she's even breathing.

"What?" I ask, forgetting what she wanted me to respond to. I get lost in my own head too often. My mom took me to the doctor to check my hearing once because I was always getting caught not listening. The doctor said my ears work fine, I'm just a daydreamer.

"Do you think they're all up in heaven or are now new people?"

"Oh," I say. I need to think about this one. Lizzie waits but has removed her intense stare as she plays with the pages of the notebook. "Yes, I think they are either in heaven or new people or something else happy."

She exhales as if she's relieved by my answer. Finally, my mom chimes in, "I think so, too, Lizzie."

SUPERPOWER #9: SYMPATHY FOR THE AWKWARD

There's that expression: it takes one to know one. The way it's thrown around elementary school makes no sense whatsoever. For instance, if one boy calls the other boy a dweeb, the dweeb would then say, "It takes one to know one." It ends up insulting both of them in the sake of just having some sort of comeback line. A good comeback line should be something that makes you look good and the other person feel like an idiot. Forget all of the, *I know you are but what am I?* and the *You're one to talk* comeback lines. They just keep you in the briar patch. You need a comeback line that makes you above not just the person being mean, but above every person in the universe. My dad taught me when someone calls you a name, like dweeb for instance, just say, "And?" It really throws the name-caller off balance. It's the comeback equivalent of easing out of the briar patch. Yet when you are in a battle of wits like that, if you can call it that, it's so difficult to elevate yourself out of it. Good comebacks always come about twenty minutes too late. But I'm getting off point here.

Anyway, the expression *it takes one to know one* has gotten all mixed up in the world. If you really think about the line, it makes sense, but you have to have insight into yourself. Lots of people roll up their fears or their sadness and never let it show to a point that they forget what it actually looks like even when it's right in front of them. Since I live in the world of nervousness, I know when someone feels awkward. I know when that kid who is calling another kid a dweeb is getting nervous he's taken it too far. While other kids might just see anger, I see embarrassment that he's in the fight and unable to get out of it. I see the little line of sweat form above someone's lip when they're unsure of what to say even though they may be saying something that makes sense. I may not know what's caused their nervousness, but I see it. I see when someone's neck turns a splotchy red over a slight embarrassment like not having enough money to pay in lunch line. I see the downward shifting of the eyes when someone answers a question wrong in front of everyone. I know when a joke has gone too far when no one else notices the person being made fun of has stopped laughing. I've even seen it with our principal as she tries to get the school to settle down during an assembly. I have a radar for nervousness since I live my life in it. That's how *it takes one to know one* works. If I have one true superpower, it's that I understand when someone feels out of place because I always feel out of place. Though I'd rather have the ability to fly, in a way, my superpower lets me relate to people I often would have no way to relate to.

Most people have a talent for letting their awkwardness go undetected to the untrained eye. People hold themselves together under extreme nervousness all the time. They have to or else we would see more people running out the door or crying uncontrollably. It helps me see other people have moments of nervousness even if they never admit it. They don't need to. It's like a breath of fresh air to me to see that not everyone has everything together nor do they always know what to say. I see it in unexpected people all the time. I see it in Lizzie as soon as we arrive at Wolfie's Pizza.

When Lizzie can't jump all over the place and tackle boys, she's easy to talk to. I can tell my mom loves her immediately. Lizzie keeps fidgeting with the fork and knife wrapped in a napkin in front of her as my mom asks her questions. She sits up straight in the booth and I see that she isn't making eye contact with my mom. My mom makes me order my own food at restaurants. I hate it. Sometimes, I won't answer the waiter and play a game of chicken with my mom. I know she hates awkward silences. Having a waiter just stare at us pushes her over the edge and she orders for me. Since this is Wolfie's Pizza, I can let her order the pizza and all I need to ask for is my root beer. Lizzie just orders water as if she doesn't want to make my mom pay for her, but my mom insists she order a soda, too. Lizzie follows my lead and orders a root beer.

"So, Lizzie, how do you like Connecticut so far?" my mom asks as the waiter leaves.

"It's okay," she says.

"Are you girls enjoying the play?"

We both nod.

"Tell me honestly, how embarrassing is your dad?"

"Your dad's the best," Lizzie says, looking at me.

"I guess," I say. "He's really popular up there. I think it's funny Mrs. Craig is his wife." Mrs. Craig is our art teacher. She wears long, floral shirts that kind of look like dresses but they go over her long-sleeved shirts and pants. A person does not need to move their arms that much when speaking, so she must love the sound all of her bracelets make when she moves them. In the play, her character is very proper in a 1950s *Leave it to Beaver* kind of way but for some reason she uses a slightly British-sounding accent and pursed lips. The director has tried to get her to tone it down, but she hasn't. She always wants to go over lines again and again with my dad. He's very good at excuses though—gotta get the kids home, losing my voice, big work project, etc.

"I think that would be a quick divorce in real life," Lizzie says.

My mom laughs. "Yes, I don't think your father can last much longer with her even as his pretend wife. She's takes it a little seriously. I, for one, would be happy if he had a second wife—someone to split the laundry duties with."

"She does that in school, too. Takes things too seriously. Like, she'll tell you to paint from your heart, but then she walks around and corrects all of our work."

"Maybe she means paint from her heart, then?" Lizzie says.

"I suppose," I say. "She ruined one of my pictures. I was painting a pretty sunset over water and then she came with her paintbrush and changed it to how she wanted."

"That's bogus," Lizzie says.

"Totally," my mom says.

"Another time, she blew up my clay mallard in the kiln."

"What?" Lizzie looks shocked. "Wait, what's a clay mallard?"

"A duck I made out of clay."

"Phew," Lizzie says.

I laugh.

"I'm sorry your duck blew up," Lizzie says with the British accent Mrs. Craig has been using.

She seems to be easing out of her nervousness when our root beers arrive.

"I *love* root beer," Lizzie announces before taking a sip, only her hand is slightly shaky and she spills some root beer down her shirt.

My mom quickly hands her some napkins. I see Lizzie's cheeks flush for a moment. She cleans herself off while I clean the table. We're quiet for a moment. "Told you I love root beer," she says and smiles. I laugh hysterically—like tears coming from my eyes hysterically, and Lizzie joins me. My mom is even laughing pretty hard.

When the waiter comes over, he gives us a strange look as he places our pizza on the table.

"So, why is this place called Wolfie's and there are pictures of pianos everywhere?" Lizzie asks him, still laughing.

"It's for Wolfgang Amadeus Mozart."

"I didn't know he made pizzas, too," Lizzie says which makes me laugh even harder.

Over dinner, Lizzie tells us all about her brother. He's an amazing athlete. He doesn't even try, but he's just one of those kids that's naturally good. He played football and basketball in his old high school. When he moved here, he wasn't sure if they would let him try out, but he did and even became their quarterback though he's a sophomore. She says less about her dad and mom, but talks a bit about her favorite vacation ever when they lived in Oregon. I guess they went to a beach there one weekend on a spur of the moment. Her mom just wanted to go so they piled into the car late one evening and drove. Even though it was cold and they stayed in a small musty cabin and hadn't realized they needed to bring their own sheets and towels, she said it was wonderful. They would bundle up and walk on the beach and look for rocks. Her mom said they could bring bikes next time, as well as sheets, but they never did.

We never get dessert at restaurants. My mom loves baking so she never thinks restaurant desserts are worth it. "If I want to eat a stale piece of German chocolate cake, I'll do it at home where at least I can add some Hershey's syrup to it if necessary." I'm not sure she's ever actually done that, but I would love to try it. She orders two chocolate cake slices for Lizzie and me. By the time we return to Lizzie's house, we see a light on inside and a beat-up car in the driveway so I know my mom feels better about leaving her. I've told her some kids are just allowed to be home alone, but I think if she could, she'd invite them all out to dinner.

Back at our house, I'm in a good mood. I have chocolate on my face and feel the sugar pushing through my veins. I know I have to go to bed, but I have so much energy—the energy that tickles your skin because you're happy. I dance around my room, practice somersaults on my bed and blast Kenny Rogers. I know my mom will scold me for not getting ready for bed but at the moment, it's worth it. On my fifth somersault, I go over the edge of a bed with a loud thud. I turn down the music and wait. There they are—footsteps coming up the stairs. I scramble into a nightgown. My mom knocks and tries to enter, but I have locked the door. She knocks again, giving me one more second to be all set for bed. I jump into my bed and get under the covers, and then put my hand out to unlock my door.

"Come in," I say sleepily.

My mom enters. "Nice try," she says, but she doesn't seem too angry. "How well have you gotten to know Lizzie?"

"Kind of well, kind of not well," I answer. Her question sounded important.

"Well, I think it's lovely that Miss Lotti chose you as her pen pal."

"Miss Lotti thinks I can help her, so that's why she chose me."

"Did she tell you why she needs help?"

"Um, because she just moved here and no one likes her, I guess."

"Really? What's not to like?"

"Well, she can be annoying, like really loud and hyper. Plus, the popular girls don't like her and she isn't doing anything to change that."

"Oh. If you could see past that, I think your friendship could be very important for her right now. I don't know if she told you or not, but I think it's best if you know. Her mother died last spring."

Her words feel like a punch in my stomach. My mom hugs my shoulders. I can't imagine, nor do I ever want to imagine, losing my mom. Sometimes at night, I think about that, but I always picture it as a time way off in the future when she's old and gray.

"I don't want you to worry about me, honey, I'm not going anywhere," she says, sensing my thoughts, "but Lizzie needs a friend now more than ever. I'd like to try to help her, too. Her father works long hours and she has no family nearby."

"She has a brother though, remember?" I offer.

"Yes, she told me that when we left a note for him on the door before going out to eat. I think he's pretty busy with his own life at the moment."

"We have time though," I say and I mean it. I mean it not in just the way of wanting to make my mom happy with me, but because if I can't be the most popular girl with lots of friends, maybe I could at least be a really good friend to one person who seems to like me.

SUPERPOWER #10: BELIEVING IN SYMBOLS

When I was younger and didn't want to go to school, my parents would bribe me. I noticed it stopped one day after I realized they found something that worked better than records, candy, or toys. I kind of wish they hadn't found it out so I could have records, candy, and toys, but they did. I have to say, my parents were pretty smart to notice something that I had not about myself.

I truly believe in symbols. By symbols, I suppose I mean signs from nature or good luck charms or tokens I've kept from a good day. So, I don't mean cymbals that go crashing in a band or something. Anyway, my mom and dad started giving me their old good luck charms on days when I felt nervous. "Hold this rock in your pocket all day for good luck," my dad said when he let me have the rock he took from outside Ebbets Field when he got to meet Jackie Robinson. "Keep this bookmark in your backpack to keep you from getting nervous," my mom said handing me a paper bookmark she made. I keep a small shoebox full of these items. Some my parents have given me, others I have collected. In the box are the following: a small eraser from the day I actually raised my hand and correctly answered a question, a teeny tiny plastic bear from a birthday party I attended, a silver dollar given to me by the Tooth Fairy, a magic button from my mom's old coat, and my movie ticket stub from *E.T.* Deep down, I know they're just objects but I think shy people start to see objects as helpers in the fight. Just like how some baseball players won't change their socks during a winning season, shy people attach value to objects to help us through the day. While I'm actually enjoying being in the play now, I still get butterflies in my stomach before every play practice. For that reason, I've been on the lookout for more good luck charms. Today, I have a perfectly round rock I found in our driveway.

April and I went to rehearsals an hour earlier than needed since my dad had to go. My mom said she could drive us later, but we both want to get there for our own reasons. I love watching the play. April loves watching Jeffrey. My dad is actually good on stage. To April's relief, he's seen as one of the cool adults. It's not much of a stretch for him to play a dad to a teenager, but he's funny in an easy way. My superpower has never once detected nervousness from my dad. Even though he says he gets nervous, I've never seen it. He's so comfortable on stage without hogging all of the attention. Whenever Annabeth has to play a part with her pretend mom, Mrs. Craig, it's obvious my art teacher wants to be the center of attention. She says her lines straight to the audience instead of to Annabeth or my dad. The director keeps trying to get her to stop that, but she says, "All of the greats break the fourth wall," which no one understands. One, does she think she's one of the greats? Two, it's awkward to see her pause before each of her lines, turn to the audience and then say her line in her Mary Poppins accent.

This evening, I can tell Mr. Freeley can't take it anymore. He opens one of the auditorium seats and puts his clipboard on it. As he pushes his hair back, the seat closes up and his clipboard falls to the ground. He picks it up and puts it on the seat again. Again it falls, he picks it up again, this time cursing under his breath. He's about to lose it. I can tell and so can my dad, apparently. My dad rushes over and picks up the clipboard and steers the director out of the auditorium.

"My heavens," Mrs. Craig says to the audience. "What, pray tell, was that about? Poor gent has lost his mind." I actually think you could hear the swish of all of the eyes rolling in the auditorium.

Annabeth is still on stage with her. She shrugs at the boy playing her younger brother. Then she leaves the pretend family room and flips onto her bed in her pretend bedroom and pulls a book out from under the pillow. It looks like an actual window into her real room. It's as if any second, her phone will ring and she'll talk with her friends or do her homework. Mrs. Craig remains on the stage and practices her singing. The younger boy scrambles off stage to find his mom.

April is actually sitting next to me since none of her friends are here yet. She's doing her homework, but every few minutes, her eyes sneak glances around to see if Jeffrey is there. She and I checked the schedule. A scene between Annabeth and Jeffrey is supposed to be rehearsed tonight. One of her knees is bouncing. "This will take forever now," she says.

"Your homework?" I ask.

"No, the whole rehearsal. Mr. Freeley is having a hissy fit which will probably move all of the rehearsals back so everyone will be here soon."

"Who will be here?"

"All of the other townspeople."

I don't understand but she seems pretty annoyed so I know not to ask anymore.

"There's Jeffrey," she says. Her eyes light up and she closes her notebook. She waves, but he has those popular-people eyes that you think have seen you, in fact, you are sure they saw you, but then they go blank and you don't receive a wave back. It's similar to the empty-eye stare but more condescending. Shy people can't pull it off without looking like they're having a stroke or something. Standing up and waving to someone who doesn't wave back to me is a crawl-into-a-little-space-moment but April only has a moment of nerves which I see in the way she fixes her hair before taking the slight in stride.

"He didn't see you," I say, trying to help.

"Obviously. Watch my stuff." She puts her notebook in the seat of her chair so it, like the clipboard, falls through. However, she doesn't seem to notice as she walks toward Jeffrey. I pick up her notebook and look at the seat. What don't people get here? It's an auditorium seat. They don't stay open for flimsy notebooks and clipboards. Heck, I've seen a few kids get swallowed up by them with the legs folding up to their chests like kid-chair sandwiches. Am I really to watch her stuff all night or is that just a goodbye? I hear my name and look up to the stage to see Lizzie and Annabeth calling to me. It's really a cool moment. They're waving me up to Annabeth's room.

I stuff April's notebook into her backpack and bring it with me up to the stage. I have to admit, it feels pretty cool to be called up to stage by Annabeth. I try to hide my smile, but can't. "Jenny!" Lizzie gives me a hug. "I made this for you." She hands me a barrette with long pink and blue ribbons braided through the middle then falling inches below to stay with your hair. They've become the symbol of friendship around my school. You give them to friends and then they give you one back. Mostly, they have become a symbol of who is popular and who is not. Girls like Jennifer keep their entire collection of barrettes in containers in their desks. I've seen girls hand them to Jennifer but I'm not sure if she's ever given one to anyone. Maybe to Susie. My mom made me one.

"Hi Jenny," Annabeth says and scoots over on the bed. "Have a seat. I'll put the barrette in for you. You have gorgeous hair."

I sit and she starts playing with my hair.

Lizzie jumps up and starts singing the song Annabeth has to sing in her bedroom. She's acting just like Annabeth does and singing loudly. Annabeth is cracking up. Lizzie doesn't know all the words so she just makes things up along the way. She finishes with a bow to the few claps around the auditorium.

"You could be an actress," Annabeth says.

"Maybe," Lizzie says. "But then I might have to kiss a boy like Jeffrey. Yuck." We look over to see Jeffrey in the corner of the auditorium with girls, including April, all around him as he holds a guitar.

"True," Annabeth says. "You also get to kiss boys like Charlie." Lizzie and I smile. He's cute. Personally, I'm not ready for real crushes but I love the idea that Annabeth and Charlie might be in love. I feel a push on the top of my head. "There. It looks so pretty with the ribbons in your hair." She swivels in front of me. "And now I can see your pretty face, too."

"Can you do this?" Lizzie is walking in a handstand.

"I'll try." Annabeth tries a handstand but her legs go past her head and she catches herself in a backbend. "Nope. Can't do it. Not sure I can get up."

Lizzie handstand-walks back to Annabeth, then uprights herself and gives Annabeth a hand. "There you go."

The auditorium doors open and my dad and Mr. Freeley are back.

"Guess that's my cue," Annabeth says.

Lizzie and I make our way out into the seats. I see Jennifer and Susie in the front row. Had they been there the whole time? I hope so. If they saw that Annabeth knew my name and likes both Lizzie and me, maybe they would think they we were cool. I walk with a little sway so that the ribbons move back and forth. When we get a few seats away, I can hear them laughing. I stop my new walk. I follow Lizzie to the aisle where she sits on the floor. I realize when it's just us that I don't know what to say to her. I know I should say something about her mom but nothing feels right.

"My grandfather died once," I say. Lizzie looks at me.

"Did he die again or just the one time?"

My face flushes. I knew I shouldn't have said anything. I didn't know my grandfather all that well since he died when I was only three, but it still makes me sad. I can't imagine how Lizzie wakes up every morning.

"Sorry, bad joke," Lizzie says. "I'm sorry to hear about your grandfather."

"I'm . . . my mom told me about your mom. I'm sorry."

"Thank you," Lizzie says. I realize this is probably when a normal friend would give her friend a hug or handshake or something. I move my hand to put it on Lizzie's shoulder, but then stop, feeling awkward. "I understand. It's strange, isn't it? No one knows what to say to me. I kind of want to hug everyone and tell them it's okay. I'll be okay. But the people who know just look at me like I'm a sad little sick puppy. Whenever I do talk about it, people just nod and don't say anything at all so I don't know what's the best thing to do anymore." She lies down on the floor.

"I wouldn't do that," I say and point to the gum on the carpet nearby.

She sits up. "Will you promise me something? That you won't feel sorry for me? I don't want a friend just because they feel sorry for me. And if I ever bug you or get on your nerves, just tell me, okay? I think I got on my mom's nerves."

"Oh." I'm one of those people who doesn't know what to say.

"So how did you handle it when your granddad died?"

"Well, I was really little. It makes me sad though. One time, I wrote him a note and put it on my windowsill. The next morning, it wasn't there."

"What did you say in the note?"

"Things about how I missed him." I had never told anyone I left the note. I remembered waking up in the morning and seeing it wasn't there and feeling this magical feeling like maybe he came and took it. It wasn't until later that I suspected my mom of taking it. I never asked though. Sometimes it's better to believe in magic than know the truth. "You know, I think all kids probably get on their parents' nerves though," I say. "I know I must get on my parents' nerves all the time. That just happens but that doesn't mean they don't love us."

"You get on your parents' nerves?" she asks. "You seem like the perfect daughter."

I laugh. "I'm not sure there is such a thing. Plus, you're fun and energetic and outgoing. You're probably closer to being a perfect daughter than me."

"Maybe our combined personalities make the perfect daughter then," she says. "I miss my mom a lot. Sometimes I like to think she's just back home in Oregon and will be coming here soon."

"Townspeople. Townspeople. All townspeople report to the hallway." Coach Jay's bullhorn takes over the room.

"Guess that's our cue," I say, trying on Annabeth's words.

Lizzie wipes the little tears from her eyes, jumps to her feet and pulls me up. We shuffle over with the mob of talkative townspeople, all in their little pockets. The grandparents all seem to know each other and are always the first to be where they need to be when Coach Jay calls us. They're followed by us, then some of the high school kids. April's friends are always the last. There's not many people my parents' or Miss Lotti's age as townspeople. Most of the grandparents are nice to us. One woman always has mints or butterscotch candies that she gives to us. I kind of feel like a pigeon when she does that though. She takes them out of her pocket and shakes her open hand at us to offer the candies. I half expect her to drop it on the floor while Lizzie and I pick it up with our beaks. Her husband always smiles at us and asks about school.

"Okay everyone," Coach Jay says. "Tonight, we have a lot on our plates. We'll have a big dance number in the beginning of the play. And, for a play made for teenyboppers, we have a serious shortage of teenybopper dancers." She walks over to April's group. "To remedy this situation, you are all now my dancers. Congratulations!" They groan. "I can see you are all super excited. Fantastic. To make things more interesting for all of you, once he's finished on stage, Jeffrey said he would teach you all the dance."

This news silences them. It's a genius move by Coach Jay.

"For the rest of you," she swivels around and looks at us, the too young and the too old. "You will be dancing, too, don't worry." One of the grandfathers grabs his wife's hand and they tango to Coach Jay and back to the cheers of their friends. "Our own Fred and Ginger. Let's work that in somewhere." She writes something in her clipboard. "For the rest of you, it's a simple step. Learn it, love it, don't mess it up." She puts down her stuff and stands in front of us after having us spread out an arm's length apart from one another. "Here we go. It's the good old jazz box. Right foot in front of left, left foot steps back, right foot steps back, left foot steps back. And repeat."

I'm a terrible dancer. I didn't know that until right now. Lizzie gets it down quickly because she's not afraid to mess up.

"Here, watch," she says and breaks each of the ridiculously easy steps down for me. There, got it. Coach Jay has us add arm movements. First our right hand waves, then our left as if we are saying goodbye to Birdie. It's so simple, but actually really fun.

"What fast learners I have," Coach Jay says, calling us all back to attention. "Practice the dance while singing the opening song and then we'll try it on stage later this week. Now, where are my precious teenyboppers? Let's go. Follow me."

April's group follows behind, somewhat willingly. I stay with Lizzie as we keep practicing our dance with the grandparents. Jennifer and Susie left as soon as Coach Jay did so now I can practice without feeling like a complete goof. Lizzie and I shout out the parts of the song we know and act as if we're so sad to see Birdie go. We pretend-cry and end up laughing so hard my face hurts by the time my mom comes to drive us home.

I feel guilty about it, but it's hard to shake the part of me that still wishes I could be pretty and popular. My mom made arrangements for Lizzie to stay here for a sleepover while her dad works this weekend. I know it makes me a terrible person, but I wish this friendship had formed with Jennifer. This thought is what goes through my head as I clean my bedroom so Lizzie will have somewhere to sleep. With my personality, I would expect myself to be neater. I take great pride in writing neatly, and keeping my desk neat at school, but my room is really messy. I know some moms care a great deal about their daughters' bedrooms being neat. April must have taught my mom that it's not a battle worth fighting because my mom never scolds me about my messy room. Every week, I'll see the narrow line of a vacuum paved through all of my clothes and stuffed animals on the floor.

I spend too much time daydreaming about Jennifer and I being best friends. I don't even know why really. This is something I think that Dr. Sedac should have been able to solve for me.

From the outside, I can see that Jennifer and I don't have much in common. She's not nice and she tries to make everyone else feel bad about who they are. So why am I wishing that she was the one coming over for a sleepover? It wouldn't even be fun. I guess I want the chance to show her who I really am. I have this vision of Jennifer seeing the true me, whatever that is, and then liking me. Yet in the vision, I'm not even the true me. I'm not quiet, I'm not shy. In fact, I'm full of energy and interesting conversations and great at making new hairstyles and applying nail polish. Maybe these aren't necessarily thoughts but daydreams.

In reality, when my mom calls up to me that Lizzie is here, I'm happy. If she told me Jennifer was here, I'd be nervous. I look at my room and realize I didn't get very far with the cleaning. I spent too much time in my head as April always tells me. Another good thing about Lizzie coming here instead of Jennifer is that I don't think Lizzie will care that my room is a mess. My dad calls a true friend someone you don't have to clean the house for. At least that's what he says to my mom when he springs it on her last minute that he's invited someone over for dinner or to watch a game. My mom wishes he had less true friends so that maybe he would help clean the house occasionally.

I bound down the stairs and see Lizzie walking up, holding her pillow and a small paper bag while a boy with one of those high school jackets they wear in *Happy Days* follows behind her with a bag slung over his shoulder. My mom opens the door wide. I slide under her arm.

"Hi Lizzie!"

She gives me a hug over her pillow.

"Hello, Mrs. Watts. I'm Lizzie's brother. What time should I pick her up tomorrow?"

April has appeared behind my mom. She looks freshly lip-glossed.

Then my dad comes out of the garage. "Hey, are you Scott Cray?"

"Yes, sir," he says, but he doesn't say it with much confidence. He looks down at the ground.

"Great season," my dad says. He looks a little star struck. "My buddies and I go to all the home games. We had a great time watching you."

"Thank you, sir."

"Playing basketball now, I hear? Double threat, huh?"

"Hopefully." He seems to be loosening up a bit. "Had a tough game last night but we're hoping to do well in the tournament today. So I really appreciate you watching Lizzie. I hope she won't be too much trouble."

My dad takes the bag from him. "I'm sure we'll manage just fine," he says and winks at Lizzie.

"Bye Scottie," Lizzie says.

"Be good, shorty."

Aren't we all supposed to have a cool older brother like that? Though, he acts more like her dad than her older brother. Do all brothers act that way with younger sisters? Brothers are such a foreign concept to me. I can't help but think if I had a cool older brother that was the star of the football team, I would be cool by relation. April is in the cool group I think, but she's definitely more of a follower than a leader. The problem with being a follower is you are always one step away from exclusion. Before Scott even gets to his car, April runs for the phone, dials, then stretches the cord to her phone spot where she has set up a beanbag chair and blanket. She likes to think she deserves privacy there, but she's still in the television room so it isn't like we can't hear her. A visit from Scott Cray at her house will definitely keep her in the group for now. "You'll never guess who was just here," she whisper-shrieks into the phone. I think she's hoping this makes it her cool by relation.

Lizzie laughs. "My brother makes girls cuckoo. Sorry."

I've never actually had a sleepover. Lizzie and I just look at each other for a moment. I'm not sure how to start.

"Can I see your room?" Lizzie says helpfully.

"Yes! Follow me."

I push open my door and see my room as she must: shag pink carpeting with green walls and a large square mirror from the people who lived here before us that seems to be attached permanently to the house. In the corner, I made a quiet spot for when I can't sleep and filled it with my books and a few Afghan blankets my grandmother knitted for me. Then, it's pretty much stuffed animals around the floor with one wall full of posters of *Star Wars* and *E.T.* I tried copying April's wall that she has filled with *Tiger Beat* folded posters. For a fleeting moment, I'm nervous that my room looks babyish. Jennifer so would not have approved. Lizzie on the other hand is smiling.

"Thank goodness," she says, and flops down on my bed. "I thought your family might be one of those super neat freaks. I'm always afraid of breaking things or messing up vacuum lines with my footprints. So what should we do first? Can we go see Bloody Rock?"

"Um, well, my mom won't let us go there."

"She could come with us," Lizzie says.

After cleaning the kitchen and television room and then forgetting twice about our request, my mom is finally ready to go with us. Lizzie runs down the small hill that leads from our porch to the landing where our swing set is. She does two cartwheels and one backflip along the way. I expect my mom to tell her to be careful, but it seems obvious Lizzie knows what she's doing. I would most likely bash my head into a rock trying to do any of those moves. "Is it through this little path?" she calls to us.

"Yes, just wait for us," my mom says and starts to move faster.

Lizzie waits and when we arrive, she bows and then says, "Walk this way, please, madams." Then she starts walking, jiggling her arms over her head and kicking her legs out high with each step. She looks back at us. "I said, walk this way." My mom starts jiggling her arms. I just laugh and move my arms a little bit.

It's not a long path so my mom quickly gets in front of Lizzie so that she sees when the trees end and where the cliff begins. I get that being a parent probably can make you worry, but seriously, even I can see this cliff isn't much to worry about. Yes, it would hurt if you fell, but if you aren't near the edge, you aren't going to fall. When we get near the clearing, my mom sits down on a rock and tells us to do the same as if merely standing feet away from a cliff could make you fall. I don't think we'll be taking any family trips to the Grand Canyon. Lizzie asks if she can peer over the cliff. My mom goes with her so she can look over it. I'd be embarrassed by my mom's worry if Lizzie seemed to mind, but she really doesn't.

"It's not as far down as I thought it would be. Where's the blood?"

My mom laughs. "There's no blood. I think the boys next door just made that up."

"No, there really is blood, look there," I say, pointing to the red marks.

My mom crouches down and looks at it. She tries to touch it with her finger to brush it away, but it doesn't. "Hmm. Well, it's red but I don't think it's blood. It's probably paint or something."

"Think about it, why would there be a paint splatter out here?" I say it just like Robbie would.

"Well, I don't know."

"What about the story that goes with it?" Lizzie asks.

"What story?"

"The one about the witch," I say but judging by my mom's blank look, she has obviously not heard this story. So I tell the story and I'm pretty positive I haven't forgotten any detail but I may have added to it. It's been haunting my dreams at night making my fear list now include witches living behind my house. I've yet to come up with a solution to handle this fear, but my temporary fix is Scotch tape on the bottom of my locked windows; just two pieces per window corner so that my parents won't worry about me. I, however, have worried about finding them chanting with a witch downstairs pretty much every night since I heard the story.

"Isn't it a creepy story?" Lizzie asks my mom.

My mom is looking at me strangely. "Where did you hear that?"

"Robbie's older brother told us."

"Told who?"

"April, Terry, and me."

"Oh," she says as if it all makes sense. "Was Terry terrorizing the boys again?"

"No. She thinks they're cute but they don't have enough brain cells."

My mom laughs. "Well, I don't want you two to give that story any more thought. It's awful really. If you want to know a good scary story, have you heard the one about the crowbar left on the car handle?"

"Let's hear it," Lizzie says.

"No!" I say. "I can't add any more scary stories to my life!"

"Okay, okay. I'm the one who will suffer if I scare you too much anyway. So, is that story why you wanted to see this spot, Lizzie?"

"Yes. I like to try to figure things out."

"What do you think then?" I ask.

"I'm not sure. I thought the cliff would be higher. I think if the ground were all snowy like the story says, it wouldn't have killed them when they fell, but if she hit her head first, I don't know. Tough one."

"It's kind of morbid to think about," my mom says.

"What does morbid mean?" Lizzie asks.

My mom looks flustered. "Just not something very happy. I hope it wasn't true."

"Me, too," Lizzie says. "I like it better when bad things turn out not to be true. Or if the bad things are true, there's a happy ending we just don't get to see."

My mom puts her arms around Lizzie, hugging her like she does April and me. "Is there anything else you are trying to figure out?" My mom's voice is delicate. Lizzie nods.

"What makes someone so sad, they can't live here anymore?"

"I believe it's just something about the way their mind works. But that isn't what happened with your mom. It was just an accident."

Lizzie nods and chokes back her tears. I haven't moved. I notice the cold wind and hear the rustling dead leaves around me. The tops of the trees in front of the cliff shield us from the street below. What was life like in this spot one hundred years ago? How many people have cried here before Lizzie? It feels as if this spot has a soul. I don't think it was the witch. If it's a soul here, maybe it's Lizzie's mom looking for her.

"What is that?" Lizzie asks, pointing below. My mom and I look but don't see anything. "It looks like one of those fancy dolls."

"I'm sure it's not . . . " my mom starts and then hesitates. "Actually, I see it. I don't know what that is."

"Greetings, Watts family." We all jump. "Didn't mean to scare you." Robbie is coming through the path dragging a large bag behind him. He heaves it forward and begins taking out its contents. A Speak and Spell, a child's plastic record player, an umbrella, Reese's Pieces and some root beer. "There we go. What brings you all out here?"

"Robbie, take a look down there," my mom says. "What's that face thing down there?"

Robbie digs in his bag and grabs binoculars. "What do we have?" He comes closer and lies down on the rock.

"Don't get so close," my mom says. He doesn't listen.

"I don't see anything."

"Can I use them?" Lizzie asks.

"Sure. And you are?"

"This is Jenny's friend, Lizzie."

"Her brother is Scottie Cray," I add trying to showoff, but Robbie either doesn't care or has no idea who I'm talking about. Or, he may not be listening to me.

"I see it," Lizzie says. "It has writing on it but I can't tell what it says."

"A mystery," Robbie says. "I'll check it out. Wait here."

"Robbie, don't hurt yourself. I'm sure it's just a piece of trash," my mom says.

"This is so exciting," Lizzie says, grabbing my arm.

"Well, I'm sure it's nothing." My mom doesn't sound convincing. We wait a few minutes listening for Robbie who has trekked back into the woods. Then we hear him stumble below us.

"I'm okay! Where is this thing?"

Lizzie directs him to it. "Walk straight, now go to your left, I mean right, now do a jumping jack and a twirl." Robbie follows all of her commands.

"Here it is," he says. "What do we have?" He brushes the leaves away, revealing a small statue with a pile of rocks around it. "Creepy."

"Maybe you should come back here, Robbie."

"Mrs. Watts, exactly what do you think is going to happen to me?" He stands and looks at her. He's really not that far away from us. My mom stays silent so Robbie continues his detective work. "Help! Help!" Robbie acts as if he's being pulled to the ground. My mom places her hand over her heart. Lizzie and I stare at her in disbelief.

"Are you actually falling for that?" Lizzie asks.

"Oh," my mom said. "Robbie, cut it out. My nerves are already shot up here."

"Had you though! It looks like one of those saint things Mrs. Brown used to have in your yard. Maybe it's Saint Elizabeth Ann. She gave my mom one, too." Mrs. Brown lived in our house before we did. Occasionally, my mom will find something small of hers and deliver it to her in the home for older people she lives in now.

"You have your own saint," Lizzie says to me. "What's a saint?"

I don't know either.

"A saint is a person that did such good work in their lives that the Catholic Church declares that they are a saint. Something like that at least. Robbie, how did you get down there?" my mom asks. Lizzie, my mom, and I try finding Robbie's route down which means getting whacked by branches and twisting our ankles on rocks and hearing my mom mutter a few times how maybe we shouldn't be doing this. But when we finally crunch our way through the leaves to Robbie, the curiosity takes over. My mom crouches down and moves more of the leaves away from the rock.

"Well, what a discovery," my mom says. She gingerly wipes more leaves away, then kisses her hand and places it on the saint. "Looks like it says St. Anthony carved along the bottom. We've had a saint looking out for us this whole time."

"St. Anthony?" Robbie said. "Don't know that one."

"Oh, he's the saint you pray to when you lose things or for lost souls," my mom says. My mom and Lizzie clean off the statue and seem somewhat calm about this finding. I do not. I see Robbie fidget with his hair and look around. He's scared, too—or bored, my senses don't work that well with teenage boys. Why did Mrs. Brown leave it here? Is the witch story true? I don't think she would trek all the way here if the witch story weren't true. I've always had suspicions about Mrs. Brown. Why did she leave so many strange objects around her house? We've found small porcelain unicorns and little lockets. One time, we even found a glass bottle with a note inside. Once April and I found a treasure map that led to a fake diamond necklace. My dad had a theory that she did it so that she would have us as visitors all the time. My mom is less skeptical. She thinks she was just a collector with odd decorating senses. However, whenever my mom goes to return an item, she brings Mrs. Brown a cake and coffee and spends hours with her.

"I'll have to tell Mrs. Brown we found another treasure of hers," my mom says.

"Wait, there's writing," Lizzie said while clearing a small plaque near the foot of the saint. It's really dirty and looks weathered, but we can make out some painted writing.

Robbie leans in, stepping on Lizzie's hand.

"Foot, foot, foot on hand."

"Sorry!" Robbie moves his foot and crouches down more.

"I can't read it."

"Here, dig it up with this stick," Robbie says.

"No, wait," I say. I don't think it should be moved. "Mom, do you have a tissue?" My mom always has a tissue. Knowing what I'm thinking, she kneels down and wipes away some of the dirt on the plaque.

"It says, 'For all those lost, once again found.'"

"I don't get it," Robbie says. "Who's lost?"

"It's beautiful," Lizzie says.

"I always thought there was something strange about Mrs. Brown," Robbie says. "What's with all of her little hiding spots around the neighborhood? I think it's . . . witchcraft! Dun dun dun!" Robbie puts his arms out straight and his fingers in the sign of the cross.

"You watch too much television," my mom says and laughs.

"Just how old is this Mrs. Brown?" Lizzie asks.

"No one knows," Robbie says with an accent that makes him sound mysterious.

"Robbie," my mom says. "She's not that old. I think she just had her seventy-ninth birthday."

"Seventy-ninth or two-hundred-and-seventy-ninth?" he asks, not letting up his crazy witch hunter act.

"Anyway, she is just a sweet lady leaving little activities for kids."

"Wait, what's that?" I ask. It looks like a little latch near the bottom of the plaque. I pull it. What we thought was just a plaque is actually the top of a box.

"There's a letter in it," Lizzie says.

"Or a body?" Robbie says.

"Oh, stop," Lizzie says. "Here, Jenny, you open it. It looks really old."

The envelope is sealed with a wax emblem. I could not have been more excited unless this had been a sealed scroll. As soon as I touch the wax, it releases from the paper. I gently remove the letter and open it.

Excellent work. You have found Clue #4. Two more trea-

sures await you. To find the next clue, look for a wooden log painted blue.

"The old street sign," Robbie says. "Is that thing still there?"

"Near the bus stop, that's right," my mom says. "That is blue. Well, it looks as if you three have a treasure hunt on your hands."

"Wonder where the first clues were," Lizzie says. "How do we get to the bus stop from here."

"Right through the trees over yonder you'll find the path," Robbie says, pointing.

"Aren't you coming?" Lizzie says.

"You two go ahead and tell me what you find. I've got important work of my own. But if the treasure involves money, just leave my cut at my front door." He grabs his bag and barrels his way back up the cliff.

"I'll walk you two to the bus stop and leave you on your adventure," my mom says. "Just don't go too far."

My mom leaves us to walk the street back to our house while Lizzie and I find the old street marker underneath the brush. The wood is pretty rotten and each year, the blue fades more and more. I love how you can find old things like the marker. I'm not sure when it was from, but at some point in time, it was important before they installed the tall metal street sign. We don't see any clue though. Lizzie and I brush away the fallen leaves until we see the dirt. I feel with my hands to see if there's anything right at the surface. Nothing.

"Maybe it blew away?"

"Wait," Lizzie says. "On the marker, look!"

A small arrow is painted on the very bottom of the rock,

pointing to a section of the ground. We start digging with our fingers. It doesn't take much time until we hit something.

"Get a stick," Lizzie said. I hand her one. She goes around the top of the object until she can pry it out. It's another box—smaller than the other one but with something painted on it as well. Since it's been under the dirt, the words are even harder to see. Instead of a quote though, this one says, *Mack's Hardware*. Inside, we find a handful of shiny pennies and a smaller envelope, again with the wax crest. I let Lizzie open it since I did the last one.

Look at you: You found a clue. This is Clue #5, and you made it alive. (I tried, but nothing else rhymes as well with five). Find your last clue on the path just above you. It's a shiny large rock with a star mark on top.

"I know just where that is," I say. "Follow me."

I lead her up our path. Though it's probably impossible, I think I know almost every rock along the way. I know the large shiny rock since it's my favorite spot. In fact, that's where I keep my collection. The scrapings on its top always looked like a triangle to me but I guess it looked like a star to Mrs. Brown. We get to the rock, slightly out of breath with flushed faces from the cool wind.

"See." I show her the rock. "It has that shiny stuff you can kind of peel off like this." I grab a small piece of the rock to show her.

"Cool," she says. "Have you ever seen the treasure here?"

"Nope."

"Think it's at the bottom?"

"I know," I say, "let's look for another arrow. You look on that side and I'll look here." We both take our sides and kneel down, brushing dirt away from the bottom of the rock.

"Over here," she says. A small arrow is at the bottom. We start digging until we find a small box again.

"Let's open it together," Lizzie says. "Count of three: one, two, three."

We lift the box open. Inside are gold safety pins with crocheted stars and smiley faces attached.

"Read the letter," I tell Lizzie as I look through the pins.

"It says, '*You did it. I'm so proud. Hope you had fun. Take a treasure. And for the last one: Remember to make someone else's day—make them smile.*' That's sweet. When did you move here?"

"When I was in kindergarten."

"So this treasure hunt must have been here for years."

"I guess so."

We lay out the safety pins on the rock to choose one for us, one for my mom, and one for Robbie. I'm pretty sure Robbie will throw it away, but Lizzie and I agree that he did help us.

"This is a pretty cool spot," Lizzie says, stretching her legs out.

"It's where I keep all my rocks. Here, look." One by one, I move my rocks over for her to look at them. "This is the path I use to get to the bus stop. April used to use it, too, but some days she doesn't. Did your brother ever get mean when he entered middle school?"

"Not especially," Lizzie says. "He got kind of quieter, more like you actually. He would stay in his room and listen to music. Once he found that he was good at sports, I think that helped him. He'd practice for hours and lots of times, I would play too, or watch. It's kind of just him and me so he couldn't get too mean."

I find all of this interesting. I can't imagine what April and I would be like if it was just the two of us. Lizzie doesn't speak much about her father. It sounds as if she and her brother are the only ones in the family left now. I pick up my favorite sparkling rock and give it to her for keeps. I know I'll miss it because I'm way too attached to objects that shouldn't mean anything really. I always wish I were the girl who didn't care when classmates borrow one of my pencils and never give it back. One: how do they not have a pencil? Two: If I ever had to borrow a pencil, I would remember to give it back. Three: It's not cool to ask for the pencil back. You look like a weirdo if you act all emotionally attached to a pencil.

At least with this rock, I can tell Lizzie understands its importance and won't just act like it's nothing. She gives me a quick hug after double-checking that I really want to part with it. I shrug and say I don't need it because really, I don't. It's just a rock but it will be like a symbol for her about our friendship and hopefully will make her happy. I get the feeling under all her cartwheels and boy tackling, she could be happier.

We bury the boxes again so someone else can do the treasure hunt and then make our way to Robbie's to leave his prize.

"Do you think she left more treasures in your house? What is a saint and what do they do? Can we search for more of her things?" Lizzie has a million questions as we make our way back home.

SUPERPOWER #11: LOVE OF VACATION

I know everyone loves vacation—a chance to try something new or relax. For shy people, it's a huge relief to go for a few days without dealing with any of the usual stuff we deal with day in and day out. No worries about not knowing what to say or having anyone pick on you. It's wonderful. Plus, if you do anything the week before a holiday break, it's forgotten about immediately. With that thought in mind, I'm preparing to speak in public Monday morning, hoping for a good small moment. I like small moments of victory. Occasionally, I try to do something to get that feeling of pride in myself. I'm feeling pretty good when I enter school that day. My first sleepover worked. I was nervous Lizzie would make fun of me for my stuffed animal arrangement. She didn't. When she saw what I was doing, I could tell she didn't want to call attention to it at first, but then she sat up and asked, "What's the deal here?" I was going to shrug it off and pretend I had no idea what she was talking about, but she wasn't asking in a judgmental way. So, I explained it all: the vampires, Darth Vadar, the attic, now the witch. Instead of making fun of me, she borrowed my stuffed frog to go over her neck.

We had searched the house for more of Mrs. Brown's hidden saints or treasures. First we made a map of my house. When we came up with nothing, we made treasure hunts for each other, hiding my Princess Leia figurine with clues to find her. Lizzie even got April to play along. She actually knocked on April's bedroom door and April actually let her come in and hide Leia. I never found it. However, after Lizzie told me where it was, April let us hang out in her room with her. We listened to records. Lizzie danced on April's bed and April just laughed. Then April actually did our hair and nails. I kind of think it was so Lizzie would go home and tell her brother about my cool older sister, but I didn't care. I barely spoke thinking my words might break the spell. This morning, April seemed annoyed that my pink nail polish was already chipped and she didn't let me walk next to her to the bus stop, but she did say goodbye to me when her bus came.

Lizzie and I drew pictures of the saint statue with the plan to tell both of our teachers about it. Miss Lotti lets us talk about our weekends on Monday mornings before we start. Usually, the same people share about their weekends and I think it's just Miss Lotti's way to get those kids to calm down so we can move on to our work. My story is actually interesting, I think. Maybe everyone thinks that though. I'll tell all about Bloody Rock and then finding the saint and most likely, I'll throw in how I had a sleepover so everyone will know I have friends outside of school. When Miss Lotti asks for hands of who wants to share something from their weekend, I raise my hand with confidence. She only calls on four people each Monday. The good thing about being quiet and shy is that teachers will call on you when they see you raise your hand. The bad thing about being quiet and shy is that when you do want to talk, everyone listens a little more closely. The stakes are higher. If you only raise your hand once a year to share something about yourself or to give an answer to a question, you had better make the story interesting and the answer correct. Miss Lotti calls on me first, then three other people which leads one of the usual kids to act all put out that he doesn't get to talk about his fishing trip with his grandfather for once. Seriously, he keeps telling the same fishing story.

I walk up to the front of the classroom so sure of myself. My ponytail is swinging behind me with Lizzie's barrette tucked right over my ear as a good luck symbol. I know Lizzie is probably telling the story to her class right now, too, and that gives me strength. Then I turn to face my class. Yikes. Why did I raise my hand? I give one little "um" and then Susie raises her hand while stating that she can't hear me. Miss Lotti tells her to wait and smiles at me. I begin the story I had rehearsed in my head over and over. I used my dad's trick of visualization even. He told me to imagine myself giving a great speech and how I will feel afterward. At the moment, I'm hoping not to feel like a fool.

"So, behind my house is a path that leads to a big rock."

"What?" "I can't hear you." "Speak up." Miss Lotti tells everyone to be quiet and smiles at me again. I've lost my thought. I look at Miss Lotti. She reminds me about the path and rock. Right.

"The rock is called Bloody Rock."

"You name your rocks?" Susie asks and laughs.

"Head down, Susie," Miss Lotti says.

"I didn't name it. I don't know who did. It was named hundreds of years ago." I realize my story may be too long and decide to cut out the whole witch thing which is probably a mistake since that's the most interesting part but my heart is racing and I don't want to pass out up here. "Anyway, I went there on Saturday and my friend who was sleeping over found a saint in the leaves." I flash the picture I drew toward them and then I walk back to my desk quickly and slump down. Tyler Miller, a boy in my class who reminds me of Robbie, taps me on the shoulder. He sits behind me and over one row so he is leaning way over his desk.

"I didn't get to see the picture."

I hand it to him. The next speaker, Eddie, is already talking about a hockey game he went to. I wait for Tyler to give my picture back. I can barely breathe as I fear he'll keep it like the six pencils he's "borrowed" this year or he'll make fun of it. Nothing good ever happens when you try to live out loud. I should know better. It's not meant for me to do that. I suffer through stories of hockey, another classmate's gross twenty-four-hour stomach flu and Jennifer talking about her part in the play without mentioning I'm in it too. My knees keep shaking. Is he crinkling the corners? He's not very clean. Is he smudging the crayon? Finally Tyler taps my shoulder again. "Cool picture, Freckles." I take back my picture and smile slightly. Is that a compliment with an insult? He smiles back though so I think it was all a compliment. My speech didn't go as planned, but I feel pretty good again. Miss Lotti even stops me before I walk into gym class and asks me to eat with her today so she can hear my whole story. By the time recess rolls around, I feel ready to take on the world.

I ask Anna to play two-square with me. She's not feeling as confident as I am but she's too nice to say no. She looks at the swings longingly. I know it's safe and away from everyone else and you can quickly get off of it while looking like you were tired of it anyway if anyone comes over who looks like they might want a turn. I feel bad making her come with me, but at that moment, I feel I have enough confidence for the both of us. I run and get the ball. It's pretty cold outside today so most of the girls are huddled near the school. The boys are playing kickball on the blacktop. Anna and I should be in the clear. I don't see anyone looking at us. We play and we laugh and we run and our cheeks are windblown. Why can't recess always be like this one?

When the teachers call us back to class, Anna and I are skipping. Things with the popular group don't look so happy though. A bunch of girls are crying and they all have muddy pants. Miss Lotti looks annoyed. All of the girls are talking at once. Finally Jennifer speaks and they all get quiet.

"I slipped on the ice and fell back into the garden which made my pants dirty. Susie was a good enough friend to then get her pants muddy so I wouldn't be the only one with muddy pants. We expected our other so-called friends to do the same, but they didn't. So Susie helpfully just placed a bit of mud on them so that they wouldn't have to actually fall and now all of them are being babies about it."

Moments like these make it so hard to be a kid. Sometimes you can see things so clearly the way an adult would. Parents really don't understand what we're dealing with here. Do people they work with chase them around with mud to make their pants dirty so the popular worker doesn't feel bad? I don't think so.

Jennifer and Susie seem to be the only ones who think their actions made any sense. Miss Lotti makes them apologize. They sit with crossed arms and evil eyes for the rest of the day. Miss Lotti ignores them. I feel grateful right now that I'm not friends with Jennifer and Susie. I also kind of wish they would have these arguments more so that Anna and I can have most of the playground to ourselves.

I tell Lizzie and Annabeth all about the Muddy Pants Incident when we meet at play practice. Annabeth is flipping through a *Tiger Beat*. I have to admit, I'm telling the story because I think it's what girls do. Jennifer and Susie always have their heads together talking about other people. I hope this story makes Annabeth like me. Usually I don't speak much when I'm around her. I don't exactly feel good about retelling this story so I'm trying to report it just with facts so it doesn't sound like I'm insulting Jennifer and Susie. In fact, I don't even use their names; instead I just say it was two girls in my class. Lizzie listens to me intently. She thinks the whole thing is hysterical.

"Wait, so how muddy were her pants?"

"Just a little."

"On her bottom?"

"Yes."

"And she thought everyone should have matching bottoms?" Lizzie laughs so hard she's holding her stomach and tears stream from her eyes.

Annabeth closes the magazine. "Ugh," she says. "I hate when

girls do stuff like that. Are they the popular girls?"

I nod. I'm sure Annabeth probably would have already guessed I wasn't one of the popular girls, but I hate admitting I'm not one.

"It's just not right," Annabeth said. "You go to school to learn and then you're stuck dealing with people who want to take you down all the time. People in my school make fun of me sometimes since I do these plays. Why shouldn't I do something I love to do? Who made them king and queen?"

It's happening. I'm having a deeper conversation with meaning. Now, what should I say? Lizzie helps out.

"Well, no one likes me at all in my school," Lizzie says.

"Why is that?" Annabeth asks. She looks totally surprised.

"I don't know. I had friends at my old school and I guess I just expected people to like me here, too. Maybe I expected it too fast though and I overstepped or something. The first day, everyone was trying to be my friend as if I was a new toy or something. Then, the next day, everyone acted as if I had cooties."

"Well," I say, "I've studied this. Sometimes, a new kid comes to school and everyone wants to be their friend and others come in and no one wants to be their friend. You really just follow the lead of the popular kids in deciding who gets the warm welcome and who doesn't. Sometimes, the new girl will be perfectly nice, but a threat to the others. And then sometimes, the new girl will be popular at first until the popular group feels threatened."

"Plus, I pick my nose," Lizzie says.

Annabeth laughs. "You do not."

"Well, I was just happy you and Jenny liked me," Lizzie says. "Jenny was my Obi Wan. Help me Jenny, be my friend, you're my only hope." I love a good Star Wars reference. I'm laughing with Annabeth. "Anyway, if Jenny didn't work out, I was going to have to make up an imaginary friend. His name was going to be Bartholomew, by the way. He was going to like everything I liked except for running. I was going to have to train him in that." She starts laughing. "Come on Bartholomew, pick up the pace!"

"See how creative you are?" Annabeth says. "If no one likes you, that's their problem."

"People say that, but it doesn't make it true," I say.

Annabeth and Lizzie stare at me. "I just mean, it hurts when people don't like you for no reason. It feels like it is your problem. Like there's something wrong with you while they seem like they're better than you. No matter how much you try to get them to like you, they just won't."

Annabeth nods like she gets it. Lizzie keeps staring at me. Finally, she shakes her head. "Who are these people who don't like you?" She's punching one hand into the other. "I get that I'm not everyone's cup of tea because I don't care to be, but you do care and you're nice to everyone so just who are these people? Bartholomew and I are ready to rumble."

Coach Jay saves me on her bullhorn. Annabeth is wanted up on stage and the townspeople have to come up as well. It's the first time the townspeople have actually worked on the actual stage instead of the hallway. Tonight we learn the dance to the scene when Birdie comes to town causing all of the girls to faint. Basically, it's the same dance from the opening number, just without the hand movements, no singing and slightly less space. I asked my mom why girls always faint in movies. I've never seen someone faint in real life. She said their girdles were too tight.

I'm not sure what those are but I'm hoping I don't have to wear one when I grow up. I would, however, love it if the poodle skirt and saddle shoes came back in fashion. In this scene, Charlie is the star. He has to sing in front of everyone and be like Elvis Presley. When he sings, all the girls are supposed to be so in love with him that they get all googly-eyed.

"Oh my gosh," Annabeth says as she jumps up and fishes Binaca Blast from her little white purse. She sprays it in her mouth, tries to smooth her hair, and then pinches her cheeks. "This is it. Just wait until you hear Charlie sing. After that, we have to practice the kissing scene which will be so wonderful, but awkward. Hopefully more wonderful than awkward. Wish me luck."

I feel nervous for her as she bounces off the stage. I'm nowhere near the point where I want to kiss boys yet, but I can appreciate how she must feel right now.

Coach Jay is physically moving people around the stage like Barbie dolls. She asks each older person if they're here with a significant other. If they aren't, she laughs and says how she's running her own *Dating Game*. "I think you two look like a realistic couple. Wait, she looks too good for you. Kidding!" The grandparents are laughing and joking as they get their new spouses. Some even give out hoots and hollers at the new couplings. None of them are embarrassed.

Coach Jay then goes looking for kids to act as grandkids for the grandparents. She wants the kids younger than us but able to leave their parents' sides. Most of the younger kids are total hams so that works and the grandparents immediately light up with their new grandkids. April and her group are next. They don't like being separated or singled out but Coach Jay is so loud, she doesn't care. She moves them around and picks out boy-friends for a few and groups of friends. April doesn't end up with a boyfriend. Instead she gets put with the group that Coach Jay says is going to be the nerdy teenagers. They all laugh when she says it, but they laugh rather quickly before tightly closing up their mouths. That's not going to go over well with April. Next she gets to Lizzie and me and then pushes us over toward Susie and Jennifer. "You're kid fainters, right?"

"Just me," Jennifer says.

"Just you? Why is that?" Coach Jay asks.

Jennifer's face tightens. "That's what you said and you chose me based on my faint. These three are supposed to catch me since I auditioned and got the part." Susie nods.

"Okay," Coach Jay says, as if she doesn't remember any of her fainting auditions. "That could work. Yes, I think that will look cute then."

Jennifer exhales. I can tell she's relieved her part is still her part and her part only. We stand there as Coach Jay moves more people around.

"So, is Annabeth your sister or something?" Jennifer asks Lizzie.

"No, I only have a brother."

"So, how do you, like, know her then?" Susie asks. She has a way of asking questions that make you feel as if you have done something wrong.

"I just met her at the play." They look at Lizzie and say noth-ing. "So, do you like being in the play?"

They don't answer her.

"I just don't get how you two are, like, hanging out with her now," Jennifer said.

"Okay," Lizzie says.

"Okay what?" Susie asks.

"It's okay if you don't get it," Lizzie said.

"You're weird," Jennifer says.

"I think Annabeth is just being nice to you because she feels sorry for you," Susie says.

"Possibly," Lizzie says. "People do feel sorry for me sometimes."

"So do you want people to feel sorry for you?" Jennifer asks.

I feel like crawling away.

"Not especially."

"Cause that's why she's being nice to you. Just so you know. Because of your mom. You know? How she died?" Susie says.

"I had heard about that, yes," Lizzie says. I can see she's at her breaking point. Her fists are clenched but she keeps her face looking kind and patient like a kindergarten teacher dealing with a bad kid.

"I would never want that to happen to me. I love my mom," Jennifer says.

I know the next thing here should be someone saying something nice and caring to Lizzie, but Jennifer just lets it hang in the air.

"Well, hopefully that won't happen then," Lizzie says. "That would be awful for you."

Susie and Jennifer nod. Lizzie's fists slowly unclench, hoping it's over.

"We should practice the faint," Jennifer says. "Everyone's hands clean?" She laughs.

Lizzie eases up and says, "Maybe we should check you; I hear girls are throwing mud on each other at your school."

Oh no. I feel the wind as Susie and Jennifer both snap their heads in my direction. "What did you tell her?"

Lizzie quickly senses she did something wrong. "Hold on, she didn't say anything to me."

"Don't lie." They hold their gaze on me.

"I mean, she didn't tell me who got mud on them," Lizzie says. "Was it you? How terribly awful that the other girls wouldn't fling themselves down in the mud for you. I guess they're not good friends."

The girls take a breath and seem unsure of what to believe but they go with it and I'm grateful for Lizzie's save.

We practice catching Jennifer over and over. My arms feel like they might break off. Susie keeps correcting my faint-catching skills telling me I'm being too mousey when I'm supposed to be strong. Lizzie suggests that I be the fainter since my arms aren't strong enough, but I think she's just messing with them. When Charlie comes in, he doesn't have a microphone yet, so it's just his voice and his guitar. Annabeth said he has a great, unexpected voice that's deep and soulful. Though his voice is slightly quiet, he commands the attention of everyone on the stage. It's an amazing thing when you see true talent up close. Everything kind of stops.

Coach Jay pulls him over to all of his "marks" where he needs to go so that the specified girls can faint. Jennifer's cue to faint is after he comes over to her and pinches her cheek. Though he's normally pretty quiet, he comes to life as Birdie. After four run-throughs, we learn how to exit the stage. We need to take our time and walk off set as if we see a friend we wanted to talk with, not just like actors whose scene is finished. I'm half-listening to her but mostly peeking back on stage to see the director with Charlie and Annabeth. I'm expecting the kiss to be a huge moment, but instead, it's done quickly mostly as a formality so they can see where they need to be on stage and the lighting. All the same, after Charlie pecks Annabeth on the lips, he turns away to listen to the director, but I see Annabeth smile.

Since this practice is our last before Christmas break, Mr. Freeley and Coach Jay call us all back on to stage. We know we're having a party since they asked people to bring in cupcakes and fruit. In the world of the theater though, nothing is simple. Mr. Freeley and Coach Jay lead us through a painful show of pretending that we all need to stay until midnight to practice and the party is canceled. No one is falling for it. Just let us have the cupcakes and cut it out. Finally, they end the charade and have some of the stage hands wheel in four tables filled with cupcakes, hot chocolate, candy shaped like Santa, sugar cookies and fruit. On cue, the lighting dims as tiny paper snowflakes drift down from the rafters. A spotlight highlights the front side of the stage where Charlie is ready with his guitar. Annabeth sings "Have Yourself a Merry Little Christmas" in a voice as delicate as the snowflakes. The directors walk around handing out candy canes. Okay, that was pretty cool. All parties should start with snowflakes falling from the ceiling. Lizzie makes snow angels on the floor.

"Come on, Jenny."

I pull her up. "No time for snow angels, there are cupcakes."

Christmas carols are now blasting through the speakers. The

dim lighting allows me to happily stuff my face with cupcakes and dance around with Lizzie without feeling anyone looking at me. I actually sing, not loudly, but still, I sing and dance—in public—and for once I'm not worried what anyone might think of me. Lizzie and I spin around until we feel dizzy and fall to the ground. It's a small moment of feeling completely happy—the kind I appreciate the most in the world. With a break from the world for a week now, everything feels right.

SUPERPOWER #12: RECOGNIZING SMALLNESS

The worst day of the calendar for me is January 4. It marks the end of the holidays. The time between Halloween and New Year's Eve is the best. The promise of Halloween, Thanksgiving, Christmas and all those little breaks from school keep me sane. When it's all over, all that's left is a long stretch of school with no interesting holiday, sorry Easter. The thought makes my legs feel like lead. All of the candy and cookies disappear from my house. The house feels battened down for the time of year when the weather is freezing so the teachers load up on homework and you're left with lots of indoor recess. Indoor recess sounds like it should be fun, but those two words really don't go together. Outdoor recess is time for getting away from people in your class and swinging. Indoor recess means you can sit on the carpet with a book while the boys continually get reprimanded for wrestling. Sometimes we play games like 7Up or Quiet Ball. Those are okay. In 7Up, I always win because no one thinks I will pick them. It's a little unsettling to have to stay up at the front of the room for so long, but it feels good to win. Plus, it puts my spy skills to use.

We spent Christmas at home and then visited Terry and my aunt and uncle in New York. While we were there, we met Terry's new boyfriend. He was okay. Actually, he was pretty great—a lot like Charlie but more outgoing. It's just hard to have to share my Terry time with some boy. Then April kept questioning the two of them how they started dating, how did they both know the other one liked them, what you should do if you like someone. Terry and her boyfriend disagreed about what to do. Terry believed April should keep getting to know Jeffrey as a friend and let things happen naturally. Her boyfriend thought April should be direct. "Guys like to know if someone likes them," he said. I could tell which perspective April sided with and it made me nervous. Jeffrey isn't the kind of guy you tell that you like. I did find out through all of her questioning that at one point during the Christmas party, Jeffrey had his arm around April. The whole thing made me nervous—April with a boyfriend? Yikes and gross.

When Terry's boyfriend wasn't with us and April wasn't hogging the whole conversation, New York was great. Usually when we visit, our parents splurge and take us to a Broadway show, but this year, the only family-appropriate show for us was *Cats*. Genetically-speaking, we're not cat people. My dad outright hates them, my aunt believes they're evil souls left walking the earth in purgatory. The rest of us would just rather not sit around a dark theater with humans acting like cats. It sounds like a nightmare. Instead, we walked around Times Square; saw all of the window decorations in the stores on Fifth Avenue and the Rockefeller Tree. I have to say, New York is probably the best place for shy people. Everyone walks so fast and there are so many people—no one has the time to notice anyone else. Once you get past the fear of being in a place so huge and busy, I think it's a shy person's paradise.

"I think I would like living here," I said to Terry on our last night. "When I'm older. It's close to Connecticut, too."

"I don't know," Terry said. "I love it here, but sometimes I wish I had what you had—space and trees and cute little shops."

I thought about this as I was close to falling asleep. Terry gave me her bed while she sleeps on the floor. It's what she's always done. April always takes a couch in the main room where she can watch television.

"Hey," Terry whispered. "Still awake?"

"Yes."

"You seem happy. Not that you weren't always happy, but you seem happier. It makes me happy. I'm glad you decided to be in the play."

I smiled.

"You're a great kid," Terry said. "I hope you've started realizing it."

Tears welled up in my eyes. They don't make anyone better than her. I wish I knew how to tell her that, but I didn't. When I got home, I wrote her a letter hoping she'd sense how important she is to me.

While the first day back after break is always a downer, I keep trying to hold onto that happy feeling Terry saw in me. The trouble is, I don't know what I did to make myself look noticeably happy. Luckily, on the first day back we're all too sleepy to do much so the day passes without much effort. I have play practice tonight that I'm really looking forward to so that helps this day, too. Lizzie and I made a plan to start making scavenger hunts. Right after Christmas but before we went to New York, my mom took Lizzie and me to visit Mrs. Brown. Lizzie had so many questions about Mrs. Brown, my mom offered to take us. At first, I crossed my fingers Lizzie would say no. I'm not sure Lizzie is the kind to ever say no to that kind of offer. Like, she has no problem sticking up for herself and saying no to people like I would, but I don't think it would ever cross her mind to say no to an activity. I could probably ask her if she wants to peel potatoes with me for five hours and she would show up smiling with a potato peeler. If someone came and stole that potato peeler from me, she would find that person, knock them down and give me back the peeler without breaking a sweat. Not that visiting Mrs. Brown is as bad as peeling potatoes, but it's not my favorite thing to do. First, she lives in one of those places that are called a home, but it's more like a one-story apartment building with a receptionist, nurses, people in wheelchairs and the constant smell of bologna. There's nothing homey about it. The walls are painted a pale pink and the furniture is a pale blue like some strange baby nursery for adults. It's as if they were afraid to commit to the fact that men and women would be living here. If I were them, I think I would use cozy chairs and have the place painted in fall colors and smelling like apple pie. My mom usually drags April and me there once a year. Mrs. Brown is nice, it's just I never know what to say and I get so bored there, I stop paying attention and start daydreaming. April and I always feel like we're the lamest entertainment show when we visit. All of the people, from the receptionist to the residents, call out to us the second they see us.

"Here they are," they'll say.

"My, just look at them. Such beautiful girls."

"Hey, hey, here comes trouble."

Nothing makes you feel like you have no personality more than strangers who act super excited at your mere existence. I always smile awkwardly while April kind of smirks. We are not worthy of this welcome. I hope they never see how April and I really just count down the minutes before we can leave. Lizzie, of course, was different. If they ever need a mascot there, Lizzie should be it. Somehow before leaving—and I should note leaving wasn't something she was in a rush to do—she got into a wheelchair race with some of the men and split a piece of pumpkin pie with them. She saw a woman playing checkers by herself in the game room and joined her. I wasn't sure we would ever leave. The visit with Mrs. Brown was a lot more, well, alive, too. Turns out, Mrs. Brown is pretty funny. She met us in the lobby and walked us back to her little apartment.

"I don't want anyone to steal my visitors," she said which I thought was a joke but as we walked the halls with her, she hustled us along quickly before anyone else could snatch us as their guests. "Leave them be, Bettie, they're here for me," she said to a woman offering a candy bowl. "There's time for jokes later, Melvin," she said to a man wearing a cape and holding a magician's hat.

"These people are vultures sometimes," she said as she settled us into her apartment and closed her door halfway. "That should keep them out for now. If I close it all the way, they'll just keep knocking. Here girls." She handed us a plate of Andes

Mints. I'd never seen these anywhere but there. They're always the highlight of my trip. Lizzie started right in on the conversation. "Thank you for the scavenger hunt. We loved it."

"Which one was it, dear?"

"The one that leads you down to Saint Anthony."

Mrs. Brown walked over to her bookshelf and picked out a folder. "Let's see then," she said as she sat down, licked the tip of her finger and combed through the papers inside the folder. It's a move I've seen all my teachers do at one time or another. Was she a teacher? I really knew nothing about Mrs. Brown and felt pretty selfish that I never bothered to find out anything about her.

"Here we go," she said. She hummed to herself as she looked over the paper. "So you found the pins at the end? And the pennies? And a box of ribbons?"

"We didn't find the ribbons," Lizzie said. "Jenny and Mrs. Watts were showing me Bloody Rock and we happened to see the statue so we missed the first part of the hunt."

"Oh, well, that's okay," she said. "It starts at the rock garden if you are ever interested in completing the whole hunt."

"I've been in that rock garden thousands of times and never saw anything," my mom said.

"You need to look like a child, dear," Mrs. Brown said and smiled.

"So, what else is in the folder?" Lizzie asked.

"Don't think I'm crazy, but I am," Mrs. Brown said. "Years and years ago, I started making little scavenger hunts around town. I like to stay organized, so I took notes about each one. It's nice to find out when someone found one. I didn't realize until lately, that I should have left my name so people could let me know. It didn't matter when I was leaving them, but now I'm so curious about it. But as they said, curiosity killed the cat so I should just leave it be."

"Why do you do that?" Lizzie asked. "I mean, I think it's awesome, but what made you do it?"

"It makes me happy," she said. "My daughter lives with her family all the way in California and my son moved with his wife to New Hampshire. When my husband died, I felt lonely. And let me tell you, I was feeling so sorry for myself all the time. For years, I organized a scavenger hunt for the children's hospital. Well, after my husband died, I was too sad to do it. My friends could have left me alone to wallow, but you know what they did? They marched right on over and made me organize the scavenger hunt so I wouldn't disappoint those kids. I'm so glad they did because some times, you just need a project to stop living inside your head and get back out in the world. And let me tell you, seeing how happy those kids were made me feel worthwhile still. I guess I wanted to keep up that feeling so I just became the crazy scavenger hunt woman, leaving little trinkets all over the place. Sometimes I would just leave a trail of pennies on the ground or other times I would put beautiful flowers from my garden on cars parked in parking lots. If I heard of something bad happening somewhere or someone who had fallen on hard times, I would leave something pretty there or bake bread for someone. I figure this hobby was better than becoming a crazy old cat woman."

She and my mom laughed. I didn't know about Lizzie, but I think she was thinking the same thing I was. Right before us sat a folder filled with scavenger hunts for us to find. Mental telepathy is not a shy person superpower, but I was trying my hardest to mentally tell Lizzie to use her boldness to ask for the folder. Please, please work.

"So did you leave Saint Anthony there because of the witch story from Bloody Rock?" Lizzie asked. Okay, that is a good question, but please ask for the folder next since I don't feel right doing it. What if she says no.

"Yes, I did."

"You heard of that story?" my mom asked. "How did I not hear of it until recently?"

"I meant to put it in the house brochure when you bought it," Mrs. Brown slapped her knee and laughed loudly. "Wouldn't that have been a hoot. 'Must see house, comes with own witch story and bloodstained rock'. Can you imagine?"

"I don't know if I think it's blood-stained," my mom said, trying to erase any darkness from my childhood whenever she can.

"Sometimes I could hear noises after I was in the house by myself. I didn't hear them when my husband was alive but then, when the house was so still, at night, I could hear like a creaking. After I put the saint down there, I didn't hear it again. I figured I put that old witch back where she belonged. Either that or my husband was pranking me and decided I'd had enough."

The skin on my arms felt prickly. Noises? Like witch sounds near my house where I live? Ghosts of husbands that once lived in my house playing tricks? I'm never sleeping again. My mom made the face she made when she didn't believe someone but was too polite to disagree. It's kind of like the smile you'd find painted on one of those creepy porcelain dolls. Porcelain dolls are also part of my fear basket. Combine Darth Vader, a bunch of porcelain dolls, a cackling witch sound, vampires, ghost husbands and put them all in my attic and you have just crafted my worst nightmare.

"Feel free to say no, but would you mind sending Jenny and I on your scavenger hunts each week? We could come visit and you can look in your folder and give us a clue about where one starts and then we can tell you if anyone else has done it or not." Yes! Excellent plan, Lizzie.

"I suppose that would be nice," Mrs. Brown said. "I could agree to that, but I'd like to ask you two a favor as well. See, I still help the children's hospital with their annual scavenger hunt. I haven't given that up yet. I would love to have your help running the stations there."

"Can we, Mrs. Watts?" Lizzie asked. Of course she was excited. I was excited about being helpful, but nervous about being in a hospital.

"I don't see why not," she said. "I think that would be lovely. Put April and I down as a helpers, too."

"Maybe Jenny and I can make friendship bracelets as small prizes, too."

"How kind you two are," Mrs. Brown said to Lizzie and me though I had done nothing to show that I was kind except sat there quietly as I always did. "The kids would surely love that. I used to sew the girls their little purses or make hug coupons out of doilies for them. My hands don't work quite as well these days though." She showed us her hands which, while older looking than my mom's, look graceful with long delicate fingers that you could just tell made some cool projects. When we left her apartment, Lizzie gave her a hug. I think that she basically adopted a new grandparent.

Since Lizzie and I didn't get a chance to get together another time over break to make any of the bracelets, we're going to do some of them at the play practice tonight. My mom and I went to the craft store and bought all sorts of yarn. January 4 is actually turning into a good day. School went well and my wish came true that Coach Jay didn't need us townspeople for too long so Lizzie and I have plenty of time to work on our projects. We had to do one run-through of the opening scene before they let us take a break so they could work on Annabeth and Charlie's scene. Annabeth told us she would help us later. At my suggestion, Lizzie and I set up in the back aisle away from people. It was my idea. I didn't want Jennifer and Susie to ask what we were doing. They might think it's stupid and I don't feel like feeling embarrassed today. When I was in Terry's room, she played for me a song by Frank Sinatra. I had heard it before, but she told me to really listen to the lyrics. In fact, she had the lyrics written on a notebook paper and tacked to her wall. The one part that really struck me was the part that goes like this: "Some people get their kicks, stomping on a dream." Well, today, I don't feel like having Jennifer and Susie stomp on my dream. We don't get far making the bracelets before we hear lots of footsteps.

"Stay down," Lizzie says in an army voice. "I'll check it out."

We peer over the seats and see Jeffrey and his friends walking toward the last seats in the auditorium followed by April's friends and Jennifer and Susie.

"What's happening?" I ask Lizzie.

"I don't know," Lizzie says. "Psst, Susie."

Susie looks over at us and makes a face. Lizzie motions her over.

"What's going on?"

"Quiet, Jeffrey is going to read like the funniest thing," she says. "Some girl wrote him a love letter. It's hysterical." She walks back to the group.

I feel my stomach sink. Lizzie and I move closer.

"I wasn't sure if I should write this letter or not," I hear Jeffrey reading in a high-pitched voice as he holds his hand over his heart. "I just can't live with myself though if I don't tell you that I think you are great. I know I'm a few years younger than you, but maybe we could hang out."

He continues reading and I scan for April in the crowd. She's standing behind everyone and she's not laughing. Her eyes look misty and her face is red. "I think you are the cutest boy I've ever seen." He flips his hair and bats pretend eyelashes like a cartoon character. In the crowd, you hear his friends saying how great this letter is and others are yelling how he has so many loser girls after him. "I'll just die if you don't go out with me." All of the sudden, Lizzie pushes through the crowd and grabs for the letter, but Jeffrey moves it away from her and laughs. She keeps reaching, but he's like the matador and she's the bull. He reads as she keeps grabbing it until one of the boys lifts her away. "I know you are the coolest boy in school and I'm a nobody, but if you just got to know me, you would find that we were made for each other. Please don't break my heart. Love, April Watts." Everyone gives a how-sweet sound as if they are looking at a baby. April's friends act that way, too. No one is helping her. April runs away.

I can't move from my spot. I don't know what to do. Lizzie fights her way free and yells at Jeffrey.

"You made that letter up," she says. "If you didn't, you should be so lucky as to have April Watts give you the time of day." Then she snatches the letter away as Jeffrey pats her on the head and leaves with his friends and April's friends following him.

"It didn't even say any of that!" Lizzie yells after him but no one listens to her. I'm not sure where April went. I don't see her when Dad comes looking to take us home. Lizzie and I searched all over backstage. Lizzie is fuming. "Even before I knew that your sister wrote that letter, it's just not right being that way. If someone has a crush on you, you should be happy, not try to break their heart like that. He's such a jerk. He made most of it up, too. I shouldn't have read the letter but all she says is that she kind of likes him. You know what Annabeth told me? Jeffrey tried out for the part of Birdie but didn't get it and he threw a big fit, even making his parents come yell at the director. I hate people like that." As I listen to her, my embarrassment for my sister mixes with Lizzie's anger making my blood boil.

My dad is fed up since he has no idea what happened and mostly thinks she is just hanging out with her friends somewhere. I want to tell him everything, but I also don't want to repeat that scene ever again. Like a lot of my embarrassing moments in life, I want that one to fizzle away as if it never happened. Watching your older sister be made a fool of feels like something that should never happen—like it goes against the laws of nature. Older siblings and parents shouldn't be made fun of or yelled at in front of the youngest family member. Like when someone honks the horn at my mom when I'm in the car. I know she's a slow driver, she knows she's a slow driver, so you know what horn honker? Cool it.

I collect our supplies, no longer in the mood for the project as Lizzie and I decide to search for April. We never find her. Lizzie hands me a bracelet from her wrist to give to April for her before she goes home. She tells me to make sure to tell April that Jeffrey Greeson is a jerk. My dad and I look again in the auditorium. He's muttering the whole time about how he's starving. When my dad is hungry, that's the closest I ever see him get to being mad. Finally he pokes his head outside and looks toward our car. April is leaning against it.

"Great," my dad says. "Just leave the building and tell no one where you are. It's only spaghetti and meatballs night at home."

We walk to the car and he just tells April to get in. I don't know if she saw me when Jeffrey was reading her letter or not. I stay silent the whole way. My dad never stays angry for long so he ends up humming. April has her body turned fully away from me, with her head resting on the window. I can't look. It breaks my heart. As we pull into the driveway, we see the lights of the house on. It's a feeling I never take for granted. I love coming home. I love seeing a light on knowing my mom is in there making dinner. Dorothy is right—there's no place like home. At home, there are no Jeffreys or Jennifers or Susies to deal with. I hope April feels that way, too, but she jumps out of the car the second it stops and walks toward the back of the house.

"What?" my dad asks me. "Where is she going?"

"I'll find out," I say. "Go eat."

I run behind the house. It's pretty dark but the lights from our house and Robbie's make it easy to see. April is down on the swing set, sitting on her old swing. She's not swinging now though. It's the saddest girl on a swing set I've ever seen. She's huddled under her windbreaker which my mom always says isn't warm enough for Connecticut in winter but she insists on wearing it because middle schoolers are never cold and parents are always wrong. When she sees me, she looks away sharply. I slow my walking. I was running since I was nervous about the witch and Bloody Rock. I sit down on my swing, hoping I don't disturb her. She's like a bunny. If I make too much motion and try to get too close, she'll hop away. We sit in silence. The wind carries the sounds of our house to us. The sink running in the kitchen, the creaks of our porch. I stare up at my bedroom window.

"What are you doing?" April finally speaks.

"I wanted to see if you were okay."

"Why wouldn't I be?"

Really? Okay. "Because Jeffrey Greeson is a big jerk."

She nods, now knowing I know.

"I didn't even write half of the stuff he read out loud, you know. I mean, yes, I wrote some of it, but he started making stuff up. He made me look like a fool."

I don't know what to say. I stay quiet. I feel hurt, too. I feel like Jeffrey Greeson did this to both of us. I know April won't see it that way though but it sure feels like it.

"I was so stupid," April says. "Of course someone like Jeffrey Greeson wouldn't like me. Why did I write that letter?"

"Maybe you thought he would want to know how you felt."

"Ugh." She tears at her hair. "I'm the laughingstock of the play now. All of my friends couldn't wait to get away from me. Now they can have a laugh about me with him and then they'll be closer to him. I gave them the perfect way to get closer."

I think I know what she means. It's what I did by sharing the muddy pants story earlier. Bonding with someone is easier over the heartbreak of someone else I suppose.

"I'll never have a boyfriend. I'll always be seen as this loser."

"I don't think so," I start to say.

"It's true," she yells. "No one will ever like me. I'm ugly and boring and insecure and I write stupid love letters to boys who don't even know I exist."

"April," I yell back, trying to get her to stop. "You're beautiful. You're the most beautiful girl I know. When you aren't being so mean to me, you're also the funnest person I know. Jeffrey Greeson is an idiot."

She's silent except for the after-crying sniffling. "Funnest isn't a word." Exasperated, I stand up to leave, but she grabs my hand. "Sorry."

I sit back in my swing.

"Do you really think I'm beautiful and fun?" She looks away from me when she asks this question. I know her heart is on her sleeve.

"I really think you are beautiful and I think you used to be fun before middle school ate you up."

She laughs. "Middle school isn't as easy as elementary school."

Elementary school did seem like a breeze for April, so I'll let her have that one, but personally, I'm praying middle school will be better than elementary school has been. It hasn't been a picnic, that's for sure.

"Do you think Jeffrey really is a jerk?"

"Yes. And he's not that cute."

"What do you know about cuteness of boys?"

"I just know he's not. And he's so full of himself, always flipping his hair and looking in mirrors. Like he's God's Gift to the Universe." I mimic him playing with his hair.

"Tomorrow is going to be awful." I really wish she had known about the beauty of vacation breaks. If she had given Jeffrey the letter before Christmas break and he had read it beforehand, everyone would have forgotten by now. You don't go bold without an out. The best days to try new things are Fridays—late afternoon preferably. That's when you would ask a new friend to play with you or raise your hand for a question. You need a few days to retreat in case it didn't go your way. Other people's memories aren't as long, or at least I hope they aren't. Instead of telling her this advice now though when it won't help, I try to cheer her up.

"You're April, you're tough. You'll be fine. I wish I was as tough as you."

April looks up at the stars. It's cloudy so only a few are visible. That's one of my secret calming techniques though. When I feel really bad at times, I look way up in the sky. It makes you realize how huge the universe is and we're just tiny parts of it. So then problems don't seem so large anymore. In this case, it's a good reminder that Jeffrey Greeson not liking you probably doesn't matter much in the universe.

"Remember when we would stay out here for hours, swinging and swinging until mom would call us in for dinner and we would pretend we couldn't hear her?"

"Yes," I answer. "Duh. It was only three years ago."

"Right."

I take a deep breath, hoping what I say next is good and that she doesn't laugh at me. "I think you aren't too old to swing. I know you think you are too old for lots of things now, but I don't see the rush. It's not like you are a real grown-up yet. I feel like everyone else has read some kind of manual telling them what is now cool and what isn't. I can't even find this manual. As much as I'd love everyone to love me and to be seen as cool, even I know that if you give up too many things that used to make you happy because you think you are too cool, you lose what made you cool in the first place. Like Jeffrey. He was just a kid who was good in plays at first and then he grew up a little and thought it wasn't cool to be nice to people and hurting their feelings was funny. Lots of kids like to give up the fun stuff right away and replace it with being mean just so other kids will think they're cool. Instead, it's like they've lost their hearts."

I'm about to go into a whole thing about E.T.'s heart light but hold back knowing I'll lose her there. April doesn't look at me. She's looking at her shoes. It slightly kills me because I know what I just said was pretty deep and meaningful. When I put out something deep and meaningful, I feel like I've given out birthday party invitations—I want to hear positive results immediately and I don't want anyone to think it was strange I invited them. Finally April looks at me and smiles.

"Bet I can swing higher than you," she says. April starts swinging. My heart fills. She understood me. I follow her. "I forgot how much it can tickle your belly!" She snorts as an uncontrolled laugh escapes her.

I laugh, too, and she doesn't scold me for laughing at her. The cold air reddens our faces and the metal chains freeze our hands, but at the moment, I feel free. My hair is blowing back and forth, my legs pumping, my stomach tickling, the stars shining, the moon watching, and my April is back again—if only for now.

We swing until my mom calls us in.

SUPERPOWER #13: GETTING OUT OF THINGS

I'm not proud of this superpower but I do know a thing or two about getting out of things. Of course, I know how to fake illness though my parents are on to that one. I also know how a well-placed bathroom request can get you out of gym when picking teams so when you return, the gym teacher assigns you a team instead of sitting through the painful popularity contest that it can be. When the whole class is being punished and not allowed to take their library books home or something, I know how to ask if I can since I wasn't the one causing the trouble. You don't ask in a way that shows you aren't part of the class, but you walk to the teacher at a different time and ask if the library book rule was for everyone. They usually wink at me and say I can bring mine home if I'm quiet about it.

I guess April has seen this superpower in action because I wake the next morning to April pushing my shoulder. "Hey, tell me how you fake being sick all the time?" My eyelids are still sticking to each eye. "Come on, wake up." She flicks my forehead.

"Ow!"

"Shh." She covers my mouth with her hand and closes my door. "Sorry. I just need you to tell me how you get away with it so well. They never believe me."

"Why? Is this because of Jeffrey?"

"Yes, of course. Now, just tell me. Do stomachaches work better than sore throats? I want to stay home but don't want a doctor's appointment."

"Stomachache. But don't overdue it. Act as if you're trying really hard to get out of bed and like you actually want to go to school, but you're just in too much pain. Like when someone flicks your forehead." It feels nice to be an expert on something.

"Like this?" She flicks my forehead again. "Kidding! Thanks." She opens my door and scans the hallway. Before she leaves, she whispers back at me that this conversation never happened and tiptoes into her bedroom. I probably should have inspired her to face her fears and rip that Band-Aid right off, but I totally get it. I'd ask my parents if I could change schools if I had been April. I expect my mom to make April get out of bed to see if she feels better, and to have her get ready for school and all of the things she makes me do before deciding if I'm faking or not. Instead, she spends like two minutes in April's room and lets her stay home. Just like that. I know this is probably one of those times my dad would remind me about the boy who cried wolf, but it's still difficult to watch your sister get something so easily.

At the bus stop, Cammy asks me where April is but she says it in a way that I know she already knows about the whole Jeffrey thing even though she's not in the play. "Ugh," she says. "I told her he wasn't worth it. I should go drag her out of bed."

"What happened?" Robbie asks.

"Nothing," Cammy says.

"I didn't want to know anyway. Just being neighborly." Robbie then burps really loudly.

"That is so not neighborly," Cammy says. "Yuck, do I smell Cheese Whiz? You eat Cheese Whiz for breakfast?"

"It's delicious on toast."

"Go be neighborly over there."

"Okay," Robbie burp-talks.

"Was she okay today?" Cammy asks me.

"I think so," I say. I'm unsure how much Cammy knows and how much I'm supposed to say to anyone.

"I spoke with her last night. She said you two had a good talk and it made her feel better at least."

"Really?"

"Yes." Cammy looks down the street as the bus rolls up. "That's why I thought she would just come to school and act like she was better than all of it—which she is. Oh well. But if she pulls this tomorrow, I will drag her from her bed and make her go to school in her pajamas. Tell her that."

I know it's wrong, but being involved in some drama really gives one a sense of purpose. I imagine myself walking straight into April's room after school with two mugs of hot chocolate to discuss everything.

We need to write notes to our pen pals which feels kind of funny now that Lizzie and I see each other all of the time. I once read this story in one of April's magazines about this boy who by accident calls the wrong phone number and starts speaking to the girl who lives there. They end up talking on the phone night after night. Turns out, they both are in high school, not the same one though. Then, the girl wants to meet him in person. He doesn't think it's the best idea although he's curious too. He says how it will change everything. He tells her how on the phone, they can be their truest selves or something. Anyway, they arrange to meet at the food court. She makes sure her hair is perfect and has her friends sit at a table next to her. They wait and wait. He never shows. Later that night, she gets home and he calls. He tells her he went to the mall, but once he saw her, she knew she would never like him. Then he never called her again. I never thought that was fair of him though. However, once we started the pen pals, I kept thinking of that story. At first, I was so excited when it was only letters, but then once we went to meet, I feared Lizzie would see I wasn't popular or stylish or the most athletic. When the tables were turned though and I saw that she wasn't all of those things, everything did change. It took away any of my excitement to write to her. I was being as unfair as the guy in the story. Now that I know Lizzie accepts me completely, I'm working on doing the same.

At lunch, Jennifer and Susie call me over to sit with them. This can't be good. They tell one of their tag-along friends to scoot down so I can sit which makes that girl give me evil looks and barely enough room to fit. No one speaks to me while they nibble their lunches of cucumber sandwiches cut into flower shapes. How do they all have the same thing? Now I have something more to find embarrassing—my lunch. It's always a messy peanut butter and Fluff sandwich on Wonder bread with an apple in a brown paper bag. Please tell me my mom didn't send in a little note with it this time. I usually like those but I know this group will see my lunch as babyish. I decide to just eat my apple.

"Well, that's a juicy apple," the Mad Girl to my right says while wiping away something from her face.

"Oh, sorry," I say. I guess I won't eat today.

"Say it, don't spray it," she says but she says it to the other girls like she's Johnny Carson telling a joke to the audience.

"So," Susie starts. "How is your sister?"

My face reddens. "She's fine."

"Really?" Jennifer asks. "That was like the most embarrassing thing, like ever."

I look down at my bag.

"What happened?" asks Mad Girl. Jennifer and Susie keep interrupting each other to tell an exaggerated version of what happened. I can tell the girls around them are just acting out the response Jennifer and Susie obviously want. They open their eyes wide while covering their mouths. Some gasp or giggle. My face remains still, looking down at the lunch I'm not eating. I hate these girls right now. When they finish, they all laugh as if it's the funniest thing they've ever heard. The girl next to me says how she can't believe anyone would be so stupid to do that. Then she asks if my sister is at least prettier than me so maybe she believed she really could have a chance with Jeffrey Greeson.

"Oh," Susie says, "I forgot one of the best parts. So, Emily's pen pal is in the play. She's this really crazy girl. Well, she jumped up trying to keep Jeffrey from reading the note, but he kept batting her away as if she was a fly."

"That's right," Jennifer says and laughs. "Oh my God, it was like so funny."

"Wait," says Mad Girl. "Who's Emily?"

"It's an inside joke but Jenny is Emily," Jennifer says. Ha! Mad Girl, I have an inside joke with these girls and you don't.

I glance at my watch and say a quick prayer. Please let this lunch end abruptly because some kid let all the frogs go in science class.

"You know what, Susie?" Jennifer asks. "I do feel bad for our little Emily here though. It's not her fault her sister committed social suicide or that Miss Lotti paired her with that mental mess."

"True," Susie says and looks at me with compassion, I think. It's either compassion or she's about to eat me.

"So, Jenny," Jennifer says, "we've been thinking, you can hang with us at the play rehearsals to save you. Sound good?"

I catch Susie giving Jennifer a look as if she can't believe she would invite me to hang out with them. Just as quickly, Jennifer gives Susie a smile that tells her this invitation isn't because I'm cool, it's out of pity or she has some big master plan or something.

"Wait, when is the play? Maybe I can come," says Mad Girl, probably afraid I'm taking more than just her seat.

"It's too late, they've already made final cuts," Susie says to her. I know and Susie knows that they would probably accept townspeople all the way up until opening night and there were no cuts for our roles ever. At least I think Susie knows. At what point does someone believe everything that comes out of their mouths?

"So, Emily, what do you think?" Jennifer asks. I was hoping she wouldn't.

"Um, that's okay," I mumble.

"What?" Jennifer leans forward. I keep quiet. "You don't actually like Lizard, do you?"

And here's where I learn to hate myself a little bit more. "No," I say.

"That's what I thought," Jennifer says. "I know you're quiet and all, but I like to think you have a little more taste than that. I mean, you've been at my house so that already makes you a little cooler." She laughs at her joke.

"When was she at your house?" Mad Girl asks. Jennifer ignores her.

"Okay," I say.

"She is so annoying, isn't she?" Susie asks. "Where does she come off making you and Annabeth be part of her little pity party?"

"You should give me your number so we can finally get together after school, Jennifer," Mad Girl says. Jennifer isn't listening to her. She's glaring at me.

"So, what do you think is the most annoying thing about her?" Jennifer asks.

I feel all of their eyes on me. Oh how I wish I were Lizzie or Terry or even Robbie for that matter. Lizzie would stick up for her friend. Terry would use humor to get away. Robbie would scare the heck out of them. Can someone please drop a tray of food right now? Please, anyone?

"Nothing really," I say, but when they look as if they're really annoyed with me, I answer the question the way I think they want to hear. "She's always running or jumping. I guess that's annoying."

"Totally," Susie says.

"What else?"

"Just that."

"Oh come on, there must be something else."

"Sometimes she can be a little loud."

"Yes!" Jennifer says. "I completely see that, too. Want some of my sandwich?"

She hands me a sandwich petal. I take a small bite. Cucumber sandwiches have nothing on Fluffernutters. Still, if I'm eating, I don't need to speak so maybe my superpower will come back and I can get out of answering their questions. I make that small petal last the rest of lunch as the conversation moves away from Lizzie. Much like flower sandwiches, this group looks a lot prettier on the outside than what's inside.

"We should make a slam book about her," Mad Girl says though she has no idea who we are even talking about. No one hears her. After a few bites, Susie grabs my hand and Jennifer's.

"We should totally make a slam book about Lizzie," she says.

Mad Girl looks annoyed. "That's what I just said."

"I didn't hear you and you don't always need to be a credit hog," Susie says.

"Yeah," Jennifer says in an irritated voice to Mad Girl who then shrinks three sizes. "Jenny, you are so right, we should make a slam book at recess." While I'm happy to hear them call me by my name again, I'm dreading what "slam book" means.

"Um, I made her one. We called it a Regrouping Book," I offer hopefully. "Is that where you write out things you like?"

"Ah, no," Susie says. "You've never made a slam book?"

I shake my head.

"They're tons of fun," Jennifer says, giving me a reassuring look. "We make them all the time."

"When?" Mad Girl asks. "I'll help you next time."

"So it's a date," Jennifer says. "At recess, I'll bring out paper and crayons."

For the rest of the day, I'm their prisoner. When I try to join Anna on the swings, they come and get me. I'm definitely a hostage of some sort. At every point, one of the girls is next to me and all I want to do is stick my head in the ground. We sit on the blacktop and spread out the paper and crayons.

"I'll draw the cover while you write out everything that's annoying and weird about Lizzie," Jennifer says. "Susie, you make the pictures for inside the book."

I sit there with the crayon in my hand. My skin itches. Lightly, I write down what I told them at lunch but I choose the words that aren't necessarily bad. Instead of *loud*, I write *outgoing*; instead of saying she is always running or jumping, I write *energetic*. Okay, this isn't going to be too bad. I'm still hopeful that a slam book is somehow something nice you give to someone. Of course, slam doesn't really sound like something nice, except like in basketball—slam-dunk. Maybe this kind of book is to show someone that they are like a slam-dunk. Forget it, I know. They're not being nice. I'm just hoping I don't have to be mean along with them.

"Here." Jennifer shows me the picture. "Wait, I didn't draw her hair right, it's more mangled looking as if she never met a bottle of shampoo." She quickly scratches some brown crayon on top of a head that seems to have pimples all over it and a mouth that looks five times the size of the face. It looks nothing like Lizzie. Lizzie has one of those completely clear faces with no freckles at all and her mouth is normal mouth size. "What do you think?"

"Looks just like her," Susie says.

"Let's see what you wrote so far," Jennifer says. "Um, you're so cute. You really have no idea how a slam book works, do you?"

Susie looks at what I wrote. "Adorable."

"So, Jenny, a slam book is meant for us to express ourselves and get out all of our frustrations about someone who has been mean to us," Jennifer says. "Lizzie hasn't been nice to us. She's lucky I haven't told Mr. Freeley about her. Instead, we're doing something constructive that Lizzie never needs to know about. I know she annoys you just as she annoys us. This is your chance to get it out. I'll write out what you said at lunch and add the other things we're all thinking."

Loud, Obnoxious, Dirty, Ugly, Smelly, Mean. Jennifer and Susie are writing any bad word they can think of. I sit there, not writing, but every time they think of a new word, they tell me and I'm supposed to nod. The worst part is that I do nod.

They make me sit next to them at reading and at art class. They don't talk to me anymore since they've stapled the book together and put it away, but I'm supposed to sit near them at all times. By the time I'm on the bus ride home, I half expect them to show up at the bus stop telling me to come with them. When the bus doors squeak open, thankfully, they're not there. I feel free, yet defeated. I swing the branches hiding the trail away from my face and start walking up the path. I get to my rock collection, allowing my knees to finally buckle and the tears to run down my face. In my backpack, I've kept my Superpowers journal. I reach for it, and with a pen cross out every one of them especially the one about *Getting Out of Things*. I couldn't get them to leave me alone. I have no superpowers. Shy kids have none. We don't even stand up for our friends. I'm unfit for this place. I laugh like a mad scientist as I cross out each one. I was so stupid to think seeing my life differently would make it any better. I want to scream. My tears feel hot against my cold face. I feel so angry with myself. I pick up my rocks from my collection and start chucking them one by one down the path as far as they will go. It feels good and bad at the same time. I love these rocks and hope I can find them later, but right now something just needs to be thrown. *Stupid, Coward, Friendless, Shy*. I yell out all of the annoying things I am, creating my own verbal slam book as I throw each rock. Once they're all rolling down the hill, I feel exhausted. I start to calm my breathing the way my mom taught me. Inhale one, exhale two. Inhale one, exhale two.

I put my backpack under my head and lie down on the path. The trees are pretty bare now. I watch the leaves come down with each shiver of wind. Just breathe, I remind myself. Just breathe. The clouds stream overhead making the gray sky look foggy. You can make this right. I close my eyes and imagine all the people who have walked this hill before me and will after me. Maybe they felt like I do right now. It's just a small moment in time. I only have a few minutes before my mom will start looking for me. I sit up and look at my scratched out list. One superpower sticks out at me. It's the one I think helps the most. I take the pen and write on a fresh page, Helpfulness. Wiping the tears from my face and taking a few more deep breaths, I stand up and dust the dirt from my clothes. April. I hope she's okay. I need to help her.

I don't have time for any of this stuff. I look around and find one rock that looks interesting and restart my collection. I walk home, ready to make the hot chocolate and sit with April all afternoon. Maybe she'll even want to swing again. My mom meets me at the bottom of our driveway.

"I was just coming to check on you," she says and hugs me. I keep my face down so she won't see that I've been crying.

"Can I make hot chocolate for April and me?"

"That'd be nice," my mom says. "Not that I want you staying home, but I have to say, you're much more fun to have around during the day. April barely surfaced from her room at all."

"Her stomach must really hurt," I offer.

I knock on her door, balancing two mugs and two cookies on a plate.

"Go away," April calls.

"It's me," I say.

"I know."

I'm not giving up. I can't give up. I need this just as much as she does. Well, maybe I need it more before I end up back in the woods throwing rocks and yelling. "I have hot chocolate and cookies."

I hear her feet stomping to the door. She may have been about to remain surly, but her face softens after looking at me. "What happened to you? Come on in."

She closes the door behind me. It's been so long since she and I have been in her room alone together, I actually feel uncomfortable about where to sit. A few years ago, I would feel right at home being a complete pain to her, running into her room, day and night. She used to call me a goblin because I would run in and grab stuff of hers and hide it as a joke. During thunderstorms, I would climb into her bed to sleep. She clears off some clothes from the corner of her bed.

"Cammy told me she wants you to come back to school tomorrow," I say.

April nods. "On a scale of one to ten, how bad do you think that was? Ten is the worst."

Fifty! My dad says to always say your pain level is about an eight if the doctor asks and you're not sure. Eight is enough to take the matter seriously without sounding too dramatic. Using his advice, I lower my reply. "I'd say a six."

"For real?"

"Yes, and I think it will have moved to a two by the weekend. Plus, I think it made Jeffrey look a whole lot worse than you."

She nods. "I hope so. It wasn't very nice of him, was it?" I eat my cookie and shake my head. Her room is filled with pin-ups from *Tiger Beat* and smells of really strong perfume. "I hope one day he realizes how awful that was. Do you think he will?"

I consider this question. I've thought about it a lot in the interests of wondering how other people fill their minds. At the moment, I'm torn up because I wasn't strong enough to stick up for Lizzie. I already feel terrible. Will those girls ever feel terrible though? I can't really imagine them ever apologizing and they were pretty terrible to Lizzie. As for Jeffrey, no, I can't see him ever feeling bad about it.

"No, but I think you won't care as much one day," I say. "It's not like we ever hear Mom and Dad talking about people they had a crush on when they were fourteen, you know?"

"That's true." She takes a bite of her cookie. "Still, it'd be really nice if he felt bad."

"Will you go to school tomorrow?"

"I think so. I just do not want to see any of my so-called friends."

"Cammy is your friend."

"Yes. I'll try to stick with her for the day. She's the only one who called to check on me."

"Are you still going to do the play?"

"That I don't know. I'll see how school goes tomorrow. I don't want to be in the play if I'm just by myself."

"You could stay with Lizzie and me. We talk with Annabeth a lot. You'd like her."

"She's so pretty," April says and falls back on her bed. "I bet something like this would never happen to her. I can't believe what an idiot I was."

Things looked as if they were getting better, but I think April is going in circles. She's tearing up now.

"April, it's really going to be okay," I say, but she looks pretty sad again and I think I may not be enough to fix it. "Should we see if Cammy could come over? Maybe she can tell you what school was like today and if people were talking about it at all. I bet not a lot of them even know about it." April snorts but I think that means yes. "We can use the phone in Mom and Dad's bedroom."

"Will you unplug it and bring it here? If mom hears me crying she'll ask too many questions."

April's room has a phone jack while mine doesn't—a fact that I'm hoping will bother me when I'm a teenager as it will mean I have a social life. I open her door and peer out, making sure my mom isn't there. Tiptoeing down the hallway, I hear the television on downstairs so I think I'm in the clear. I unplug the phone and run it back to April's room.

"All clear," I say.

"You're so strange," she says. I can't expect it all to go so well with her. I plug it in, hand it to her, and then relax on her bed. She looks at me before dialing. "A little privacy?"

"Right."

I walk downstairs with our cups and I see someone biking, well trying to bike, up our driveway. My mom is looking out the window, too.

"Is that . . . Lizzie?" I look closer. The biker is now walking the bike. It's her. Now she's sitting down. "That has to be a ten-mile bike ride," my mom says. We rush out without our coats. "Is everything okay?"

"Oh," Lizzie says. She's trying to catch her breath as she stands. "Yes. Hi. Water. Water."

"Come in." I can tell my mom is nervous. I'm only allowed to ride my bike on my street with the promise that next summer I can bike the next street, too.

"Whew," Lizzie says. "That is one steep driveway. After the big hill leading up here, I thought I was going to die. Then I see your driveway. You really should think of installing a gondola."

My mom hands Lizzie a water. "Is everything okay? That is too big a ride with too many dangerous streets. I'm happy to just pick you up next time, any time. Does your brother or dad know you are here?"

Lizzie nods, but it's not convincing. "Well, I told my brother to pick me up here after his practice. I left out the bike part, but really, it wasn't a scary ride at all, just hilly."

"What's wrong?" My mom will not relax.

"Oh, I'm sorry to worry you. Nothing at all. I had some things I wanted to show to April and Jenny."

"Okay." My mom exhales. "April is hunkered down in her bedroom."

Lizzie and I go upstairs. She knocks on April's door.

"Go away."

"It's Lizzie. I have something for you."

"Call you back."

April opens the door slightly.

"Can we come in for a second?" Lizzie asks. "I know the secret password. It's Hershey's syrup."

April laughs. "Well, that's not it, but okay, you can come in for a second."

Lizzie opens her backpack and dumps its contents on the bed: a sock doll with mismatched button eyes, a letter, tiny dolls made of twisted paper, some sort of candle with a painted picture on it, feathers tied with yarn hanging from a paper plate and a sketch of an elephant.

"What on earth?" April asks.

"Okay, so I thought you might be sad today and I hated thinking of you sad. I've been doing some research at the library lately and these things are all supposed to take away sadness." She looks at us. I can tell she's wondering if she looks like an idiot—it's my look. "So, first we have this. It's called a dream catcher and was used by the Chippewa Indians to ward off bad dreams."

"Um, it looks like a cheap paper plate," April said. She holds it up. "I like it though. Where do I put it?"

"Right here." Lizzie ties it to April's headboard.

"What are these?" I ask holding up one of the little dolls.

"Oh, those are worry dolls. They make them in Guatemala."

I have never heard of this place and I'm not entirely sure it's not in Connecticut so I don't ask.

"What do they do?" April asks.

"Well, you tell it your worries and then it takes all your worries from you. You can put it under your pillow and as you sleep, all your worries will disappear." She hands one to me, too. I love it. Of course I love it. It's a symbol. She's drawn little faces and clothes on each of them.

"Next, is a candle from the Catholic store. I'm not sure how it works, but it has one of those saints on it and I figured those must be pretty lucky. I need to do more research on them, but apparently there's a saint to pray to for pretty much anything from losing your keys to losing your mind. I think you light this one so you probably should check with your mom first."

"And, the elephant picture?" April asks.

"Well, lots of cultures seem to really believe elephants are good luck. I thought you could bring it to school in your backpack tomorrow. Sorry I didn't have it for you today."

"She didn't go," I say.

"Oh, well, perfect, now you will have a lucky elephant when you do go."

"And this ugly thing?" April holds up the doll.

"That's Jeffrey."

April and I crack up.

"I know you're nervous about how everyone will treat you

so the other things are to help with that from beliefs that are all about light and kindness. This Jeffrey is a voodoo doll for when light and kindness need to take a backseat."

"Oh my God," April says. "This is hysterical."

"You take a pin or two and stick them in his arms or legs or head and he feels some of the pain he caused you."

I feel panicked. I hate Jeffrey, but inflicting bodily harm seems wrong.

"Let's do it!" April jumps up and starts rummaging through her desk drawers for a pin.

"I brought some right here," Lizzie says.

"You think of everything." April hugs her quickly and takes a pin. "Now, what do you think? Right in the heart?"

"April, maybe you shouldn't," I say.

"Don't be such a baby," April says. "One, two, three." She pushes the pin in. "That felt good. Can I pretend it's other people, too? Like my so-called friends who abandoned me?"

"Sure," Lizzie says.

"I need to call Cammy back. This is so rad. Thank you."

Lizzie puts the letter and the rest of the worry dolls back in her bag. When we head into my room, she whispers that the doll won't actually harm Jeffrey. I guess I know that actually, but it still feels wrong.

"Ever punch a pillow while pretending it was someone's face?"

"Yes," I admit.

"That doll is pretty much the same thing since I don't actually know any voodoo spells. She's poking pins in my brother's old socks, stuffed with straw."

I laugh. Then I remember how I sold out Lizzie today. I spoke badly about this person who biked ten miles to make my sister feel better just so I could be in with the popular kids. I feel sick. Am I a bad person? On the path, I had decided I would tell her what happened and hope she understood. I just didn't think I would have to tell her tonight. I'm not prepared. I squeeze my worry doll and blurt it all out with tears and everything. I'm half apologizing, half wanting her help. When I finish, she looks at me with a smile.

"You are really upset about all this, huh?"

I nod, wiping away the tears.

"It's okay, really."

"But I spoke about you meanly and didn't stop them from making the slam book."

"It hurts. I'm taking them off my Christmas card list for sure. But I understand and seeing how upset you are makes me feel like it's all okay though. You wouldn't feel upset if you really didn't care. Plus, I know how those groups can be. Sometimes it's all you can do to just come out alive. They would have turned on you if you had defended me." As she says that, her face turns red and tears now come to her eyes.

"I did hurt your feelings. I'm so sorry."

"It's not you, I swear," she says. "It's people like that. Why do people feel the need to be so mean? What's the point?"

"I don't know," I say. Lizzie still looks sad.

"Can I tell you something awful?"

I nod.

"I was once really mean. To my mom. I think about it every day. My mom had some problems. She drank a lot and wasn't very happy. She would try so hard though. I loved her for how hard she tried. I did. Really. But one day, I guess I just got sick of it. I just wanted her to be happy. To stop being so sad. My dad had to work really late all the time and my mom would just leave my brother and me home with babysitters until Scottie turned nine. Then it was just the two of us. Sometimes, my parents would come home really late and trip all over the place and argue. And then, my dad was in a bad car crash that he caused because he had been drinking. He spent time in jail even. After that, my dad stopped going out and stopped drinking but my mom went the other way. During the day, she wouldn't wake up. We'd only see her around dinnertime when she would shower and get ready for a night out. But on the day she died, she did wake up before I left for school. She had actually packed me a lunch. She told me things would change and she would be a better mom. Except she didn't get that chance."

I hand her a tissue and my bear.

"The worst part is, my face. When she told me that she would change, I know I made a face that told her I didn't believe her. Like this." Lizzie lifts her eyebrows and purses her lips. Yep, I know that face. Everyone has that face but it usually comes out when you're annoyed or when you're just April. It sounds like Lizzie had every right to be annoyed. "And then she died and I never got to tell her I did believe in her. I never got to tell her it was okay. I loved her anyway."

I stare at Lizzie, unknowing of what to say. She sniffles.

"My dad moved us here to get a change of scenery and leave all those memories behind us. Scottie and I thought my dad would turn to us and spend more time being a dad but that hasn't happened either. And I miss those memories. Even the bad ones. I miss my mom. I miss what she wanted to become and what she may never have been."

Lizzie's life is completely different than mine. Her life makes me realize how great I have it.

"You know, what I just thought of?" Lizzie asks, coming out of her sadness.

"What?"

"It's kind of like the witch story?"

"What is?"

"My mom. She was one thing that got pulled into darkness with just that one flash of light before it was just too late."

"Wow," I say, which seems very inefficient.

"Deep, huh?" Lizzie laughs.

It is a deep thought and one that makes me see the witch story in a much different way. My parents drag us to church once a month and sometimes I listen instead of daydream. Sometimes, the priest tells a story that you think is about one thing but it's really about another and you feel like you were let in on a great secret. That's how Lizzie's interpretation feels.

"I'm pretty sure these girls can drag me off the cliff though. I'm not strong like you."

Lizzie nods. "It's not easy, is it?"

"Nope."

"And we're not even in middle school yet. That's where it gets even harder."

We sit in silence for a minute. Neither of us has any answer.

"I know," I say. "We can write your mom a note and leave it on my windowsill. That worked with my grandfather. You can tell her you're sorry for not believing in her."

"Actually, I'm one ahead of you." Lizzie digs in her bag and takes out the envelope. "I wrote her and thought I would sneak it on your window so you wouldn't think I was totally strange."

"Too late for that!" I laugh which is probably totally inappropriate, but I don't normally make jokes out loud. I'm probably not supposed to laugh at them.

"Right!" Lizzie laughs, too.

I show her the spot to put her envelope.

"Well, now my brain hurts," Lizzie says. "We need something stupid to do."

"I have some old Smurf latch hooks."

"Perfect."

"I like the worry dolls," I say. "Think we should make those for the hospital kids, too?"

"Great Scott!" Lizzie says and jumps up. "What a fantastic idea. Yes, yes. We shall do that, too."

"You're nuts," I say.

"Can't crack me though."

She smiles. We work on our Smurfs until our fingers hurt and then hunt around my house for construction paper to make the worry dolls. Lizzie stays for dinner and checks the windowsill before her brother comes to take her home. I'm not sure she thought it would be gone, but I think she was just hoping it was moved a little bit.

Popular people aren't always the same way twice. You can see them one day and they decide they like you and want to be best friends. Then the next day, they act like they don't know you. Maybe I should write *Superpowers of the Popular People*. They really know what works for keeping people on their toes around them. I'm sure people aren't as calculated as I think they are, but I can't help but picture Susie and Jennifer calling each other the night before school to coordinate outfits and decide who to torment, ignore, or embarrass for the week. What they don't realize is that I have my own superpowers no matter how useless they can sometimes be. When I'm prepared, I can use my avoidance techniques pretty well. I start by packing an old copy of *Moby Dick* in my bag. For some reason, this book finds its way around our house all of the time.

As I suspected, Susie and Jennifer seem to have forgotten that yesterday, they wanted to be my friend or keep me as their pet. They leave me alone for the morning, but lots of things go down at recess. You can't count out recess. I bring the book and notebook out with me and place them on the ground next to my swing. My plan is that if they do come near me, I'll pop off the swing and tell them that my lame parents are forcing me to do a book report on this book. I think sometimes most of life is just having a plan to get out of tough situations. If you don't come prepared with a plan, you'll end up doing what you don't want to do. If you do have a plan, lots of times, you don't need it. It's like bringing an umbrella in case it will rain. If you have the umbrella, it won't rain. If you leave the umbrella at home after considering it, you'll get soaked. I can do this for the rest of the year. They leave me alone at recess, too. Luckily, I'm all clear for the day. They barely look at me.

April refuses to go to the play practice that night. My dad tries to pep talk her into going thinking she's just giving it up because she's bored. That doesn't work, so he goes into how she made a commitment and what if no one showed up. While he may have a point, April's rebuttal is better. "Then there would be no corny community play," she says. "It's not like we're healing sick babies." In the interest of time, my dad lets it drop. April gives me a mission. I'm to feel things out and see if anyone is still talking about her. If everyone has forgotten about her letter to Jeffrey, she'll come back to the play. This morning at the bus stop, she crossed her fingers and hoped that no one would ever talk about it again. "Oh, please someone let someone like vomit all over a teacher today or have something more embarrassing happen to them so people will forget about me," she told Cammy.

We're rehearsing most of the townspeople scenes at the next practice since the play is in two weeks. It seems impossible that it will be ready by then, but I don't think anyone expects greatness here. I hope no one is talking about April so she won't miss the next practice. Tonight though, they just need some screaming teenage girls which April would have been perfect for and then Coach Jay will run through stuff with the rest of us townspeople.

Lizzie meets me in our spot and hands me some Twizzlers. We put our feet on the chairs in front of us and lean back to watch. "Jenny," I hear my name and cringe. They've found me. It's Jennifer and Susie. "Hi," Jennifer says as if we're best friends. "We've been looking for you. You were supposed to sit with us, remember?" She motions with her eyes toward Lizzie, trying to convey the message of, I'm saving you from that awful girl next to you. I put my feet down and kick myself for not having a plan. How could I have been so stupid?

"Um," I say.

Lizzie doesn't look at them. She keeps eating her Twizzlers.

"Are you coming or not?" Susie says, putting her hands on her hips.

"No. Thank you. You can sit here if you like."

"Ugh, no." Susie starts to leave.

"It's just," Jennifer starts, "I thought you said she was weird and loud and that you didn't like her." My face flushes. "You said that right? I brought the book you even wrote."

Susie spins around. I don't think Susie cares to see where any of this is going. I think she just wants Jennifer to herself. When seen with an opening, she attacks.

"You did say that and made a slam book," she says.

"No offense, Lizzie," Jennifer said. "I'm just repeating what she said."

"None taken," Lizzie keeps eating Twizzlers.

"I didn't mean it," I say.

"So why did you write the slam book?" Susie asks.

Lizzie puts her feet down and asks to see the slam book. Jennifer hands it to her as if she's an innocent bystander in the whole thing. Instead of looking at it, Lizzie rips it down the middle and hands it back to Jennifer. Then she coolly slips another Twizzler out and places it in her mouth.

"So, you're saying you would rather sit here with her than hang with us?" Susie asks just for clarification that I don't want to be friends with Jennifer.

"You can sit with us," I whisper.

"Suit yourself," Jennifer says and with a hair flip, she leaves.

"Yikes," Lizzie says. "And I thought my school was tough."

My heart is beating fast and my face is still red.

"You handled that well," Lizzie says.

"I did?"

"I think I would told them off or something. You were nice and mature."

I start eating my Twizzler, thinking about what just happened. Luckily, they start rehearsing the scene so my mind will stop replaying it over and over. My dad's character has to keep interrupting Birdie and Kim, because he wants to be on television to promote his store. Everyone laughs. It's a funny thing to see my dad on stage. Any time I have one of those moments that I realize my parents are actual people with their own hopes and dreams, my heart kind of swells for them. He's so comfortable on stage and everyone loves him. He just didn't sink away into dad world and be too busy or too stern to enjoy life. Though I don't think he'd make it as a real actor, he's having too much fun not to enjoy his performance. Then, it comes time for Birdie to kiss Kim though by this point of the play, Kim no longer wants to kiss him. Annabeth is backing away from Charlie as he leans in close to kiss her, then Jeffrey comes in and punches him in an obvious fake punch sending Charlie to the ground.

"What the heck is that?" Everyone stops, trying to search out who just yelled. The community play doesn't get much heckling. "That's ridiculous."

I hear another voice say, "It's the Kred boys. What are they doing here?"

In the center of the front section, sit three of the Kred brothers including Robbie. Mr. Freeley calls out for audience members to please be quiet.

"Okay, but I think there's been some major miscasting," Robbie continues.

"Robbie Kred," Coach Jay says and shakes her head in bemusement. "If you have thoughts about the play, you can share them later."

"Thank you, Coach," he says and stands. "It's just, I think there are . . . what's the word?"

"Plausibility," his brother says with a toothpick hanging out of his mouth.

"No, no, what's the word that means you wouldn't believe something?"

"I'm saying it's plausibility," his brother repeats, pulling the toothpick out to speak this time.

"Well, whatever it is, as a test audience for you, there's no way that a girl like that would ever be interested in that guy." At first, I think Jeffrey thinks Robbie is talking about Charlie. I see Jeffrey nod.

"We actually aren't interested in test audiences, Robbie," Coach Jay says.

"I'm just saying there's no universe where a guy like that Jeffrey kid would get a girl like Annabeth Higgins. I thought they were playing brother and sister or something so I'm a little grossed out as you can imagine. Oh wait, is this one of those science fiction plays where the scrawny nerd gets the girl?"

"Okay, Robbie," Coach Jay says. "Next year, you audition then."

"I will if I can get paired up with Annabeth Higgins. One more thing, though. Are you telling us that Jeffrey Greeson gets Annabeth Higgins and can punch out Charlie Brooks?"

"That's enough Robbie," my dad says which he probably wouldn't have said if he knew what Jeffrey did to April.

"All due respect, I'm just saying what we're all thinking." He holds his hands up as if he just had to bear his soul; he couldn't help it.

His brothers stand up. They look huge. I see Jeffrey cower slightly. "What are we doing here, man?" one of his brothers asks, shoving Robbie toward the aisle. "This is bogus. Let's bolt."

"For the record," the older Kred brother offers, "I think that Birdie cat would totally pummel that kid. I kind of want to do it and I don't even know him. It's something about his face though."

"Totally," Robbie says. "He has one of those punchable faces, you know?"

"Do you like pay people to come watch this or do they have to buy tickets for it? Cause if people have to pay, I would totally put in a cool fight scene with like ninjas or something," his brother says. "That would shake this thing up and totally fill more seats that way."

Besides Jeffrey and his band of teenage girl followers, everyone else is straddling the line of finding the whole exchange funny even if it is wrong.

"C'mon, I said this was bogus," the older brother says.

"I'm just trying to help them because I don't think anyone will actually pay to see such a punchable kid win. And I think there's a huge age difference. Is he like thirteen?"

"No, I think he's like fifteen."

"Try sixteen," Jeffrey says but his voice kind of breaks as he says it, making him sound younger.

"Maybe after he has a growth spurt and his voice changes," the brother offers as if this is sound advice.

"Thank you Kreds," Coach Jay says. "Delightful commentary."

"Anything to help the arts," Robbie says and bows to her. They walk off, pushing and kicking each other.

Jeffrey storms off the stage yelling at the director. "You can't let idiots come in here like that. They're not even in the play." Now he sounds like a seven-year-old girl.

Mr. Freeley sighs. "Take five, everyone."

"Oh my God," Lizzie says. "That was awesome. Is it just me or is Robbie like totally cute?"

"It's just you," I say, but I have to admit, having Robbie on our side has been pretty great this year.

Truthfully, I hate seeing people get made fun of, so part of me feels bad for Jeffrey, but it was awesome. Jeffrey deserved it. Plus, Lizzie and I have plenty of time to make our bracelets and worry dolls since it takes Coach Jay and Mr. Freeley to talk Jeffrey into leaving the dressing room. When I get home, I tell April all about it. She keeps asking me to repeat it until she has all of the details she wants then tells me to leave so she can call Cammy. I had been hoping that while we were away, Lizzie's note to her mom would move from the windowsill. It hasn't. Before leaving for school, I opened the shade a bit so that my mom can see it. In case she is the one that took my letter to my grandfather, I hope she takes Lizzie's note, too. I don't want to know that it was my mom because I still want to believe and I want to give Lizzie that believing feeling, too.

SUPERPOWER #14: OBSERVATION

Okay, I've been in our rock garden thousands of times and never noticed the tiny painted arrow under which the first clue in Mrs. Brown's scavenger hunt was buried. However, I'd still say that being somewhat observant is one of my powers. I notice things. Sometimes this superpower isn't so great though. Noticing things is good when in a scavenger hunt or near a hidden waterfall, but not noticing things allows a person to barrel through life without thinking too much about the details. I think, at times, that's the better way to be.

Right now, I'm about to go on stage for the play's debut, and all I'm noticing is how bright the lights are and how serious everyone around me seems. All of the playfulness we've had is now gone as Coach Jay is yelling in a whisper at all of us to remember our marks. I feel beads of sweat forming on my forehead. Jennifer and Susie look like nervous people trying to act too cool to be nervous, but I know. Their mouths are clenched tightly and they're not speaking. I see Susie keep swallowing and Jennifer's eyes darting around the backstage. Lizzie looks excited more than nervous. She lightly bounces on her feet, ready to spring into the play when told to. From the stage, I can hear Annabeth singing and feel really proud of her. We're supposed to all march on stage toward the end of her song and join her last few verses. Mr. Freeley said it's a great way to surprise the audience right from the start about how big of a cast we have this year. He keeps talking about it and the play programs even mention how this is the biggest cast they have ever had. In fact, instead of just listing us as Townspeople, he numbered all of us—Townsperson 1, Townsperson 2, and so on. He didn't do it alphabetically or by any order I can figure out really. I'm always looking for hidden meanings. That's what helps my observant superpower. Why am I Townsperson 25? Was I the 25th person to sign up? Did he rank us by likability? Was that the order he remembered us in? It's killing me.

April decided at the last minute to remain in the play. She finally told my mom what happened and I think she was surprised to find that my mom was a good person to speak to. I don't think they did a Regrouping Day though. You don't offer a Regrouping Day to a serial eye roller. Whatever my mom said to her, seemed to work. April came and kept to herself until one or two of her friends decided to stay with her. It's like they all had to choose sides between April and Jeffrey without Jeffrey knowing or caring that was happening but it blew April's world up into pieces. She's over on the other side of the stage waiting to walk on with the other teenage girls while Lizzie and I are supposed to skip out together holding hands as if we are much younger than we are. Fifth graders don't really go around holding hands and skipping. We get to wear poodle skirts that my mom made for us in her sewing class. Coach Jay starts pushing us one by one out on to the stage. When she taps my shoulders to go, Lizzie grabs my hand. I hold it back for a second. My feet won't move. "Go ahead, girls," Coach Jay says and kind of pushes me. I stumble slightly, but I'm still behind the curtain.

"I've got you," Lizzie says and squeezes my hand. "Let's go live a little!"

I smile and summon up my courage. The stage is even brighter out here. I don't look anywhere toward the audience which would be breaking the fourth wall anyway. As soon as we're out there, I'm skipping away with Lizzie. Her skips are much more energetic, but hey, I'm skipping on a stage in front of people and haven't passed out from fear yet. I forget that we're supposed to be singing, too, not that anyone would notice. When Lizzie and I reach our mark at the other side of the stage, I start singing. It's wonderful. After these months of practicing, we've created our own little world here to show to everyone. My favorite part of any play is between scenes. Before the number, on stage, someone may be pretending to sweep a sidewalk and girls playing hopscotch and then when the music starts, they all stop what they're doing and turn into dancers and singers. After a musical number, people just saunter back to what they were doing as if just a few minutes ago they weren't singing and dancing.

When our song ends, Lizzie and I clasp our hands together again and skip back across the stage. After the townspeople have left the stage, the audience is clapping and all of us our talking about what a great number that was until Coach Jay runs through reminding all of us to be quiet. Lizzie and I hide behind the curtains so we can watch the play. My dad walks up behind us giving me a scare.

"Hey girls," he says. "You looked great out there." He's about to walk out onto the stage in front of a few hundred people yet he seems at complete ease like he's just walking out our front door to get the paper. "Wish me luck."

"Good luck, Mr. Watts."

"Knock 'em dead, Dad."

He gives me a thumbs up and walks onto the stage. I watch as he delivers his lines acting as if he's a high stress dad, which is nothing like him. The audience eats him up, laughing. Mrs. Craig is cringe worthy, but it kind of goes with her character. "Move along girls," Coach Jay says behind us.

We have lots of time before we're needed again so all of the townspeople have to shuffle off into the dressing room area. Lizzie and I have a few more worry dolls and bracelets to make so we find some old bean bag chairs in a corner and get to work. We don't actually know how many to make for the hospital party, but we just like making them so we thought we would make as many as we could and find other places to use them, too.

"That was so rad," Lizzie says. "I loved it out there. I can't believe how great Annabeth sounded. I can't believe we know her."

"I know," I say. It is strange to see a person behave so normally one minute and then have talent gushing out of them the next minute. She was fearless on stage. "It was great. My heart is beating like a thousand times a minute. I can't believe I was just on stage in front of people. Yikes!"

I start giggling. It must be how people who skydive feel. I'm excited, slightly sick and jittery, and so proud of myself for actually doing something. I feel pride oozing out of my pores. I can't stop my lips from smiling. I cannot wait to hear what my mom thought. I know she feels what I feel almost like Elliott and E.T.

"You have to calm down, Townsperson 25," Lizzie says in Coach Jay's voice. "We have three more scenes to get through, you know."

"What are you making all those things for?" I hear Susie's voice.

We don't answer, hoping she's not talking to us but she comes closer. She doesn't ask the question again but watches us in silence, not buying the fact that we didn't hear her. One of my dad's seminars told him that if you can use the power of silence to your advantage, you'll win more. More what, I don't know, but after she just stares at us for what feels like an hour, I cave and answer her. She knows the power of silence.

"We're making bracelets," I say, not wanting to talk about the worry dolls. They seem too vulnerable.

"Like for the whole cast?" Jennifer says showing up behind Susie and grabbing one of the bracelets from the floor. I'd be fine if she would say the bracelet was nice and help herself to one. Instead, she inspects it as if it's made of slime and throws it back into the pile. Lizzie isn't speaking. She continues her work without looking at them. Jennifer and Susie continue waiting for me to answer. It sounds strange for a quiet person, but I must say using the power of silence is not one of my superpowers here. If they stare at me any longer, I think I'll burst and tell them my whole life story.

"If they're for the whole cast, don't bother," Susie says. "Jennifer and I were planning on doing that." I don't believe her.

"So are they?" Jennifer asks. "If they are, that's our idea."

Lizzie keeps working and actually starts humming.

I can't take it anymore.

"We're making them for kids in the hospital. We're helping with a party there and thought we could give these away to the kids to make them happy." Phew.

Susie and Jennifer look like balloons slowly deflating. I realize they don't know what to say now. Making stuff for kids in hospitals isn't something you can easily make fun of people for without looking like a jerk. Even they seem to get that.

"They're probably not allowed to have that stuff because of your cooties," Susie says, hoping to goad Lizzie into speaking. "You don't want to make them sicker."

"Jenny," Lizzie says. "Look at this one." She holds up one of the bracelets. It looks like all the other ones, but her point is taken. She's ignoring them. "Think I should make more with the red yarn?"

Jennifer and Susie whisper to one another. Lizzie rolls her eyes.

"Maybe you should stay at the hospital so they could figure out what's wrong with you," Susie says to Lizzie. Jennifer lets out a gasping laugh and covers her mouth as she giggles.

Lizzie stands up. "We're making bracelets for kids in hospitals," she says slowly in a teacher's stern voice. She's not exactly mad or hurt but she sounds really annoyed. "If you don't like that, I don't care. If you don't like me, I don't care. If you are so much better than me, I'm sure you can find something better to do than watch me every second, talk about me, and make books about me." Jennifer and Susie look at her with their lips pursed. Lizzie doesn't back down. She stares right at them. "So you two seriously have nothing else to do but watch me? Like be my private audience. Perfect. I've been working on a little something." She lifts her back straight and places her right hand over her heart. "Four score and seven years ago,"

"What are you doing?" Susie asks.

"I have to recite the Gettysburg Address in class next week so I thought I could bounce it off you two since you'll be watching me." She straightens herself up again. "Where was I? Okay. I always forget this next part. Our fathers . . . "

"We do have much better things to do," Jennifer says with narrow eyes.

"But I'm not finished. There's more," Lizzie says.

"Let's go, Susie." They flip their hair as they leave us. They bump into each other as they try to figure out where that better thing they have to do may be. Is the better thing to the right or the left? Lizzie smiles as she watches them look angry at each other for not walking in the right direction. I don't think they have anything better to do. I'd offer that they could help us make the bracelets but I've found that life isn't always like an After-school Special. Sometimes mean people are just happier being mean. Unfortunately, we once went on a family camping trip. Except for the hike we took when we got there and the raw s'mores we ate in the tent as we hunkered down out of the thunderstorm that came out of nowhere, it was not fun. I did learn something useful though. Before we went, my dad bought a guidebook that talked about bear encounters. You had to keep your trash secure and out of the way. If you did come across a bear, you were supposed to show the bear that you were just a human—not a tasty treat. The guidebook said we should wave our arms and speak softly. Jennifer and Susie are the bears. I want to remind them that I'm a person, too. I'm just a person that hasn't bothered them at all and have nothing that they should want from me.

Still, I'm feeling so good after my first stage performance, I call after them.

"You could help us if you want," I say, waving and smiling.

"As if," Susie says right away.

Jennifer looks at me with, something different. Maybe it's kindness; maybe she's seen she shouldn't be mean to me. Maybe my smiling and waving look so crazy to her that she's scared of me. I don't know. It's probably that she has nothing else to do to fill her time and actually wants to make bracelets. I don't need to be their friend anymore, but I wanted them to see that they don't need to be like that. I wanted them to see that I'm just human, too. Why do people want to be like angry bears anyway?

"That's okay," Jennifer mumbles. "Thanks."

"Whoa," Lizzie says after they leave. "For a second there, I thought one of them was about to turn nice right in front of our eyes."

"I hope I didn't seem like an idiot for asking them," I say. "I just don't like all the attacks all the time. I thought maybe they would stop if they saw they could just have fun with us."

"Good idea in theory, I suppose," Lizzie says. She shrugs her shoulders. I know I'll still think about this moment a lot but seeing how much Lizzie shakes off naturally gives me hope. Maybe one day I can learn to do that more, too. Does that come with confidence? Maybe she truly never cared and was born like that the way I was born the way I am.

Our next number comes much faster than it ever has. Usually during rehearsals every scene took so long. Now, the play is flying past. This scene is the one I'm most nervous about. It's the fainting scene. We'll be upstage, close to the audience and I know the audience is meant to see us as cute. We had to wear our hair in pigtails with bows in the bottom so we're definitely supposed to seem younger than we are. As we follow the crowd back toward the stage, we're looking around for Susie and Jennifer but don't see them. I'm panicking. Lizzie is looking around for them, but she's definitely not on the mental DEFCON 3 that I am. Coach Jay gives the marching orders to set up for the scene. This time, we set up the scene in complete darkness. Stagehands move around the set swiftly as we get into our places. I'm so nervous that Lizzie and I have messed up somehow. Jennifer and Susie are supposed to be with us. As the lights come back on, I see them across the stage. Susie points at us and then points next to her telling us we're supposed to be over there. I know for sure we're not. When Charlie walks through the townspeople, he doesn't go to that side of the stage. It's a disaster. I feel all of the eyes of the audience staring at me, probably realizing there's been a mess up. I start to walk back off stage thinking we can quickly run around to get on the other side, but Lizzie grabs my hand and smiles at me. Charlie is already singing and girls are already fainting. Oh no. What do we do?

Lizzie whispers to me. "Want to be the fainter?" I shake my head. "Okay, just follow my lead then." She stands in front of me. As Charlie comes closer, I don't get to enjoy his voice at all. I'm so scared that everyone will know this isn't how it's supposed to be. However, when Charlie comes toward us, he gives us a wink and pats Lizzie on the top of her head, causing Lizzie to faint.

I try catching her, but my arms aren't exactly working. I manage to grab her and fall down under her. Lizzie lays her head toward the audience and lets her tongue fall out of her mouth to the side. The audience giggles. She's like deadweight on my knees so I stay there trapped. I figure I should do what the other catchers of other fainters do so I fan her face with my hand, pretending I'm trying to wake her. Like a professional actor, Charlie makes his way to Jennifer and Susie and he pats their heads, too. Susie catches Jennifer. Phew. It worked out. Hopefully no one noticed or maybe they liked this version better. I think I'll stay away from Jennifer and Susie now though. The bears have been provoked. Even though we did nothing wrong, somehow this will be our fault. Time to secure our food and stay away. When the scene ends, they drop the curtains. The next scene takes place in front of the closed curtains so we have time to get everyone off the stage. Lizzie jumps up the second the curtains close. Coach Jay warned all of us that after this scene we needed to be quiet as mice or else. I don't want to find out the or else part. When Lizzie looks like she's about to speak, I cover her mouth with my hand. She nods as if she remembered now. I quickly rush to our old spot and gather all of our supplies and find a more hidden spot to do our work.

"What are you doing?" Lizzie asks.

"I don't want Jennifer and Susie to bug us again."

"Right," she says. "Good plan."

"I don't know why they were on the wrong side."

"I know! What happened?"

I shrug. "You did a good job though. Did you hear the audience?"

"Yes, that was fun. Can I tell you something without you thinking I'm strange?"

I nod.

"It felt like at that moment when I was lying there on stage with my eyes closed, well, for just a second, I thought I felt my mom's presence and it made me feel . . . I don't know. Peaceful or something. I know it was probably nothing, but, maybe she saw my letter at your house."

"It hasn't moved, but that doesn't mean she didn't read it," I say. "I don't know how it works really. Do ghosts need to open letters? I mean, I think they just walk through doors so maybe they can see through envelopes."

"Exactly, so maybe, I don't know. Maybe she is watching out for me now."

"I bet she is," I say. It's never occurred to me that her mom wouldn't be watching over her. In some way, I thought everyone who loved us who dies is watching over us somehow.

"It's a good feeling," Lizzie says and starts making a bracelet with the last bit of yarn.

Our last scene as townspeople goes much smoother. We come out, do our little jazz box dance and sing. I wonder if the audience can feel how happy we all are. They must think we are crazy. I know we didn't put on a play worthy of Broadway and most of us are knocking into each other in our jazz boxes, but we're all happy we did it and the audience can rejoice in the fact that the play is over now. We take way too many bows and bouquets of flowers are being tossed up onto the stage. All of the teenagers are wearing flowers tucked in their hair. My mom has three bouquets of yellow carnations for Lizzie, April, and me.

She pulls me up into a big hug when she meets us backstage.

"You did it," she says. "I'm so proud of you." She puts me down and hugs Lizzie. "And you two were wonderful during the fainting. How funny!"

Lizzie and I barely come up for air as we describe to my mom all of the little things that went wrong with the play and ask her all about the scenes we didn't see. Annabeth runs over to us holding Charlie's hand. "My favorite pretend sister and Townsperson 17!" She pulls us both into a hug. Charlie gives us each a nod and tells us good job.

"You were wonderful out there," my mom says to both of them.

"I babysit and I won't even charge," Annabeth says. "I just love hanging out with Lizzie and Jenny so call me any time."

"I may just take you up on that," my mom says. "I can see how much fun Jenny has had here and I think you are one of the reasons."

Lizzie and I did make a few bracelets for our favorite actors. We give a bracelet to Annabeth and Charlie who actually put his right on surprisingly. We also made them for the grandparents who always spoke to us and gave us candy and one for Coach Jay. I'm a little scared to go up to her though.

Scott comes through the crowd over to Lizzie and gives her a high five.

"You sat through the whole thing?" Lizzie says.

"Got the numb bottom to prove it," he says. "Nice fainting."

"Did Dad come?" Lizzie asks.

"Um, no," Scottie says. "I think he had Bingo night at his church."

"Right," Lizzie says. She smiles, but I can see that Bingo night is a really lame reason to miss your daughter's play. I guess she can tell what I'm thinking because she shrugs her shoulders. "Really, it's okay. It hurts, but I kind of knew he wouldn't come. He told me musicals aren't his thing. And it's Bingo. I mean, come on. Bingo. You don't want to miss someone saying B9 over a loudspeaker."

"It's true," Scottie says. "Sometimes, they say G7 and it's like such a rush, man."

"You haven't lived until you've played Bingo," Lizzie says.

Scottie puts his arm around Lizzie's shoulders. "So she really is fine because she has her older brother here who sat through all of that singing and dancing instead of going to Bingo night like all the cool people."

April comes back over to mom and me. She had taken the flowers and gone off with her friends but I think the sighting of Scott Cray made my mom and me more interesting. She's acting kind of shy though. My dad comes over and squeezes April and me before patting Lizzie's head. "We did it!"

"Oh my," my mom says, reaching in her purse to find a tissue. "Time to lose the stage makeup. Close up, it's a little disturbing." She starts wiping his face.

"Who wants to go out for pizza on me?" my dad says as she cleans him up.

Scottie seems nervous to accept someone buying him dinner, but my mom insists.

"You can offer her your ten dollars," Lizzie says.

"What's that?" my mom asks.

"Scottie always carries a ten dollar bill. People are always offering to buy him food whenever we're out just because he plays football. So, he always offers to pay with this one ten-dollar bill, but no one ever lets him. He carries it with him all of the time though."

"That's kind of a family secret, Lizzie." Scottie playfully puts his hand over Lizzie's mouth. "Yuck, you licked my hand."

"Yuck is right," Lizzie says, scraping her tongue with her finger. "Would it kill you to wash your hands once in a while?"

"Well, you can keep your ten dollars as well tonight," my dad says.

As we walk toward the parking lot, April walks past Jeffrey and her old friends. "Okay, Scottie, we'll meet you at Wolfie's then," she says really loudly. Everyone hears her. Scottie looks at her and then at the group watching them.

"Sure, want to ride with us?" he says.

"Um, okay," April says.

In the real world, Scottie Cray is higher up on the popularity chain than Jeffrey Greeson. He's the star athlete without being a big jerk about it. In fact, I don't get the impression he even cares if he's popular—just like Lizzie. Even Jeffrey Greeson must know, outside of the community theater, he's no Scottie Cray. I watch Jeffrey pause for a minute to watch April walk off with Scott and Lizzie. It's not a look of regret on his face, but for a second, it's like a flash of, wait, is that girl actually cool?

When the time for the hospital party came, I was so excited right up until we pulled up to the hospital. In my lap, I had a bag filled with worry dolls and Lizzie had the bag of bracelets. I loved the idea of giving these things out to kids to make them happy but now I can't help but feel nervous. They're in a hospital and I'm showing up acting like some sort of superhero because I have bracelets and paper dolls. My mom, Lizzie and I all walk in through the entrance feeling the same way. No one likes hospitals. I have a feeling most of us feel inadequate when entering one to visit someone. Mrs. Brown is sitting near the reception desk talking with women who look a little older than my mom but much younger than Mrs. Brown.

"Here are my beautiful helpers," she says. The women look at us with warm smiles.

"Wonderful," says the one who is wearing an official hospital badge.

"I'm Vicki, this is my daughter Jenny and her best friend Lizzie."

Best friend. It's never actually been said. It has a good ring to it.

"We made bracelets and worry dolls," Lizzie says showing the woman the bags. "Think they'll like that?"

"I do," she says. "They'll love it. Come right over here and I'll show you the party room. I don't know how she does it, but Mrs. Brown got here early this morning with a bunch of her friends from the home and, well, you just have to see it." She opens a big door that leads into what is probably a meeting room usually. Shiny streamers hang from the ceiling so you have to walk through them to enter. She's made it look as if we're under the sea. Blue paper lines the walls with pictures of giant fish and seahorses. A bubble machine sits in the corner waiting. Four tables are filled with coloring pages and crayons, popcorn and drinks, one has hats with shell patterns made out of felt and a place where you can make gingerbread houses.

"It's lovely," my mom says.

"So, we'll need you two to help run our little bowling game." The bowling pins have fish faces painted on them. "Then Vicki, if you can sit at the table over there and make up name tags for everyone, that would be great. And when they leave, make sure they get one of the little bags Mrs. Brown sewed. Look at them, they look like little fish made out of jeans. She's got a gift, doesn't she?"

"She sure does," my mom says.

"Well, T minus four minutes until party time."

Lizzie and I stand in our spot and set up our bags to give each kid a bracelet and worry doll after bowling. I stand near the bowling pins, ready to set them back up each time. That way Lizzie can talk with the kids. When kids come through the door, some are just like Lizzie, bouncing in excited about everything and others are just like me, holding back and holding closely to their parent's hands. Some you wouldn't exactly be able to tell were sick if it weren't for their hospital gown or bandage. Some of the kids are in wheelchairs. One little girl has her arm up in a cast that connects to her body and looks completely uncomfortable.

The first child who came over was led by her mom. "Oh look, Julie, bowling. You love bowling."

Julie looks like she's probably about six years old. She's in a yellow hospital gown with an IV attached to a pole attached to her arm.

"Want to bowl, Julie?" Lizzie asks in a sweet voice. Julie looks at her arm. She looks so shy, frightened, and hurt, I can't take it anymore.

"Let's do it together," I say, coming over. I take the ball from Lizzie. "Okay, when you're ready, push right here on my arm and then I'll throw it." I feel my face flush, but I just want to make Julie happy. My parents were always pretending there were buttons on places so I would do things I didn't want to do. "Ready." Julie gently pushes my elbow. I pull my arm back, ready to bowl. "Oh no, you need to push the release button on my hand." Julie laughs and pushes my hand. My arm swings forward, setting the bowling ball off to hit down two pins. I'm not the best bowler. "You did it, Julie!" Julie smiles. "Want to try it again?"

We play this way until I finally knock down all of the pins. I ask her to pick out a bracelet and worry doll and she actually lets go of her mom's hand and takes mine as I bring her to the table. She looks though all of the bracelets and quietly asks me for a pink one.

"Want me to tie it on your arm?" I ask. She nods and sticks out her arm for me. I tie one on her wrist and then pick out another bracelet. "I don't want your other arm to feel left out." I tie another bracelet on her same wrist. "When that arm gets rid of that IV attached to it, put this bracelet over there."

Julie looks at her wrist and smiles. It's the most wonderful feeling.

"And this is a worry doll for you," I say, bending down to her level. "Whenever you feel nervous or worried, you can tell this doll all about it. Then place the doll under your pillow as you sleep and the doll will take your troubles away."

Her eyes light up. I walk her back to her mom. Before she

reattaches to her mom, she shows her the bracelets and then gives me a hug.

"Thank you," her mom says to me with tears in her eyes. "She's usually so shy. She really just took to you."

I nod, feeling shy again, but I can't help the smile from forming on my face. As they walk away, I see Julie showing her mom the worry doll.

Some kids are able to bowl, some aren't. The ones that are older than us don't act like they're too cool for it either. They even accept our bracelets and worry dolls. Lizzie and I try to make it so they all have fun no matter what. In the end, some of the kids come to give us hugs goodbye. We see our bracelets on theirs arms. I completely know what Mrs. Brown felt like now. I don't want this feeling to end. I felt like I mattered. The kids looked to me to forget the fact that they were in the hospital and I did it. I couldn't be shy and I couldn't stay in my head all day. It was just a little bowling game, but it felt important. As the last kid left, Lizzie and I carefully took down the decorations. We still had a bunch of bracelets and worry dolls so we gave them to the nurses. They said they would pass them out to the other hospital wards as well and to the kids that were too sick to come. Mrs. Brown gave us our own jean fish bag and felt hat.

"I'd love to help again," I say to Mrs. Brown.

"I'd love to have you help again," Mrs. Brown says. "I saw you with the kids. You really seemed to have a way with the shy ones."

My mom put her arm around me in her usual *I'm proud of you* way. Sometimes that gesture makes me feel bad because it's often for something that maybe she shouldn't be proud of me for. Like for going to school all week without faking a stomachache—really I should just go to school and not make up reasons not to like other kids do. Having her *I'm proud of you* hug today feels exactly right. This week, I was good at something that mattered, the hospital, and had fun at something that didn't, the play.

GREATEST SUPERPOWER: WHAT MATTERS

By the time we have our spring pen pal meeting back at the Cider Mill, Lizzie and I have completed two more of Mrs. Brown's scavenger hunts and made two of our own. We created 100 more worry dolls and friendship bracelets. When we visited Mrs. Brown again, we gave them to the residents at the home. I actually got the strength to bring them into school and give them to the whole class. Since the Cider Mill is open again, Miss Lotti and Miss Hansom haven't bothered with activities besides letting us run around and see the petting zoo. It's time meant for pen pals to continue getting to know each other. No one has become as close as Lizzie and me. As she runs ahead of me to chase a boy in her class, I'm struck with the thought that I almost wouldn't have had the good things that happened to me this year if I had been Emily. Had I been popular and friends with Jennifer and Susie, I would have missed out on knowing Lizzie. If I hadn't have been friends with Lizzie, I wouldn't have joined the play. I also wouldn't have found Mrs. Brown's scavenger hunt. Then I wouldn't have ever helped at the hospital party.

I see Miss Lotti and Miss Hansom sitting together on a picnic table bench. I walk over to them. My heart pounding.

"Excuse me," I say.

"Yes, Jenny." Miss Lotti looks at me in her warm way that always calms me down.

"I just wanted to say thank you for pairing me with Lizzie."

Miss Hansom smiles. "Miss Lotti told me you two would be a good match." I see her turn to look near where Lizzie is. Then I see her smile fade. "Excuse me while I tell your pen pal to stop teaching the boys how good she is at choke holds. Lizzie!"

"It's all good, Miss Hansom," Lizzie calls back. "It's just a self-defense demonstration."

That doesn't stop Miss Hansom from walking over to scold them.

"You two really hit it off in the end," Miss Lotti says.

I nod. I've kept Miss Lotti up to date on my friendship with Lizzie and everything we've done together when we have our lunches.

"Well, you've got that kind way about you. Don't ever change."

Lizzie calls over to me.

"Well, gotta go," I say.

"Have fun."

I run over to Lizzie. "Ready?"

She pulls out a folded piece of paper with our first clue. When Mrs. Brown heard we were going to Cider Mill, she pulled this scavenger hunt list from her binder. We run past Jennifer and Susie who look bored sitting on the ground, too cool to do anything.

"Watch this," Lizzie says. She does a round off at full speed. "You try."

I stop running, and then do the world's worst cartwheel. My knees aren't straight and I topple over to the side into the dirt. And then, though I know people saw me, I actually laugh.

"Perfect ten!" Lizzie said. She grabs my hand to help me up. I dust off my pants and take off running with her again.

Maybe I didn't exactly come out of my shell this year, but at least I started to like what was inside my shell. I decided my greatest superpower needs to be knowing what matters. It's not an easy one because I always think way too much about anything and everything, but it's the one that I think will be the greatest. I may be shy and nervous, but I can still matter. And I can matter in a good way, not in a look at me I'm popular way. I can matter by being a good friend to someone. I can matter by trying to make someone feel happy. I can matter by using my superpowers in the way that superpowers are meant for in this world: to help.

While the world certainly needs Emilies, Aprils, Annabeths, Terries, and Lizzies, it also needs Jennies. It's not always easy, but I've started seeing my shyness in a different way. Mostly, I'm no longer focusing on it. I'm shy. I'll work on it when I need to but in the meantime, maybe it doesn't matter so much so long as I'm happy. It makes me happy knowing I can still leave my mark on the world by doing little things like leaving pennies on the ground so someone will come along and have good luck. Or helping Mrs. Brown with all of her work around town that makes other people happy. I've come to realize, not everyone lives in the big moments as the star of the stage. Some of us are lucky enough to possess the superpowers that let us truly enjoy the small moments.

Acknowledgements

This page is for the author to extend their gratitude to the people who helped them during the process of writing. There are many people to thank for their assistance with the creation of this book.

For our parents who provided the inspiration for the characters in this book and heard Amy's voice. Our dad will always be the original "Darth Banana." Our mother's unconditional love has been our foundation.

For Jason, for supporting her through this experience. You gave her the time to put this story down on paper, and you were her rock.

For Amy's friends who continue to demonstrate true devotion.

For Miss Proctor's fifth grade class who were among the first readers. Your book reviews and letters meant the world to Amy.

A special thank you to Elizabeth Weaver for the cover art. To Alex Weaver for reminding her mom what it's like to be a shy girl in an extroverted world. To Derrick Miller of Blue Square Editing for his help editing this book and to Meg Dudek for book layout and cover design.

And finally, to our original shy girl, thank you for giving us a beautiful novel from your heart and inspiring us every day.

With love,
Amy's sisters

About the Author

Amy Gorman is the original shy girl. Growing up a quiet red-head laid the ground work for this treasured book. A book she completed the fall of 2014, a year before she passed away from her second battle with breast cancer.

Amy developed her writing skills at Lehigh University, and her degree in Journalism led her to New York City where she worked as an editor for a small magazine. Whether it was making her way through campus, or navigating Central Park, Amy forged lasting friendships on her regular runs. Craving some mountain air and more challenging terrain, she headed out west and settled in Colorado, where she earned her graduate degree in Political Science.

After finding her favorite running partner, Amy and her husband moved back East, to Ashburn, VA, so they could raise a family closer to her three sisters and parents. Though looking after her two daughters was her biggest passion, she still found time to pursue her love of writing doing freelance work.

Along with her beloved daughters, this book is Amy's lasting legacy and final gift to her cherished family and friends.

CPSIA information can be obtained
at www.ICGtesting.com
Printed in the USA
FFOW03n1840061217
43929226-42989FF

9 780999 146118